THE BEACH INN

ALSO BY JOANNE DEMAIO

The Seaside Saga
Blue Jeans and Coffee Beans
The Denim Blue Sea
Beach Blues
Beach Breeze
The Beach Inn
Beach Bliss
Castaway Cottage
Night Beach
Little Beach Bungalow
Every Summer
—And More Seaside Saga Books—

Summer Standalone Novels
True Blend
Whole Latte Life

Winter Novels
Eighteen Winters
First Flurries
Cardinal Cabin
Snow Deer and Cocoa Cheer
Snowflakes and Coffee Cakes

the beach inn

A NOVEL

JOANNE DEMAIO

This is a work of fiction. Names, characters, places, and incidents are either the product of the author's imagination or are used fictitiously. Any resemblance to actual persons, living or dead, events, or locales is entirely coincidental.

No part of this book may be reproduced, or stored in a retrieval system, or transmitted in any form or by any means, electronic, mechanical, photocopying, recording, or otherwise, now known or hereinafter invented, without express written permission of the copyright owner.

Copyright © 2017 Joanne DeMaio
All rights reserved.

ISBN: 154476281X
ISBN-13: 9781544762814

Joannedemaio.com

To my husband, Tony

*My stroll-the-boardwalk guy,
trusted coffee-break companion,
epic kite-flyer.*

one

IF HEAVEN'S A LITTLE CLOSER in a cottage by the sea, then Maris should be living in the land of paradise. This Connecticut beach community of Stony Point is peppered with all sorts of seaside homes. She considers them while standing on the empty September boardwalk. Beyond the beach's small dunes, a straight line of stacked two-story bungalows sits nestled practically in the sand. Two stories, mostly with lofts and upper-level decks, to take in the expanse of a sparkling blue Long Island Sound.

But if there's one thing that her husband, Jason Barlow, often reminds Maris, it's that paradise is open to interpretation. Because further down the sandy road, it is the rambling shingled cottage—with scaffolding still in place, with wisps of beach grass blowing in the breeze, with faded hydrangeas still holding on to summer—that catches her eye. Seemingly paradise. Like many of the cottages here this late in the season, her aunt Elsa's scrapped beach inn is buttoned up tight. But the FOR SALE sign in front of it hints at forever, rather than just for the oncoming winter.

Her aunt isn't the only person at Stony Point who feels the

need to pack up and leave paradise. Maris' own husband, Jason, did the very same thing a few weeks ago, even though he did return to their gabled cottage on the bluff.

Because the sudden death of Elsa's son, Salvatore DeLuca, set so many here adrift. Sal, who washed into their lives this summer like a cool breaking wave. He ended up breaking hearts is what he did—his mother, Elsa's; his fiancée, Celia's; and of course, his cousin, Jason's.

And Maris gets it. She does. Two years ago, Maris was tempted to turn her back on all of Stony Point, on the quirks and accidents and friends and familiarity and happiness and problems, and just sink into her denim designing, sink so deep she couldn't find her way back.

Instead, she stayed and reunited with her long-lost sister, Eva, after having been separated for over three decades.

Instead, she gave her old beach friend, Jason Barlow, a chance, and found a love like no other.

Instead, she opened her heart, rather than close it up and run again with fear.

Maris moves beneath the shade pavilion of the Stony Point boardwalk. She's given everything of herself to this little New England beach. Even more so now, having left her fashion career as director of women's denim for Saybrooks Department Store. Because she needs to be here. She needs to convince her husband and her aunt and the rest of her friends that this is where they all belong.

And, okay, maybe she needs to convince herself, too.

With no structure to Maris' schedule, the days start to blur. So while sitting on the boardwalk facing the morning's empty beach, she checks her cell phone calendar—first, to see if she got the day right. Yes, coffee with Eva on Monday, September twenty-eighth. Then she checks for a message from Eva, who should be here by now, and finds no calls, no text messages, nothing. When she hears someone walking, she looks up, but doesn't recognize the woman approaching, her oxford shoes clip-clipping on the boardwalk's wooden planks. Maris squints through the glare of the rising sun, then resumes watching the gentle waves break as the woman, apparently out for a brisk morning walk, strolls along.

Until that woman sits with a flourish beside her and lightly pats Maris' leg. "Hey, sistah," she says.

"Whoa!" Maris jumps up, staring at the woman with bobbed, layered auburn hair, and a deep side part. Auburn hair freshly streaked blonde, particularly on the long, side-swept bangs. "Eva?"

"Who did you think it was?" Eva asks while setting down her purse and a paper bag, before peeling the lid off two take-out coffees. Then, almost as an afterthought, she touches her trendy cut-and-dyed hair. "Do you like it?"

"Like it? Well ... yes! Yes, I *love* it." Maris still stands, and reaches forward to stroke her sister's hair. Eva wears a feather-print scarf over her tee and gold cardigan, not to mention a pair of distressed skinny jeans from Maris' last line. And her hair is stunning, falling just to her neck. "But I'm shocked that you chopped your long hair!"

"I did."

"Wait." Maris drops her voice and sits on the boardwalk bench. "Eva. Isn't cutting your hair so, well, so *drastically*, a rash decision?"

"What?"

Cupping her coffee close, Maris turns sideways to face her sister. "A rash decision," she repeats. "I know how much you loved your long hair. You spent a whole year growing it out for my wedding. And this is really ... different. So I'm worried you're making rash decisions. You know, in the throes of grief, like Kyle warned us."

"No, silly." Eva gives her tousled hair a casual shake then sips her coffee. "I felt like I needed a little fun in my life, that's all. This month's been too sad."

"What about your husband?"

"Matt? He didn't cut his hair."

"No. I mean, does he like it?"

"He does," Eva admits with a wink. "Says it's like being with a new woman."

"Oh, you two lovebirds." Maris eyes Eva's streaked-and-layered locks, having to touch them again. "So you *swear* it's not a rash decision, and that I don't have to worry that you'll make more. You know, like you'll move away." Her fingers drop to the funky scarf Eva wears. "Or, I don't know, take up rock climbing or something."

"Relax, I'm fine. I guess I craved a change, like you did with your job." Eva reaches into the white paper bag she brought. "Anyway, I got us goodies from the convenience store. To have with our coffee." She unwraps an array of treats. "Chocolate-dipped apple pops."

Maris takes the lollipop-looking, sinful concoction. "What are they?"

"Apple slices coated in chocolate and drizzled with caramel, dusted with sprinkles and cookie crumbs. All on a stick," she says while biting into one and fluttering her eyes closed with the flavor. "And, speaking of rash decisions, have you heard the latest?"

"Oh, no."

The Beach Inn

"Oh, yes. Elsa is now fielding not one, but *two* offers on the inn!"

"Says who? Because I was there Saturday, saying goodbye to Michael. And I hated seeing her rattling around that big cottage by herself, so I slept over again." Maris bites into her apple pop. "She didn't mention anything. Are you sure?" she asks around a mouthful of the snack.

"I am. But I guess Elsa's keeping it to herself," Eva says while taking another bite of her caramel-drizzled treat. "Tay likes to do her homework there. Because Elsa always has some homemade pastry for her, and they sit at that little bistro table overlooking the beach. So when I went to pick up Taylor on Friday, there were the real estate contracts, plain as day. Right on the kitchen counter!"

"Two offers? That doesn't sound good. What if one goes through?"

"And one potentially could. The first offer—which I only gave a quick glance—was ridiculously low. But the second offer said the buyers, a retired couple, might actually proceed with the beach inn plans."

"That's awful." Maris sips her coffee and, okay, eyes Eva's snazzy haircut again. "So what are we going to do? Just make her smile, like Cliff Raines said with his grand plan?"

"Operation Make Elsa Smile?"

"That's the one. But it doesn't seem like enough to sway Elsa to stay."

"Well, we saw what happened when we tried to force her to keep the inn. It all backfired and she pretty much just yelled at us. So ... what would make Elsa keep it?" Eva shrugs her scarved shoulders. "Maybe Cliff's right. Finding happiness here. We *have* to keep trying. The question is, how? What makes her smile?"

"It's not as simple as Commissioner Raines thinks."

"Do you have any ideas?"

"Let's see." Maris looks out at the beach. Damp seaweed shapes the high tide line, and beyond, two cabin cruisers are moored out past the big rock. And then, blue, blue, blue ... the sky and sea, as far as she can see. "We should try thinking like Elsa. You know, what does she like?" She turns to Eva. "What makes Elsa tick?"

"That's a no-brainer. *Famiglia!*"

"Yes! Oh, she was so, so happy this summer when Sal was here. How can we bring those smiles back?"

"I've got it! A photo album. We took lots of pictures at Sal's birthday party. We can put them all together and make a nice album?"

"I'm not sure." Maris reaches around her sister to the bag on the bench and lifts out another apple pop, this one dotted with pretzel pieces. "That might make her sad again, seeing all those summer memories."

"This Operation Make Elsa Smile is not easy."

Neither says anything as they each finish off their second apple pop, then sip hot coffee. There's something about late-September's empty beach—with a straggling beachcomber passing by, and the gentle waves whispering to no one, and haunting echoes of laughter and sweet times carrying on the sea breeze—that gets Maris feeling wistful, so she decides to share a secret. "I have to tell you something." She gazes still at the sea, for a moment feeling as blue as the water. "I actually have *another* operation going on."

"I know. Finding a new career. Your life plan?"

"I did work on that a little. But it's not that. It's operation something else."

"What? Something else?"

Maris nods. "Come on, bring your coffee and we'll walk. *A braccetto*, as Sal used to say."

"*A braccetto?*"

"Yes. Arm in arm." When they kick off their shoes, cross the boardwalk and step onto the sand, Maris leans close and whispers, "Promise not to tell?"

"Ooh. A sister secret."

"Pinkie swear?" They hook fingers beneath the morning's sun, beside the ocean stars glimmering on the sea.

"Tell me," Eva says, her voice low and steady.

There's a pause then, when only the distant waves break on shore and a seagull flies low, cawing into the breeze. Maris takes a deep breath and brushes back a windblown strand of hair that slipped from her side braid. "Operation Heal Jason's Heart."

"Oh no, hon."

Even sharing her private secret, Maris still feels blue, knowing that Jason's heart needs mending. With tear-filled eyes, she nods at Eva.

"What's wrong?"

"Something's bothering him, Eva. He's kind of quiet, all the time. And withdrawn."

"Is it because of Sal?"

"That's what I'm trying to figure out. Now that I'm home, I see things I didn't before. He's really grieving Sal's death, but he does *anything* he possibly can to hide it. To the point his life is practically a mania with the schedule he keeps."

"I'm so sorry to hear this. He took Sal's death that hard?"

"I didn't want to say anything, but yes. And I think this busyness is all to keep himself from slipping into that sea of darkness, like he did after his brother died. But I see it." Maris sips her coffee, feeling the salty air on her skin, praying for it to work its magic on healing her husband. "And it's sad, Eva. He's not eating right, he got into that bar brawl with Michael. I mean, fighting? It's not like Jason. And even after he walks the beach at night—which he hardly ever does anymore, even though it's his favorite thing to do—he comes home and kind of sulks downstairs."

"Are you sure?" Eva stops walking, cups her coffee close and turns to Maris. "Sometimes it's so late, you might be asleep."

"Oh, I'm sure. I get up and think he's out walking. But when I sneak a look downstairs, he's sitting in his chair, alone in the living room. Sometimes he has a cigarette, sometimes a drink."

"How can I help? You just tell me."

"Thanks, Eva. But I'm going solo on this one. At least you and Matt will be at the architect gala, right? I sent in our RSVP."

"You know we wouldn't miss it."

And as Eva tells her how Matt's taking the day off for the event, Maris looks at Long Island Sound once more. Eva's voice is soft, assuring her that they can't wait for the gala, all as the waves keep breaking, again and again, at the water's edge.

Somehow, in Maris' worry about Jason, it helps to stroll seaside here on the beach he loves. To soak it all in and maybe later, over a glass of wine outside, by candlelight, she'll tell him about these morning moments walking the driftline, listening to the sea.

The Beach Inn

"This is getting old, bro."

After he says it, Jason turns his head. When he hears nothing in response, he first looks down at the brown leather journal in his hand, skims a page of Neil's notes, studies a sketch of a historical cottage, then looks over his shoulder. Journal still in hand, he tries something else. This time, he walks to his barn studio's double slider, open to the cooler September air outside, and stops at the screen.

"Maybe you didn't hear me, Neil," Jason says then. "I'm adding a second floor to a bungalow, over on Back Bay. Lots of design possibilities. Could do a loft, peaks, floor-to-ceiling windows facing the sea." He skims a few journal pages, the paper rustling beneath his fingers. Outside, a lone robin chirrups. The day is breezy, carrying to him the sound of waves breaking on the bluff. He looks out in that direction. And what it all does is piss him off. Again. "Damn you, Neil. Where the hell are you?"

After a quiet minute, Jason walks across the wide-planked floor, straight to the bookshelves, and tosses his brother's old journal there. It's been so long since he's heard Neil's voice in the sea breeze, or in the hiss of a breaking wave, or even since he sensed his spirit beneath the night's stars, that now Jason wonders if any of it was ever real. Before his brother died, they'd been so close, every day of their lives—from when they were kids reenacting their father's Vietnam war stories, to adults working side by side out on the porch, bent over cottage reno plans till all hours—that it's hard to believe some ethereal connection doesn't linger.

But oddly, since Sal's funeral, Jason's only heard silence. Thick, impenetrable silence. So it's obvious he's on his own with this bungalow redesign.

"Suit yourself," he mutters on his way to his drafting table. When he passes the bin of Elsa's inn renovation sketches, he takes one rolled plan to the table, opens it and studies the details that his crews had been ready to implement. Problem is, now instead of a grand, three-story shingled beach inn, he's left with a paltry bungalow addition, which has a way of annoying him, too. He was ready for a big job—a challenge—and it actually feels like Barlow Architecture's taken a step backward with this latest nominal project. So he rolls up Elsa's design, tosses it aside, sits on his wheeled stool, lowers his swing-arm work lamp and begins sketching the bayside bungalow.

First up? The basic, existing cottage, which he pencils from memory. His hand draws lines and angles, moving constantly in sketch mode. Next, a sheet of tracing paper to add his own vision. He starts with an upper-level loft, giving the structure a center peak. On second thought, dual peaks are more in line with this redesign—one larger, the other, to the left, smaller.

By the time he's gone through six layers of tracing paper, he's no closer to settling on an initial concept. "Son of a bitch," Jason whispers, sweeping the papers aside to start from scratch.

"Hey, babe," Maris says as she opens the slider screen.

"Maris." Jason spins around on his stool as she walks in wearing a cropped denim jacket over a long white tee and black leggings. Her brown hair is in a loose side braid, and she's holding one of her self-help books. "You're back from the boardwalk with Eva already?"

"She's showing a house over at Sound View Beach. Thought I'd sit upstairs in my studio and research my life options." As she says it, she walks to his drafting table. Maris slips her hand alongside his still-bruised cheek, bends and leaves a light kiss on his lips before glancing over his shoulder. "What are you working on?"

"New job, over on Back Bay." Jason spreads the sketches across the table. "It would really help to see Neil's journals I told you about. In that shack Michael showed me before he left."

After picking up a couple of Jason's sketches, she sets them down. "I'd love to see that shack. Take me now?" She brushes his shoulder and touches his hair.

And even while Jason resists, even while he checks the business message on his dinging phone, then explains to Maris he was going to start on this job's initial sketches, her small smile lets on that she sees right through his bluff.

"Because I'm free," she reminds him softly.

"Seriously? You really want to go out there?"

"Come on." She hitches her head toward the door. "I'll change into jeans, grab a sweater and pack us a quick lunch."

Jason lifts his cell phone when it dings again. "Aargh. I have too much to do here."

"But you won't have another chance, babe. We'll be so busy with the architect gala at the end of the week. And today's such a nice day, so warm for September. You can take pictures at the shack and bring Neil's journals home."

He spins around on his stool and eyes the crammed bookshelves on the side wall.

"Don't worry," Maris assures him. "When we get back, we'll clear a shelf, special for the shack journals. Come on." As she says it, she takes the cell phone from his hand. "I'll call Elsa and tell her we're borrowing Sal's rowboat."

two

ALL IT TAKES IS ONE sound for Maris to get it. To totally understand the lure of Neil's secret shack. That one sound is why half the pleasure of this mysterious shingled shanty must come from the journey there.

Because once Jason raises the little outboard engine and paddles the rowboat closer to shore, she hears it. The comforting sound of those wooden oars—creaking against the oarlocks as he pulls back on them, then drip-dripping into Long Island Sound's choppy water—unknots every bunched nerve in her body. Then there's the rippling waves splishing and splashing against the boat's sides. She dips her fingers in and gives a swish to feel the salty water on her skin. If she closes her eyes, it could all be a peaceful dream.

But she doesn't close her eyes; Maris doesn't want to miss this, well, this fish-eye view of the coast. "Little Beach?" she asks when they pass a stretch of sand dotted with occasional boulders. Memories of summer nights of their youth come to her ... times when the gang traipsed through the wooded path to Little Beach, then built bonfires on the sand, shared a bottle of wine, and laughs, and good times.

The Beach Inn

"It is. Neil's shack is around the next bend."

Even then, Maris doesn't spot this elusive shack. Instead, there's a ragged beach and scrubby dunes along the coast. Plumes of beach grass, golden and tan this September day, line the sandy hills. "I don't see it," she tells Jason.

"*Pazienza*," he says while maneuvering the waters. He occasionally uses one of the oars to push the rowboat away from large rocks off to the side. "Patience, as your cousin often advised."

Once they anchor the boat and carry their totes, bags and shoes to shore, Jason leads her to a narrow, sandy trail through the dunes. A slatted storm fence, gnarled and weathered, leans against clusters of beach grass and wildflowers, swaying as they pass.

"This really isn't an easy place to get to," Maris says to Jason ahead of her. "But wow, do I already feel its attraction."

"Just wait." Jason slows, hikes their totes on his shoulder and takes Maris' hand. "It gets better." As he says it, they reach the top of a dune. This is where he stops and steps aside.

"Jason," she can only whisper. Down below, a shabby little hut sits on a desolate beach. Red and yellow and blue lobster buoys hang from its silver shingles, and hazy, paned windows look out on the sea. Maris glances at Jason, who motions for her to go ahead.

So she does, hurrying down the sloping dune toward the shack. Another storm fence is behind it, holding back more wild grasses. She rounds the side of the shack to the painted front door, its white color faded from the salty sea spray and breezes. If she thought the rowboat ride felt like a dream, this is the stuff of fantasy, straight out of a seafaring tale. Jason comes up behind her, turns the knob and shoves the sticking door open.

Open onto an enchanting seaside scene. The mustiness inside is wild and salty and private and so, so Neil. Everything about the small room has her gasp: from the sunlight spilling through the rustic windows to the wood shelves lined with leather journals, from the glass-domed hurricane lanterns to the white conch shells nestled in a tattered lobster trap.

"Jason!" Maris spins around to him standing idle in the doorway. And she sees something she hasn't seen in a long time now. A smile—a genuine, wide smile as he takes in his brother's secret world. "It is so beautiful," she says, walking to her husband, clasping both his hands in hers and tugging him inside the room.

"Fascinating, isn't it?" he asks. "A genuine hideaway shanty."

"That only Neil could've pulled off." Maris walks toward the back of the room, where carved duck decoys line a high shelf. "I really feel him here. Do you?" she asks over her shoulder, before touching a couple of old fishing poles mounted against the wood-boarded wall beneath the decoys.

"Not sure," Jason quietly admits. "Feels more like a museum, with relics of a different time, a different life."

"Oh, Jason," she exclaims, unable to stop exploring. There are threadbare chairs covered with thick, soft throws. There are dusty mugs near a two-burner camping stove. "How could you not have known about this place? Your brother really never told you?"

"Absolutely not." Jason shakes his head and sets down the empty totes. "And we can't be too long, because according to Sal's directions, we can only get out of here while the tide's high enough. Once it turns, the boat will be trapped in rocky shallows."

"Okay." Maris opens a small cooler she'd brought. "Okay, so we'll have lunch first, then pack up some of Neil's things?" As she asks, she is already setting out wrapped sandwiches and a couple of late-season peaches, as well as a bottle of water to share. She arranges it on a dingy round table, its wood finish streaked and worn. The closeness of the sea shows on everything in here: a wearing away, a salty coating, a damp mustiness.

And it has its own beauty that Maris can't get enough of. Utterly captivated, she and Jason sit on mismatched chairs at the table. Jason opens one of the dust-covered Mason jar candles there, straightens the blackened wick and lights it. The wisp of candle smoke that rises strikes Maris as very sad. Because she knows in her heart that the last person who ever lit that candle had to be Neil, and Jason must know it, too.

Life can fool us sometimes; here she thought having lunch in this magical place would help heal Jason's heart. But something about it all ... from their quiet togetherness while eating, to the sound of the surf outside, to Jason browsing the journal shelves afterward, evokes—if she had to name it— loneliness. Jason seems utterly alone in this room, even with the wealth of his brother's artifacts right at hand.

"Why don't you take a walk outside?" Maris asks from the table where she finishes her sandwich. "Near the water, on the high tide line."

Jason looks back at her from the shelves.

"It'll be nice, and feel good on your leg. I'll clean up our lunch things, then meet you there." When he doesn't move, she waggles her hand to shoo him out. "Go," she whispers.

It's only when he's outside that Maris does it; she lets herself cry. Just a little, but damn, there's something so sad about all this beautiful life left behind in a forgotten silver-shingled shack.

After packing their lunch things back into the cooler and straightening the table, she walks to the doorway and simply watches Jason further down the beach. It's obvious what he's doing, the way he'll stop walking, hands in his jean pockets, wind blowing his long-overdue-for-a-cut hair, head tipped to the sea. He's listening for Neil's voice in that untamed sea breeze, in those breaking waves splashing onto the sand. He's talking, too; she can see that. His expressions change with whatever thoughts he's tossing to the wind, tossing to his brother's spirit.

⁓

"Hey, you," Maris says as she comes up behind Jason a little later. A black sweatshirt is draped over her arm. "You seem kind of blue, babe."

"It's hard, seeing all this. Seeing where Neil thought he'd pick up the day after the motorcycle accident." Jason turns his back to the strong breeze lifting off the water and faces the shack. His hair blows, the wind ruffles his shirtsleeves.

"You're cold." Maris opens the sweatshirt she'd lifted off a wall hook, knowing full well it was Neil's. She holds it up as Jason slips his arms into it, then she moves in front of him and carefully zips it halfway. "Better?" she asks, leaving her hands on his chest.

He nods, stepping closer to her, tucking a windblown strand of hair back into her side braid.

Maris quickly raises her hand to his, holding it to her face. "Thank you for bringing me here, Jason," she says. "It's a beautiful place."

Jason looks past her toward the shack. Maris glances back, too, then steps closer to the water to beachcomb, finding a few seashells. In a moment, Jason comes up beside her and pulls a small conch out of Neil's sweatshirt pocket. He smiles, shakes his head and puts the shell in her hand.

Again, Maris does it. Silently, but insistently. She does not let go of his hand, and this time, takes it in hers *and* walks slowly backward toward the shack. When Jason resists, she tucks her seashells into his sweatshirt pocket, takes his other hand, too, and hitches her head with a small smile. "Come on," she says, still stepping backward and tugging him toward the shack. Because she knows. The last time Jason felt Neil's loss this badly, nearly a decade ago, he had nobody and was alone. This time, she wants it to be different.

Jason follows for a few steps, then stops. But he doesn't just stop; he pulls her close, raises his hands to her neck and kisses her on the untamed beach, beneath the mist of a breaking wave's sea spray while the sunshine glints off the water. Maris hooks her fingers through his belt loops and leans into him, deepening the kiss before stopping, touching his wavy hair and kissing him once more—this time walking slowly backward as they kiss, until they get inside the shack and Jason closes the door behind them.

Jason notices as she peels off his sweatshirt. He notices how Maris doesn't let up. Before they make it to the cot at the side wall, her fingers unbuckle his belt and tug up his shirttail, then quickly unbutton the shirt and slip it off his shoulders. The beauty of it is that she accomplishes this all while kissing him.

And all before they even sit on the cot's thin mattress. By the time they do, he's pretty much undressed, and she finally stops, sitting beside him. Breathless.

So he waits to see what his wife's next move will be, surprised at this turn his day has taken. Maris doesn't let him down. First, she slips off her fisherman cardigan, then lifts off her long white tee and sets them both on a chair. When he traces a finger along her collarbone and moves to slide her bra straps off her shoulders, she lets him, for only a second. Then she leans back, unhooks the bra and when it slips off, she takes his hand once more. This time, she kisses it first, then lowers it to her breast, her eyes dropping closed at his touch.

But his hand doesn't linger there; instead it rises to her wind-tousled side braid. His fingers slip off the elastic, but again, she stops him. Her hands remain on his for the moment she leans close and kisses him, before she pulls back and slowly, one strand at a time, unwinds that thick braid herself—her fingers silently weaving through the silky strands until her brown hair falls freely. The whole time, her dark eyes never stop watching him.

The wind lifting off the water rattles the shack's front window, and Jason looks away then. For a moment. When he looks back at Maris sitting there, half naked, her long hair unkempt and tousled, he raises a hand behind her neck and lifts it through that thick hair, gently tugging upward as she goes with it and lies on the mattress, leaving the rest for Jason to finish. Leaving her jeans for him to unzip, her panties for him to slip off, her legs for him to draw his hands along, her back for him to slide a hand beneath, pulling her close as he moves on top of her and kisses her deeply.

She leaves it all to him, he knows, in this raw seaside

moment, in the shadows of his brother's mysterious, run-down, shingled shack.

Maris isn't sure the last time she's seen Jason sound asleep. *Yes, Neil,* she thinks while gazing through the shack's shadows at the lanterns and baskets and random dusty seashells. *That salt air cures what ails him.* At least, for now.

She shifts to her side on the cot and watches Jason sleep; watches his chest rise with each easy breath of salt air; watches his arm casually tossed across his eyes. Eventually, with a feather touch, she strokes the length of his body, starting where his left leg is amputated just below the knee. Her fingers lightly trace the skin above Jason's prosthetic limb, massaging his thigh, then rise up along his belly, crisscross his chest to the contour of his shoulder, then move up to his jaw, stopping on his fading bruise. It's nearly impossible to see now, beneath the three days of whiskers covering it. But she knows. That bruise is another hit he took in his life, one that threw him for a loop when Sal's good friend, Michael Micelli, landed a blow there. Now her touch tries to soothe Jason, or his heart, in any way it can.

And Maris sees, beneath his arm over his eyes, the way Jason's mouth smiles. So she leans over and kisses his neck, slowly, her mouth and tongue teasing him. And it gets him to shift that arm of his off his eyes so that his hand touches her face and runs down her neck to the soft of her throat before brushing along the curve of her breasts.

"I love you so much," she whispers.

"You're making that very clear, sweetheart," Jason answers

as his hand rises to her hair, tangling through it. And apparently catching sight of his wristwatch as it does. Because he sits up quickly beneath the light blanket and straightens the watch on his arm. "Damn," he says.

"What's wrong, babe?" she asks, stroking the gnarled skin on his back—another permanent reminder of his long-ago accident.

"The tide. Oh, heck." With that, he grabs his jeans from the chair, gets them on and pulls his tee over his head. Then he rushes outside, leaving the shack door open behind him.

While he's out there—pacing at the water's edge, looking out toward the horizon—Maris puts on her jeans and V-neck top. She's just straightening her star necklace when Jason comes back inside.

"Son of a bitch," he says as he closes the door against the sea breeze.

"What's the matter?"

"The tide turned. We can't get out of here."

"Really?"

"There's no way. Sal wasn't kidding, in his note, when he said to be aware of the tides." Jason walks to the cot-side chair and lifts off his long-sleeved shirt, putting it on over his tee and buttoning it up as he talks. "Because the tide's going out now, and the boat's practically beached on the rocks."

Maris watches him as she sits on the cot and straightens the light blanket beneath her. "You mean, we can't leave?"

"No. Not for *hours*. I'll have to cancel my late appointments. Where's my cell phone?"

"Oops," she whispers. "I left the phones at home, in the kitchen, so that you could unplug."

"What? We have no phones here?"

She shakes her head and goes to him, straightening his collar. "Calm down. It's okay, Jason."

"But clients will be waiting for me."

"Shh. You'll tell them something later, that you were delayed, maybe. And we can go through the drawers and shelves here, while we have the chance. Don't worry."

There's a long silence before Jason talks. Talks and backs up a step, dipping his head down to meet her eye. "Did you plan this?"

She won't go there; won't start arguing with him. Not after the beautiful time they just had, making love so close to the sea.

Instead, Maris shrugs and walks across the room to the wall shelves. "You seem really stressed lately, and all I thought was that it might help to visit here," she casually tosses back to him, then plucks a journal from a shelf and thumbs through the salty pages. "And this shack's so intriguing, Jason," she says, keeping her voice soft, "that I don't mind having a few more hours to explore. Too bad it's so hard to get to. With your leg, wading in the water and sand is difficult." She keeps skimming the pages to give Jason time to accept the reality of the situation. Yes, they're stuck here. "And now we might not get back at all, with the water getting choppy in the colder months."

Jason sits at the round table where they had lunch. "Winter will do a job on this shack." He looks around the shadowy room, apparently resigned to the fact that they're stranded. "Sal, man, that Salvatore. I can see that he fixed it up the best he could. He must have come here all summer, either alone or with Celia. Cleaned the wood floors. Painted. Even put one of his mother's curtains on the front window."

Maris looks over at the topper gathered along the frame, its white linen sun bleached.

"But one bad storm can take this all out to sea." Jason glances toward the tattered wood door. "Then it's simply gone, just like that."

Just like Neil was, Maris knows. And Sal. There, and brimming with exuberant life one day, and gone the next. Just like that.

"Wonder if I can move it."

"What?" Maris asks, watching Jason get up and survey the room. He walks from one side to the other, as though calculating measurements.

"I don't know. Brace the walls, elevate it and get it onto some kind of barge?" His fingers toy with Neil's typewriter keys, then pick up an old pair of drumsticks. "Tow it over the water?" he asks while giving a rat-a-tat with the sticks.

"To where?"

"Stony Point. Set it up on the other side of our barn studio, maybe."

"Jason. A barge? You'd need some magic connections to get *that* job done. Which would be easy, compared to then getting Cliff and the Board of Governors to approve it all." Maris lifts an empty tote and begins setting Neil's leather journals inside it. Some she lingers with, brushing a seagull feather bookmark, or running her palm along the salty coating on the leather covers.

All the while, Jason is poking around the room, exploring the nooks and crannies, she supposes, in case it's the last chance he gets. They are still in the heart of hurricane season, after all. And one bad storm might be enough to erase this shack from the beach. Maris lifts another journal, this one with edges of photographs sticking out from the pages. "See?" she asks while carefully tucking them inside. "It's not so bad having me around. We go on adventures together!"

Jason is at the shelves toward the back, opening drawers in a small cabinet beneath them.

"What do you think?" Maris holds up a journal and a tattered copy of H. A. Rey's celestial guidebook, *The Stars*. "This?" she asks, raising one higher. "Or that?"

"Both."

"No room."

"I can't decide," Jason says, glancing over. "That star book went everywhere with Neil, practically burned a hole in his back pocket. So bring both."

"We'll sink the boat!" What she doesn't say is that she's also sneaking in some of Neil's personal things—a pen he'd have used, a small nautical steering wheel that must've washed ashore, a navy coffee cup.

"Maris, oh my God." Jason stands at an open drawer in that cabinet. He holds a narrow box in his hand and is lifting pages from it; one, then another. "Come here and check this out."

There's something in the way he says it that gets Maris to drop her tote and hurry over. His voice has an urgency, and an excitement that's been missing for too long now. So she stands beside him and skims the top page in the box, then lifts out a handful of pages and slowly fans through them. Finally, she looks up at Jason, who is nodding as the reality of what they've found starts to sink in.

Maris looks at the papers again, then to Jason. "Is this what I think it is?"

three

ONE THING KYLE BRADFORD KNOWS is this: When summer wanes, so does the loving. Gone are the carefree, breezy days of sandy feet, salty hair and sweet love. No more shower-cabana interludes; no more scent of suntan lotion rubbed onto Lauren's skin; no more kids at Parks and Rec, giving him and Lauren an illicit hour to sneak here and there. No blue skies over the sea, no swaying beach grasses, no cawing seagulls serenading them.

On Tuesday morning, he winds his way through his closed-floor-plan, traditional Cape Cod, a house getting smaller by the day now that the kids are back in school. The kitchen table is covered with homework papers, alongside the bottle-and-can-drive flyers Lauren made. It all reminds him that in a few weeks, Kyle has to help Evan's third-grade class with their annual car-wash fundraiser and he needs to solicit auto soap, wax and detailer donations. So the house feels like it's shrinking, as are his and Lauren's daily schedules, with no more room for easy loving.

Instead, he makes his way to the coffeemaker on the counter and multitasks, opening a notepad of fall menu ideas for the diner and skimming his latest entries. What he wouldn't give for a few more hours in the day.

While sipping his coffee, a noise wafts through the walls; it's quiet, but rhythmic. And achingly familiar. So he takes his steaming cup and follows the sound, opening the door to the garage—which is now part art studio as they bust the seams of this tiny house.

"Hey, you," Kyle says over the sound of ocean-wave music playing from a wireless speaker. Waves slosh and roll onto shore, and if he closes his eyes, he and Lauren are settling in for a sunny morning on the beach at Stony Point. Not standing miles away in Eastfield, in a damp garage surrounded by concrete and drywall, with oil stains on the floor and a dim ray of sunshine making its way through the dusty window. Summer livin' is only a daydream, now. Kyle walks over to Lauren's table, which is covered with pieces of driftwood. "What are you working on?" he asks over his steaming coffee.

"Stormy seas." Lauren lifts a large piece of brown driftwood and dabs a frothy whitecap on a breaking wave. She wears faded jeans and a black tank top with a blouse half-buttoned over it, her sleeves cuffed back, her hair in a loose bun. Silver chains hang around her neck. "I'm channeling the beach through its soundtrack. Making new artwork to sell at the diner," she says, nodding to the music speaker while her brush bristles swish on the wood. "Shouldn't you be there, cooking breakfasts?"

"Rob's covering for me," Kyle answers. He sets down his coffee cup and pulls his wallet from his pocket. "I'm getting a haircut this morning."

"Go a little shorter this time, and tell the barber to spike it."

"Will do." He lifts his wallet higher and thumbs through

the dollar bills. "Want to make sure I've got enough cash." A white slip of paper catches his eye, and he pulls it out. "Damn, I forgot about this. And I definitely can't read it, either."

"What is it?"

His fingers toy with the tightly folded-up paper. "When Michael Micelli was here, he cast the deciding vote for the diner name."

"Oh, good! So Sal's friend will be your tiebreaker, which is very fitting." As she says it, Lauren holds the driftwood at arm's length, squints, then swirls her bristles across the whitecap again.

If only Sal had been here, instead of Micelli. Sal would have made the answer so obvious, and fun, too. Kyle sets the folded paper on the edge of Lauren's art table and stares at it. "That diner name is tearing me up. The Driftwood Café, or Dockside Diner. I changed it for you, after all, Ell." He picks up a finished driftwood piece, this one of a blue crab nestled in the muddy bank of a lagoon. "Because of your driftwood painting, you know. Maybe I think too much, but what's it mean if I change it back to Dockside Diner? That I don't love you? Or don't appreciate what you do?"

"Kyle. Relax." Lauren dabs another brush in gray paint. "The diner name's not personal. It's business. And either way, we'll still sell my driftwood paintings there."

"Well then, what do you think the current name says to people? The Driftwood Café. Is it a casual diner, or a trendy eatery? Grilled cheese? Or specialty coffee? Lately I've been losing sleep over this."

"I know. You toss and turn all night." Lauren presses the back of her hand on her cheek, then brushes away a wisp of blonde hair. "But seriously? You don't have to do anything with the name, until you're certain. Business is okay for now."

"Exactly. For now. That's the problem, because I have to be forward thinking, too, or else the place can stagnate. That's what the Italian said. Keep things fluid, man. Always have a little undercurrent going on." Kyle picks up the deciding ballot and cups it in his hand. "Heck, I can't even think about it anymore. It's exhausting me."

"It is! You do look tired. Right here," Lauren says, tapping his face beneath his eyes. "I see some shadows."

"Really?" Kyle touches his hand to his face, then opens his other hand—the one clasping Michael Micelli's deciding vote. The one holding his life's answer, ready to set him on the right course. He considers it, pauses, slaps the paper back down on Lauren's art table and heads out the garage door to his old crapper parked in the driveway.

"Kyle!" Lauren grabs the scrap of paper. "We can look together …"

"You see what Micelli voted," he calls over his shoulder as he puts his key in the pickup's door lock. "And tell me later," he adds while settling in the driver's seat. "I'm off to the barber."

─⌇─

Elsa reknots her tie-front chambray blouse, then finds her leopard-print reading glasses in the kitchen drawer. Finally, she sits with her coffee and reads the buyer-feedback emails real estate agents send after showing her cottage to their clients. Like the latest: *Not enough natural light.* For crying out loud! She glances at the sunshine streaming through her large kitchen window, where her herbs wither and languish in mini red pots on the sill.

With a shrug, she turns back to her laptop emails and full coffee cup on the table. But her gaze wanders to the far side of the table, where Kyle's gift basket of inn guidebooks is perched. She looks at it for only a moment, though, then scans the potential-buyer comments again.

For mere seconds this time. Only until she stretches her arm across the kitchen table and inches that gift basket closer. One of the books features a quaint inn on the cover. Faded blue-slatted shutters frame its white paned windows. And beneath the windows, two bistro tables are set outside on a patio—just like hers, outside her kitchen! On the book cover, lavender tablecloths drape over the tables, and pretty dotted pillows look so comfy nestled on the bistro chairs.

Okay, she likes that idea and so reaches for the guidebook to give it a better scrutiny. Because comfy pillows would make comfy guests. On the book's cover, clay pots of red geraniums line the brick patio, and a basket of rolls sits with coffee cups on each sun-dappled table. Oh, she could easily spend a morning right there, nibbling on warm bread and sipping fresh-brewed coffee in the sunshine! Can't potential buyers see *this* vision when they tour her rambling shingled cottage? With a little elbow grease, picture it on the cover of inn guidebooks like this?

Goodness knows, she has—countless times over the past year—before things unexpectedly changed. So she trots out the side kitchen door and looks at her own bistro table with its two chairs, trying to *see* it the way potential buyers might. Finger to her cheek, she steps back and considers staging the table with linens and fall flowers. It could help secure a sale for anyone interested in transforming the cottage into a seaside bed-and-breakfast. And she knows the perfect autumn tablecloth to use. Actually, it would be fun to change the linens seasonally.

"Whoa, Nellie. Hold your horses," Elsa whispers to herself while walking back inside, with only two glances back at the table. "It's time to move on from that dream."

Instead she plucks a yellow highlighter Kyle included in his gift basket. She fiddles with it, then begins paging through the guidebook, looking for pointers to help visually stage her shabby cottage for a sale.

"Like that," she murmurs, adjusting her reading glasses to peer at a photograph of white Adirondack chairs lined up along a picket fence laced with climbing beach roses. Maybe she'll stop at the nursery later, the one with an antique pickup parked in front. They use the truck as a giant planter, with cascading flowers spilling from its every nook, window, truck bed and cranny. Surely that nursery must have Adirondack chairs on clearance now that the summer season is over. Who knows? The sale of her beach inn could be as close as those enticing chairs.

The funny thing is that while reviewing the chapter summaries, it's obvious she's already done much of what's included in these guides. Some of it comes from her business savvy acquired while owning her Milan clothing boutique. It's amazing how much of that knowledge is still relevant.

It's About More Than Money, and *Write a Strong Business Plan.* "Check," she whispers, "and absolutely check." The business plan Sal crafted couldn't be any stronger, with every angle covered, and then some. Over the summer, she'd listened to his typing fingers for hours, long into the night, as he prepared that extensive document.

So she skims the full-color inn photographs further. The

glossy images are remarkably similar to what she'd envisioned here—before her son died just weeks ago, when her dream of a beach inn died, too. The book's pages are filled with airy balconies topped with lazy-spinning ceiling fans; bedroom décor in a striped, coastal style; vases of wild daisies on nightstands; grand Sunday dinners served in seaside dining rooms much like her own. Oh, how Jason had hoped to open up her dining room wall with floor-to-ceiling windows facing the distant beach.

She sees it all in the guidebook's pages, her beach inn come to life, until there's a sound of a sharp knock, followed by Jason's voice.

"Elsa?" he calls out as he opens the front door.

"In here, Jason," she answers, sliding the book aside before standing and leaning toward the doorway with a wave. "In the kitchen!"

Jason walks down the hallway, straight to the kitchen table and sets down a blueprint tube along with an oh-so-familiar white paper bag. Which he promptly opens as Elsa rushes to the cabinet for two dishes. She sets them on the table right as Jason lifts cinnamon-powdered doughnuts from the bag.

"You've certainly made my day," Elsa says while lowering her reading glasses to ogle the sinful breakfast. "How are you this morning, Jason?"

"I should ask you the same thing." He drags out a chair and sits before peeling the lid off his take-out coffee.

"I'm doing okay." Elsa slides her doughnut dish closer. "It'd be nice to have this outside on our bistro table." She secretly glances at the pretty bistro tables on the inn guidebook, with a twinge of ... okay, envy! "Like we did all summer, remember? But it's chilly out there today."

The Beach Inn

"This works, in the kitchen."

There's something unexpected about this visit, making Elsa a tad wary. From across the table, she eyes Jason. He wears a black-and-white plaid button-down—his silver dog-tag chain showing at the collar—and dark, casual jeans. Lord knows when a razor last ran down that face of his; it's covered with a shadow of whiskers. And wait! She leans imperceptibly closer. Yes, he's still got that lingering bruise, beneath that scruff. Just like Michael Micelli had last weekend. So it's true, though neither Michael nor Jason would speak of it: The two of them actually fought. Wondering why, she sits back, still studying Jason.

"What are you looking at?" he asks.

"What?"

He nods to the table.

"Oh. These?" She pulls over one of the glossy books. "It's inn stuff. I'm browsing advice books," she says while lifting her still-warm doughnut and biting in because she simply cannot resist. "You know, how-to guides," she says around the warm, sweet dough.

"Aha!" Jason flips through the pages of city bed-and-breakfasts and country lodges and beach inns. "I knew it."

"No, no. It's not what you're thinking. I'm not changing my mind and opening an inn here."

"You sure? Because it seems it." Jason turns another book and takes a better look.

"No. It's just that, well, okay. I did receive an offer on the place. Yes, that's it," Elsa says with a determined nod. "An offer. Mm-hmm. And it's from someone who might actually move forward with the inn idea. So I was thinking, maybe, you know, *they* could use these books."

"Seriously?"

Elsa can only nod as she sinks her teeth into another hunk of her doughnut. She even convinces herself that's the only reason she paged through the inn books. Yes, to give them to potential buyers. That's it and nothing more. Anything to just sell this place.

"You received an offer?" Jason asks. "From who?"

"A retired couple," Elsa explains, holding up a finger while she takes a drink of her coffee to wash down the doughnut. And that much is true, so she's not lying. But something about the couple's intent sparked her own, too. "Said it's something they've always wanted to do ... run a Connecticut bed-and-breakfast and live the good life by the sea. *La dolce vita*." What she *doesn't* say is that she felt a pang of that same darn envy when she heard those words from the real estate agent. That envy that's apparently been niggling at her lately. She tosses another glance at the pretty bistro table settings on the guidebook cover. "The interested couple thought this place could work."

"So they've never done this sort of thing?"

"No. Both worked careers in corporate America. They want to get away from the rat race, slow down to seaside pace."

"Doesn't sound like a feasible plan to me. No experience, no inn knowledge?"

"You have to give people a chance, Jason."

"Which is why I'm here so early on a Tuesday morning. To give you one more chance and issue you an ultimatum with *your* inn. It's time that you give me a final yes, or no."

"But I already did that, a few weeks ago, and my answer is the same. Yes, I'm selling this big old cottage ... with its drafty windows and creaking floors and leaking roof and dried-out shingles." Just saying all that tires her. The work necessary to make this future inn shipshape seems insurmountable. And convinces her, again, that selling *is* the right decision. "With my son gone now, it's much too much of a project for me. You know that." Elsa grabs the white paper bag and lifts out a second doughnut. As she does, Jason goes to the cutlery drawer and returns with a knife, which Elsa takes to cut the doughnut in half. "So why would you think my answer's *not* final?" she asks while setting his half on his plate.

"Because I've done intense prep work for renovations here, and maybe you're not aware that it's *not* too late to add you back to my schedule. I can fit your job in, right now."

When he pauses to sip his coffee, Elsa sees how he's scanning the kitchen: from the faded, painted cupboards to the scuffed-up floor to the dated appliances to the seashell wind chime clinking outside her window. It's so apparent that he's itching to gut this space and open it all up.

"The thing is, some of my contractors have time available, Elsa. And you *can* change your mind about selling this significant property. It's okay." He reaches for his architect's tube, slides out a blueprint and unrolls it on the table, using her inn guidebooks to anchor the blueprint corners. "Before you go ahead and commit to leaving this place behind, why don't you review these renovation designs again? Just to be sure."

"I told you my mind's made up, though." And it has been. Maybe if new buyers move forward with a beach inn, she'll feel better about leaving the cottage in someone else's hands. "And I *do* have interested parties."

"Just take a look. It's really beautiful, what we collaborated on and came up with. Do you remember the hours we sat out on that bistro table and talked this over? Especially the added turret with views of sunlight sparkling on the sea. Perfect for your Ocean Star Inn?"

Elsa can't help herself. The whole past summer when Salvatore was here, and alive, she and Jason finalized these amazing design plans while Sal finalized the business end of things. So she pulls the blueprint over and adjusts her reading glasses to scan it. "It *is* beautiful, I'll give you that."

"So you're agreeing to stay? And move forward with your inn plans?"

"No! No, that's not what I'm saying. But what you *can* do is use these designs." She pauses to look at them again. "For the new owners, if I accept their offer." Still, her eyes don't veer from the precise, methodical numbers and lines shaping her stunning turreted inn facing the distant sea. Jason's astute vision rises straight and tall, imposing in its seaside character. Every room is labeled, dimensions duly noted, from the covered porch to the turret's balcony. They came so close to realizing her dream. "I can pass your name along to them, and include your designs in the sales contract." Then, and only then, she hesitantly looks over at Jason, who is watching her with a steady—but angry—gaze.

"Really?" He squints a little, tipping his head, not wavering in his stare.

"Come to think of it, this is actually very good timing, Jason." She slides the blueprint across the table to him. "Your designs can be helpful to the sale. And the sooner it sells, the sooner I can move on with my life."

"You don't get it, do you? That is *not* how I work. My architectural designs are *custom-made* for each client, filled with very personal meaning. As you well know, I work really closely with my clients to distinguish their properties. What works for you would *not* work for a retired couple coming on board."

"But I thought that since you already completed the work, you'd make an exception and use these plans. Hand them over to the potential buyers. Why let them go to waste?"

Then? Nothing. Jason is absolutely silent, the room thick with his tension. There's a shift, too. A change in his expression. It's enough for her to give him a hopeful smile to lighten the air around them.

"That's your decision, then?" he finally asks.

"Yes," she answers with a sigh while setting her reading glasses on the table.

Jason takes the last hunk of his cinnamon-dusted doughnut and presses it into his mouth. He slowly chews, swallows, nods, and rubs his knuckle on the old scar running along his jaw, a scar now hidden by, well, it must be several days' worth of whiskers.

It's almost painful, the way Elsa sees every move he makes. Because each one, in Jason's stony silence, seems amplified.

Finally, he stands up, carefully takes the blueprint and slowly rips it over and over into pieces, leaving tiny blue-lined scraps scattered across her kitchen table. Then, without looking at her, he turns, walks down the hallway and straight out the front door, leaving it open behind him.

"Jason!" Elsa calls out, scraping back her chair and running after him. She stops in the front doorway when she sees Cliff Raines approaching. He's carrying a large garden pot with a mum and purple fountain grass towering out of it. And he's close enough for her to hear every single word exchanged with her nephew-in-law.

"Hey, Jason! You make Elsa smile today?" Cliff asks, turning to watch Jason storm past.

And though she can't see Jason's face, Elsa hears his voice as he steadily walks away. It actually alarms her, the emotion in his words, leaving her with a pit in her stomach.

"She's all yours, Commissioner." Jason gives a callous wave to the side. "All yours."

four

MARIS DOESN'T COME OUT HERE often. Between the cobwebs and dust and hedge trimmers and rakes, not to mention Jason's keep-out attitude, their backyard shed is not one of her favorite places. But later that afternoon, she finally ventures into this shadowy space, after putting it off with the hope Jason would get home early and do most of this.

Instead, she's on her own, working her way around the lawn mower and leaf blower to the dusty shelves in the back. Because *that's* where the shed turns into a beach time capsule; it holds all Jason's nostalgic summertime memories with his brother. The old metal minnow trap they'd toss into the creek at high tide. The sand pails, still with sand and crabbing lines in them—the thick string coated with salt and dust, with little sinker stones tied on the end. She can just picture Neil and Jason as kids, wearing shorts and striped summer tops, their hair moppy in the sea breeze, their backs bent over a tidal pool at the end of the beach. She's sure they carefully deliberated *thee* best rocky crevice into which they'd drop their baited line.

And of course, bait was never hot-dog pieces, or chicken scraps. Oh, no. Real crabbers plucked snails off the bottom of damp boulders, found a good-sized stone and smashed open the snail shell, then tied the snail onto the end of their crabbing line. *Real crabbers use real bait*, Jason's often told Maris. She thinks of that line as she scoops a seaworn rock out of one of the pails, knowing precisely what it was used for.

Which has to be why Jason is so protective of this shed space. It's a shrine, of sorts, to his childhood.

But given the circumstances, Maris hopes he won't mind her poking around. She squints through the shadowy dust, brushing away strands touching her face. At least, she *hopes* they're dust strands, and not cobweb strands attached to some monstrous shed spider. She persists, though, until there are two piles of beach gear and seaside souvenirs stacked outside the shed door.

It can't happen soon enough that Jason finally pulls his SUV into the driveway, the vehicle's tires snapping twigs and tree debris on the pavement. Maris brushes her hands on her jeans, hurries out of the shed and waves him over.

"Can you give me a hand loading this into your truck?" She motions to the minnow traps, nets and pails.

"What's going on?" he asks from the driver's window, all while turning his SUV around and backing up to the shed.

"Lauren called. She needs to use this stuff, for the diner."

"But it's *my* stuff." As he says it, Jason gets out of the SUV and raises the liftgate.

"Right. Collecting dust in this old shed. And all this beach gear still *is* yours—put to good use elsewhere now."

"I still don't get it. Put to good use for what?" Jason asks while gently setting his and Neil's grimy minnow trap in the SUV, handling the metal contraption as though it holds the finest jewels.

"It's a secret. Lauren said we'll see when we get there. So let's go." Maris grabs her purse from the deck.

"Now?" Jason asks while tossing the last of his sand pails in the vehicle. "We're bringing it now?"

Maris walks around the SUV and gives him a light kiss. "Uh-huh. Now."

"What about dinner? I'm starved."

"We're having dinner at the diner, too." They both get in the SUV and Maris turns to Jason in the driver's seat. "It's all part of a surprise for Kyle. Who, may I remind you, was your best man."

The sun is setting, and long shadows fall across the beach roads. Jason drives the winding streets to the railroad trestle and they leave Stony Point behind, heading to The Driftwood Café.

"*Is* my best man," Jason explains to Maris. "To hear Kyle say it, which he often does, once a best man, always a best man."

"Well that's nice, don't you think?" Maris reaches over and touches Jason's face in the dark SUV.

"Yeah ... Just wish this was some other night, because I'm really beat."

"I know. But let's say you're doing this for your lifelong friend from the beach."

"Fine." Jason stops at a traffic light and taps his fingers on the steering wheel. "It's just that I thought we were staying in tonight, and looking through that box we found. Of Neil's."

"I already did, all day. And Jason?" Maris shifts in her seat and leans close as the traffic light changes and Jason drives again, passing beach boutiques and a small harbor still filled with boats. Evening's waning sunlight paints it all pale gold.

"What your brother did—it's so amazing! Neil wrote a *novel*. A beautiful, seaside novel!" she tells him as he hits the blinker and turns into the diner's parking lot. "I skimmed it," Maris lets on. "But I want to read it slowly, from the very first page. With you."

By the looks of things, Lauren's got some big surprise planned. Matt and Eva are here, and Nick, too. And if Jason's not mistaken, Cliff's car pulled in right behind him.

But it's Lauren rushing out of the diner to greet everyone, unable to contain her excitement, which clues Jason in. Oh yeah, she's got something cooking. As he and Maris get out and head to the back of the SUV for their gear, Lauren is already taking a carton from Eva's arms.

"It's staging stuff. Celia left it behind when she went home to Addison," Eva tells her. "She used it in the cottages I listed, so it's all got a nautical, beachy theme. You'll put it to good use?"

"Oh, how I wish Celia were here. I miss her so much."

It happens then, the way it sometimes does. A thought, a mention, a song … it brings back Jason's memory of his dance with Celia a few weeks ago. But the reckless touches and looks of that sultry night have a way of making the dance haunt him. He regrets it all. So he watches Lauren, wondering if Celia told her about their drunken liaison.

Apparently clueless to Jason's life, Lauren spins around and squints at the long, silver diner. The windows are illuminated, and glass fishing floats hang inside each one. "Celia would know how to instantly transform this place back to the

Dockside Diner," she tells Eva.

Jason grabs Maris by the arm and tugs her close. "What? Is she serious? We're overhauling the diner ... *now?*"

Maris nods and whispers, "Seems it. Kyle was so tormented by this decision, Lauren must have went ahead and made it for him."

"Tormented? That's putting it mildly. He's so afraid to make a change, it paralyzed him." Jason lifts a box of crabbing nets and pails out of the SUV. "It's all he's been talking about. But just talk, no actual move to change things."

Maris takes the box from him. "Then I guess you're doing your best man a favor he *really* needs. Lauren must be redecorating with this old beach stuff."

Before he can say more, Jason notices Cliff walking through the dark parking lot. His arms are loaded down with a tangled mess of salty, seaweed-laced swim rope and faded, colorful buoys from the Stony Point supply shed.

"Hey, Jason!" Cliff calls out as he heads his way. "What the heck did you ever say to Elsa this morning?"

"What?" Maris asks, looking quickly to Jason. She steps closer. "You saw my aunt?"

"She was pretty upset when you left," Cliff goes on, "crying while piecing together scraps of a shredded blueprint?"

"Jason? A destroyed blueprint?" Maris sets down the box of crabbing gear and puts both hands on her hips. "Come on! We're trying to convince Elsa to stay here, not chase her away!"

Jason looks from Cliff on one side of him, to Maris on the other. "Later. Okay, sweetheart?"

If ever he'd been granted a reprieve, it happens right then. Sweet mercy, Jason is saved from a heated interrogation on the one subject over which Maris gets very sensitive: her aunt. And the last thing either of them needs right now is any sort of argument, especially one with Maris' wrath. Lauren saves them both.

"Welcome, friends!"

Everyone in the parking lot turns to Lauren standing beside the entranceway to the diner. She's got on distressed jeans, a black tank and loose blouse over it, and old hiking shoes. Jason reckons that she's ready to do serious decorating tonight, and he's sure there's a buoy-hanging, shelf-building, swim-rope-draping itinerary involving all of them.

"I'm glad you guys could make it here," Lauren continues. "Kyle is at home with the kids, helping them with homework and *thinking* I'm at book club. So oh boy, do we have a big surprise in store for him. And one which I'm sure he'll say is a rash decision!"

Nick gives a sharp whistle from the back of the crowd as another car's headlights sweep across the parking lot. Jason's surprised to see that it's his own sister, Paige, and her husband, Vinny—who is lifting a cardboard carton brimming with beach towels and a faded canvas tote, as well as flippers and a boogie board. It's obvious that Lauren went all out for Kyle, calling in the beach troops.

"So thank you for your support," Lauren continues. She walks back and forth in front of the gang while giving Paige a big wave. "Because reviving the original Dockside Diner *does* feel rash. But with you all here now, it also feels a little bit right."

five

"It'll be hard to replace this truck, even with the cash from Sal. Because, man, this is like the old days," Kyle says early the next morning as Lauren drives him to the diner. He pats the dusty dashboard. "You and me, cruising the beach roads. Remember?"

"Lots of memories in this pickup. But I barely have a moment to think of them, we've been so busy lately." Lauren downshifts as they near a stop sign. "Like today. With my mom getting the kids to school so I can go straight to Elsa's after dropping you off."

"Rumor has it she's fielding a few offers on her cottage," Kyle tells her. "Then the old Foley's joint will be lost to us forever."

"Exactly. So we all have to kick Operation Make Elsa Smile into high gear. Something's got to convince her to stay at Stony Point. Which is why I asked Mom to bring the kids to school, so I can get to Elsa before she signs any contracts."

"Why can't the kids just take the bus? Then you wouldn't have to bother your parents, especially letting your mom use *your* car, leaving me without wheels all day."

"But her car's still in the shop. *And*, Evan can't take the bus, not carrying his science-project poster. The one that left silver glitter all over the table?"

"Constellations, right. Believe me, I know everything I need to know about Pegasus and Orion, after helping him glue on stars last night. You sure picked a good day for book club. Got you out of that celestial mess."

When Lauren turns onto the main drag, leaving their Eastfield neighborhood of small ranches and Cape Cod homes behind, Kyle settles in for the twenty-minute commute. Traffic picks up here, even at this ungodly hour with the sun barely breaking the horizon.

"I have a surprise for you," Lauren says after changing lanes. She hands Kyle what looks like her sleep mask. "Put this on."

"What?"

Lauren shakes the mask at him while she drives. "Just do it, okay?"

"Fine." Kyle gives a long look at the plush, pale blue mask and stretches the elastic around his head before tugging the fabric over his closed eyes. "What's this for?"

"You'll see."

In her voice, he hears a smile *and* some anticipation. Without being blindfolded, he might not have noticed it, but his hearing is heightened with his eyes covered. "I kind of like this, being blindfolded. I read in a magazine how blocking your vision activates other senses."

"Seriously?"

"It's true. I actually feel very tuned in to you like this." He reaches over and pats Lauren's leg. And yes, by the touch of the fabric on the skin of his fingers, he knows she's wearing her cropped gray pants with the raised seam along the front. His fingers lightly stroke the fabric, moving up toward her thigh.

"Is that all you think about?" Lauren slaps his hand away. "I'm driving, Kyle."

With a shrug, Kyle sits back and relishes these new blindfolded sensations. "We could try this in the bedroom. It sometimes feels like we missed out on some fun when we first got married. You know, with everything that went down."

"Maybe we should renew our vows. Next year is our big one-oh. Ten years, honey."

"Good idea, yeah. We didn't exactly have the dream wedding," he says, air-quoting the word *dream*.

Lauren slows the truck—Kyle feels the change in forward motion. And the click-click of the blinker means she's about to turn into The Driftwood Café's parking lot. She stops, though, so without seeing, he knows there is oncoming traffic she's waiting to clear. Finally, she swings the truck to the left, and he feels it lurch over that dip and rise of the parking lot entrance.

"You know, Ell," Kyle admits from behind the sleep mask. "I do have a suspicion about what you might have done. For this surprise of yours. Something to do with the diner name?"

"Shh. Now don't peek."

If she only knew he's enjoying this too much to bother looking. Instead, he quietly sits blindfolded in the passenger seat as she parks the old pickup, gets out, walks across the gritty pavement to his door, opens it and lets in a rush of cool morning air.

"Ready?" she asks.

When he nods, he feels her hand take his to lead him slowly

across the parking lot. They walk side by side up the stairs to the entrance door, where Lauren stops and turns the keys in both locks.

"Okay," she says while holding the door and guiding him in. "After you."

Kyle walks past her, stepping into the diner and waiting while Lauren locks the door again. He hears it, the locks clicking back into place. She moves behind him, puts her hands on his shoulders, first, as she stands on tiptoe and leaves a soft kiss on his cheek. Then her gentle fingers move up his face and carefully lift off the sleep mask.

There's only silence as Kyle takes in the sight. Or time travels, judging by the wonder that meets his eyes. What happens next hasn't happened in years. Kyle used to say that it wasn't necessary for him to die to go to heaven. All he had to do was stand in front of the big stoves at the Dockside Diner.

And here he is, finally, again. In heaven, as evidenced by the large painted sign anchored by roped dock pilings on either side: DOCKSIDE DINER.

"Yes," Kyle whispers while punching the air and taking a step for a better look. Vintage anchors lean against his diner's far wall, while buoys strung from rope hang around them. Other buoys—weathered red and blue and yellow—hang from the ceiling like pendant lights throughout the room. A big fishing net dotted with starfish and seashells drapes along a back wall, where a seaside display of sand pails and a boogie board and a faded minnow trap, all nestled in sun-faded beach towels, lines the wall shelf.

Time travel, indeed. If he's not mistaken, Kyle stepped back through the years to the nostalgic Dockside Diner, all salt-encrusted and beach casual and oh, so right.

"It's just a start." Lauren's voice is soft, behind him. "Everyone helped."

"Everyone?"

"Last night."

He turns to her then. "From your book club?"

"No, silly!" Lauren steps beside him and fixes a strand of his newly spiked hair, mussed by the sleep mask. "There was no book club," she says while dabbing at his hair. "It was Jason, Maris, Eva, Matt. Cliff, too. Oh, and Paige! Paige and Vinny."

"No shit. The goombah was here?" Kyle cannot take his eyes off the room. The Driftwood Café has simply been erased, with the new down-home décor mooring The Dockside in its rightful place once more. "I cannot believe you did all this. This is ... *huge*. But, wait. I mean, this happened kind of spur of the moment, right? So heck, is it one of those rash decisions I keep warning everyone about?"

Lauren shrugs. "Rash? You've been stymied for months about your diner name! Now you can breathe easy, Kyle. No more sweating it out day and night. Which means no more sneaking those smokes with Jason—cigarettes you can now quit. Cold turkey, a patch, gum. Whatever it takes."

"Wait. So you're telling me Micelli's vote, it swung the decision this way?"

"Kind of. Sal had something to do with it, too."

"Sal?"

Lauren nods. "Look," she says, pointing to a picture frame hanging near the entranceway.

Kyle walks over to the frame made with thin pieces of grayed driftwood, so unmistakably crafted by his wife. Beneath the glass, Michael Micelli's deciding diner-name ballot is displayed, front and center. Creases still show in that paper from where Kyle had tightly folded the scrap before tucking it into his wallet. He never once opened it.

Now, he finally bends close to read Michael's framed message.

Dockside Diner. Endorsed by Salvatore DeLuca.

"Over the summer, Sal must've told Michael about this place. And about your diner-name dilemma," Lauren whispers behind him.

Kyle's eyes tear up at what he sees next. Above Micelli's ballot message is a photograph of Sal from a summer day when he waited tables here. In the picture, Sal stands with a tray of breakfast dishes raised high. And he wears a white half-apron left behind from when the diner belonged to Kyle's old boss, Jerry. The apron is clearly screen-printed with the words *Dockside Diner*, with a small anchor tipped on either side of the words. Kyle hasn't seen that apron for two years now, so Sal must've rummaged deep in the supply closet to find it that day. As though he knew the right name all along.

"It's from last July," Lauren says as she comes up beside Kyle. "And when I read Michael's vote, I prayed I still had the photo, which I did. I took the shot of Sal with my cell phone, just for laughs. You know, showing Mr. Wall Street schlepping tables, which he so loved, Kyle. Check out that smile."

Kyle looks again, speechless, but a bead of perspiration lines his face.

"Dockside Diner is definitely Sal-approved. So don't worry." Lauren takes his hand and walks him to a red-cushioned stool at the counter. "Just sit and relax. Because this is only a start. We'll get to the rest one step at a time."

"The rest?"

"Sure. A new website, social media, Chamber of Commerce ribbon-cutting."

"Oh, man." Kyle grabs a napkin from the counter and dabs his forehead.

"Do you like it?"

It was always meant to be; it's obvious by what his friends accomplished last night. Kyle swivels the stool, stands again and looks around the beach-casual diner. "Love it, especially that your painted driftwood display is still a part of it all," he says, taking in the swim rope garland around it, and fishing net laced with starfish and seashells on the wall behind her work. "I can't believe I ever doubted this."

"Now *there's* a smile if I ever saw one." Lauren touches his face, then stands on her toes to kiss him. Her hands wrap around his waist as she kisses his chin, then his mouth.

As she does, Kyle pulls the sleep mask from his pants pocket and slips it on her head. "Here." He tips up *her* chin and kisses her again. "Put this on."

"Wait, Kyle." She touches the mask perched on top of her head right as he pulls it down over her eyes. "What?" she whispers.

"Come on, doll," he tells her, taking her hand and leading her straight beyond the kitchen to his back office. "We've got one more rash decision to tend to."

⁓

Here it is the very last day of September, but the warm air drifting in the open bedroom window feels more like July air, steamy and damp. The caw of seagulls feeding out beyond the bluff drifts into the room, too. Maris strokes Jason's face, running her fingers along his whiskered cheek, down to his neck where she traces along his dog-tag chain. As she does, feeling the length of his naked body beneath hers, he reaches up and sweeps her long hair back behind her shoulder, where his touch stays as he watches her. Though they'd just made love, she gives him a little more, kissing him once, twice, then again, deeper this time, until she feels his grin beneath her lips.

"Now there's a smile if I ever saw one," she whispers through another kiss, before rolling off of him and settling beside him beneath the bedsheet.

"I love you," Jason tells her, turning on his side and still touching her hair, her shoulder, his touch moving down her arm.

"You're not half bad, yourself," Maris answers, her fingers toying with the hair on his chest. "Mr. Barlow."

"That's it?" he softly asks, planting a light kiss on her forehead. "Not half bad?"

"Not bad at all," she murmurs while dragging her fingers down his belly.

Jason watches her, then reaches over and pulls some of her hair forward, letting the silky strands run through his fingers. "You know, I'm getting used to you being home. So I hope you're not highlighting too much in those career how-to books."

"Why not?"

"I'm finding I like having you around. Don't need you running all over the world again."

"Jason." She cups her hands around his whiskered face and kisses his mouth, feeling his arms reach behind her bare back as she does. "You're so good to me. But you have to be nice to other people, too."

A quiet second passes before he answers. "Elsa?"

"Mm-hmm."

"I'm losing my patience with her, Maris. Your aunt's decision to sell her inn is so drastic, and set in immovable stone, when we all know she needs to stay put. Doesn't she get it, the whole rash decision thing?"

"Listen." Maris runs her fingers through Jason's a-bit-too-long, wavy hair. "You're a special man who I love very much, so I hope you'll hear me out." When he simply nods, she continues. "Two years ago, after so much time apart, I met you again. And you were stubborn and obstinate. Moody, too. I understood you were still getting over the traumatic accident that cost you so much. Your brother, and my God, half your left leg. But remember, when I ran into you that summer, it had been seven *years* since Neil died. Years."

Jason rolls over onto his back, but still watches her talk.

"It's only been a month since Sal died. Elsa's son. One *month*." She stops when Jason drapes his arm over his eyes. "Oh, no you don't," Maris says, lifting his arm off his face. "Talk to me, babe."

He takes a long breath and Maris sees his eyes drop closed as the sea air fills his lungs. "You would not have wanted to know me one *month* after losing my brother. I was bad news."

"Exactly. Which is why I've been sleeping over at Elsa's some nights. I hate thinking of my aunt alone and sad in that dark cottage."

"The nights were the worst after Neil died. Awful to get through."

"Right. So you be nice to Elsa. Even now with that serious offer on her place."

"Which she seemed really interested in closing the deal on,

annoying me enough to rip up that blueprint."

"Tsk." Maris lightly slaps his chest, then leaves her hand there and strokes his skin. "No, we have to make her *happy*. To make her do what Sal would want her to do. Smile."

"I know. *Sorridi*." After a moment, Jason looks at Maris beside him, then looks toward the lightening window. "Hey, what time is it, anyway?" he asks while reaching across her for his cell phone on the nightstand. "I'm late!" Sitting up, he grabs his robe from the foot of the bed, then turns to Maris still lounging beneath the cool sheet. "Ever since you quit your job, I'm always running behind."

"I thought you liked having me around," she says as her hands reach to tie his robe.

"Oh, I do, sweetheart." He kisses her hand, then leans over and grabs his crutches propped against the bedside chair, and heads to the bathroom. "But eventually I've got to get out of here," he says as he walks across the bedroom. Then, quietly, "*Avanti tutta*."

As Maris thinks of Sal and whispers, "Full speed ahead," she hears the shower starting, and so Jason's Wednesday begins.

Elsa raises her watering can and sprinkles her new pot of mums from Cliff. Her favorite part of the pot, though, is the tall purple fountain grass, with its wispy seed heads swaying in the gentle sea breeze. Just as she tucks a strand of hair behind her straw sun hat, a voice calls out, "Yoo-hoo! Elsa?" So she looks around her potted plumes of decorative grass blades to see Lauren rounding the front corner of the inn.

"There you are," Lauren says as she nears. After setting down her art gear, she touches the purple fuzzies on the end of the fountain grass. "Wow, look at that. Can you believe it's fall already?"

"Not today, I can't. What a warm day it is. But all the days blur, lately. Some days I wake up and it still feels like July. I even catch myself putting on a pot of decaf for Salvatore."

"Oh, Elsa. I know how you feel. I do, really." Lauren reaches over and affectionately clasps Elsa's garden-gloved hand. "Your son got the biggest secret out of me this summer. And so I think I can tell you the secret, too." She gives Elsa a small smile as Elsa lifts her watering can again. "I used to feel the same way you do, after Neil died."

"What?" Elsa stops watering, the spout dripping on her sandaled feet. "Jason's brother?"

"Your son was a smooth talker," Lauren explains while nodding, "in such a sweet way, though. And I told him some of my past. It's an old story, and done now. But trust me when I say I *get* what you're going through after losing someone you love. And that's why I'm here today. To distract you." She picks up Elsa's hand again and starts to tug her toward the beach. "Come paint with me. *En plein air.*"

"French, is it?"

"*Oui, madame.* It means ... in the open air. You're supposed to paint outside, right in front of the landscape. You immerse yourself in the subject and bring it to your easel."

"I'd like to, Lauren, but I'm busy." Elsa sweeps her hand to her hydrangea bushes and potted mum.

"The plants can wait. Because I really need some fresh watercolors for an upcoming craft fair. Come on." Lauren grabs her gear and hoists it up under her arm. "I brought a special easel for you," she says over her shoulder while heading straight to the secret path behind Elsa's inn.

By the time Elsa finishes watering her mum pot and gets to the narrow beach path concealed by tufts of dune grass, she sees Lauren's flip-flops kicked off in the sand there. So Elsa shrugs and does the same, leaving her sandals behind and heading barefoot along the hidden path, then crossing the warm September sand. Two portable easels are already set up seaside.

"Look!" Lauren glances back at her, then points to the deep blue water of Long Island Sound. "Ocean stars, Elsa!"

"Did you plan this?" Elsa stops at the water's edge and feels the gentle wind touch her face as the water shimmers beneath drops of sunlight. "Timing your visit with the sparkling sea?"

"What? No! Of course not."

When nothing more is said, Elsa turns to see Lauren immersed in her pre-painting routine: sun visor donned, denim shirtsleeves cuffed, small rag tucked into cropped gray pants pocket. Then she moves to Elsa's easel, clips on a blank white paper, fills her water tray from a bottled water, and stands a few brushes in the brush holder.

"Here." Lauren motions Elsa closer and gives her a paintbrush. "Hold your brush like this." She sets Elsa's fingers halfway up the brush. "Now try to capture what you see in front of you. Your paints are on the tray, below. Water's there, too. Feel free to change brushes, mix colors and try different techniques."

So beneath the midmorning sun, Elsa does something she's never done before: paints in the outdoor air. Much of her past year here in Stony Point has been spent doing things for the first time: reuniting with her two long-lost nieces; reliving sweet memories of her sister, June; buying her fixer-upper cottage; deciding to renovate it into a beach inn.

And now, this. Painting *en plein air*. Elsa swishes the bristles on her paper to capture the blue of the rippling water.

"You're really good," Lauren calls out a few minutes later. "A natural!"

Elsa steps back and considers her painting. She's varied the shades of blue in the water while leaving tiny dots of the white paper unpainted, giving the illusion of ocean stars floating on her watercolored sea.

"I'm going to miss coming here after you sell," Lauren says when Elsa steps closer to glimpse her painting. "When I worked on your staircase mural during the summer, I loved sneaking breaks along your private beach path and standing in this quiet spot. Or even painting from your yard, seeing the water beyond the dune grass." Lauren turns toward the outcropping of rocks and boulders on the point, then brings that gray to her painting. "What beautiful views, everywhere you look here."

"I'm sure you and Kyle will find a beach home soon. Maybe it'll have a view, somehow, too." Elsa returns to her easel and mixes up silver paint to add to her clouds over the water. "Have you ever considered my place?"

"Out of our price range, Elsa. And *out* of the question! But listen to this funny story, girlfriend. No lie, yesterday Kyle came in the garage," she says, then pauses and turns to Elsa, "aka my *studio*." That word, she air-quotes. "And he caught me listening to my ocean-wave *music* for inspiration. In our concrete garage!"

"Oh my." Elsa keeps dabbing now, feeling more and more like a natural. She can get used to painting outdoors like this, breathing that salt air the whole while. "I do hope you can find a home with a more suitable painting studio."

Their brushes keep swishing then, as the warm breeze lifts off the water. Every now and again, Lauren ventures to Elsa's painting and helps her give a shadow here, a highlight there.

"Have you seen Celia at all?" Elsa asks as Lauren shows her how to flick silver paint on her paper. Tiny specks of silver land on her painting, glimmering wonderfully.

"No. I drove by her cottage coming here this morning. Do I ever miss her, so much. If Celia were here, she'd probably do a little painting with us, too."

"I'm sure." Elsa takes her brush and tries flicking a bit of silver over her ocean stars. "Anyway, will you and Kyle be at Jason's architect gala Friday night?"

"Wouldn't miss it. Can't believe it's only two days away. My parents are babysitting, so Kyle and I will finally have a date night that does *not* involve house-hunting!"

From the corner of her eye, Elsa notices Lauren setting down her brush and carefully wiping her fingers with her rag. When she keeps glancing over at Elsa, it's an aha moment. Here comes the real reason Lauren stopped by this morning.

"I'm not here to pressure you, Elsa. Really. But I want you to know that I lost Neil here, in the thick of a secret love affair we had."

"I kind of thought so, when you mentioned him earlier."

Lauren nods. "But, the thing is? I also healed here. And you can, too. You don't have to leave."

"Lauren—"

"Wait, listen. Let me explain something." Lauren walks closer and takes Elsa's hands in hers. Her gray eyes hold the sad story that Sal must've gotten out of her one quiet day this summer. "Kyle and I should have avoided Stony Point altogether, you would think," Lauren begins. "After what we went through in our late twenties, with me eventually leaving him—for Neil. But this place actually brought us even *closer* after Neil died. Two years ago, we rented a summer cottage and faced those difficult memories. And Kyle? Well, Kyle put back the pieces of my life, right here *at* Stony Point."

Elsa can't help it then, seeing the way Lauren tears up. She gives her friend a hug and holds her by the shoulders. "Don't you worry, dear. I'm here, for now. I'm here."

"Good." Lauren smiles, finally, and catches sight of Elsa's ocean star watercolor. "And look at what you've painted! It's so pretty, I want to grab a picture to show Kyle."

So Elsa steps beside her easel while Lauren digs her cell phone out of a tote. Actually, Elsa wants to be photographed *while* painting, so she raises her brush and dabs the paper. In a moment, a breeze lifts the brim of her straw sun hat, and she looks over at Lauren. It's a moment when, surprisingly, Elsa feels a hint of happiness brush across her life like a faint streak of her *en plein air* painting.

Lauren raises her cell phone and snaps the picture of Elsa dabbing at her ocean star watercolor. "Now there's a smile if I ever saw one!"

six

THE WATER WAS THE COLOR *of steel; smooth as it, too. Too smooth, hinting at a storm to come.*

Of course, Maris thinks, sitting beneath the lantern-chandelier at the dining room table—the calm before the storm. To see where Neil's taking this chapter, she lifts the manuscript page and reads quietly, with a sip of coffee.

Because this Thursday morning, she actually snuck out of bed earlier than Jason. She slid from beneath the bed covers so as not to wake him during her secret rendezvous. Yes, an illicit affair. That's what it felt like as she took a quick shower and tiptoed downstairs. In the kitchen, cabinets were lightly opened and closed, silverware carefully plucked, mug and plate silently lifted. If Jason knew what she was up to, he'd put an immediate stop to it. So she can't be too cautious.

Finally, with the coffee percolating, Maris noiselessly turns to her tryst with Neil's waiting seaside saga, the novel drawing her in like some literary undertow. Her pile of self-improvement books are of little use now, other than to barricade herself behind while sneak-reading this forbidden manuscript, page by delicious page. Savoring every sultry sentence in the wee morning hours.

When she hears Jason coming down the stairs with Maddy close at his side, Maris reaches for one of her career guides and *does* use it for self-help—helping her out of a thorny dilemma. Together, she and Jason started reading Neil's manuscript aloud in bed at night, and Jason doesn't want her finishing without him. So she opens *The Perfect Job: Fulfillment or Fantasy* on top of the manuscript, expertly concealing Neil's typewritten pages.

"I'm taking Maddy with me to work," Jason mentions while rushing through the dining room to the kitchen.

"Okay." Behind her, Maris hears him lift a piece of driftwood from the bucket by the door before packing kibble and dog treats into plastic containers. Next he unzips his black duffel on the kitchen counter and loads his work gear into it.

"What are you up to today?" Jason asks.

Maris jumps at the nearness of his voice, and at the hint of suspicion in it. He's come up behind her, looking over her shoulder at the mess on the dining room table. Highlighters and notepads and job guidebooks are strewn about—the perfect camouflage to her covert literary affair. "I'm doing some browsing." It's the truth, actually. Especially if she doesn't specify that the browsed reading material is Neil's.

"I told you," Jason reminds her while giving her shoulder a squeeze, "don't be reading that manuscript ahead of me."

"I'm not." She grabs her copy of *Career Conundrum* and holds it up. "Next, I'll be charting my inner compass."

"Okay, good."

After a second, she feels Jason's light kiss on the top of her head. It's enough of a sensation to briefly drop her eyes closed with the pleasure of it.

"Heading over to Sea Spray Beach this morning," Jason tells her.

"Oh, to see Ted?"

"No. The Nantucket-style reno. One of the peaks will be in stone, and I need to review the front elevation with the owner."

"Is that the one with the stonework blended right in with the shingles?"

"That's the one. But I'm making a quick stop at the Woods teardown first. Reviewing the new owners' site plans with the contractor," Jason says while turning back to the kitchen, lifting the coffee decanter and filling his travel mug. "The whole place is gone, imagine? Completely leveled."

"Just like old Maggie. Remember how she would whip out her binoculars and spy on families on the beach? It was so creepy, Jason. And then she'd steal their things, given the chance … a sand chair, a kite."

"She even swiped some of Neil's journals, back in the day. Got her hands on his writing."

"And what did it amount to?" Maris asks. "Nothing. Maggie lost everything. Karma, I guess, especially when you're doing things you shouldn't be."

"It's not surprising." Jason sips his coffee and runs his knuckles along his scarred jawline. "Because my brother had another saying he'd toss around."

"What's that?"

"Karma's only a bitch if you are."

"Isn't that the truth. Every choice we make circles back again."

Jason checks his watch. "Listen, sweetheart. Got to run." He lifts his cup to Maris. "So I'll see you at dinnertime."

"Don't work too late," Maris says over her shoulder. "You need to rest for the gala tomorrow." She gets up and watches him through the back slider as he loads everything into the SUV: his black duffel, Maddy's supplies, and of course, the dog.

───

It's not until Jason actually backs out of their long driveway that she does it. That Maris trots to the dining room, sweeps aside her how-to guides and grabs Neil's manuscript. After one more check out the window to be sure Jason's gone, she laces up her oxfords and runs outside, off the deck and across the still-dewy lawn to the barn studio, which she unlocks while finagling the manuscript box in her arm.

Quickly she heads inside through Jason's studio space, the wide-planked floor creaking beneath her steps. Climbing the wood stairs to her loft, she pats the mounted moose head on her way to the worktable Jason made for her. He used actual planks of wood from the barn's walls, the dark wood pitted with aged tree knots, as well as nicks from her fabric scissors and rotary denim cutters, all of it beneath flecks of silver paint she'd spattered on sample jeans. As she always does before beginning a project, Maris traces her fingers over the initials Jason carved in the table, *J + M*.

But today, instead of manipulating fabric there, Maris spreads out early chapters of the typed manuscript and finds passages describing the characters: a group of beach friends gathered when a hurricane brews on the Connecticut shore. As if straight out of the story, the manuscript pages are seaworn from the years hidden away in Neil's shack. Some pages are warped by the sea's dampness; others left with a salty film on the paper; others with grains of sand embedded in the creases.

With the manuscript arranged on the table, Maris opens her sketch pad, pulls out her pencils, sets her hand to a blank page and visualizes Neil's words. It's the first design work she's done since being unemployed.

In no time, her sketch lines bring the novel's latest chapter to life. That sea, steel gray and still, is the backdrop to a young man in a casual button-down shirt, jeans and boat shoes. He stands on a cottage deck. Her quick charcoal lines depict his dark, wavy hair, but the lines showing his loose button-down and jeans are fluid. There's a casualness to his style as he leans on a deck railing while watching a woman walking the beach. But Maris rough-sketches only a small portion of the deck's cottage, enough to merely suggest the structure. It's a technique she's always brought to her fashion sketches: Let the viewer's eye finish the image.

With each pencil stroke, an intriguing connection grows between fiction and fashion. Her drawing feels like a form of storytelling—the sketching creates a visual outline, noting the characteristics, setting and plot of Neil's novel.

Which gives Maris an idea. She flips the manuscript pages back to the first chapter, intending now to sketch-outline the entire beach story as she reads it.

While drawing scenes, it's almost eerie how what she sees, Neil sees. How his story captures Stony Point in passages set on the sandy boardwalk, and on a sunset's high tide line, and on the mysterious, misty lagoon. There are cottages and bungalows, their porches and paned windows and shingled walls achingly familiar to Maris as she realizes what Neil did.

He brought every bit of their beloved Stony Point to the pages of his novel.

seven

ONE THING JASON DIDN'T TELL Maris is that before anything else, he plans to make peace with her aunt. Elsa will long be in the clutches of grief, and he'd been too harsh, ripping up that blueprint at her table two days ago. It's been on his mind since then.

So twenty minutes later, he's hoping that waving a white bag from the convenience store might accomplish the same thing as waving a white flag of surrender. When Elsa opens her cottage door moments after he knocks, he raises the white bag in his hand. "Egg-sandwich truce?"

"Jason!"

Already, success. Jason sees it in her instant smile, and in the way she clasps his face, giving his whiskered cheeks a pat.

"Wait. I brought company," he says while balancing a tray of take-out coffees, too, as he backs up a step.

"Maddy!" Elsa exclaims now, rubbing the scruff of the dog's neck, okay, almost the same way she rubbed the scruff of Jason's face.

"Let's try this outside," Jason says. "At the bistro table?"

"Perfect." Elsa grabs a thick sweater from a coat rack by

the door, as well as her cat-eye sunglasses from a shelf there. "A little sunshine will do me good."

Together they walk alongside her tall, shingled cottage. When Jason glances up at it, he notices a thin white starfish propped in her dining room windowpane.

"No hard feelings about the other day?" he asks over his shoulder.

"No. We're just two hotheads, you and I."

"That's one way of putting it." Jason sets the coffee tray and bag on the bistro table behind the cottage. He lifts out the paper-wrapped egg sandwiches, ketchup packets, mini paper salt shakers, napkins. As soon as each item hits the table, Elsa is on it, meticulously lining up their goods. "Dig in," he tells her as he swirls ketchup on his cheesy egg, then pats down the croissant top while keeping an eye on Maddy settling in the shade of the hydrangea bushes.

"Mmm. So good." Elsa chews and sits back in her chair, seeming to savor the surprise breakfast.

"Elsa," Jason quietly says before eating. "I'm very sorry about the other day, when I lost my cool with you."

"I understand. I'm more sorry that you destroyed that lovely blueprint."

"It was only a copy, so no problem." Jason sips his coffee. "But I shouldn't have pressured you to change your mind. You're grieving, and it's not an easy time for you."

Elsa looks out toward the sea, raising her face slightly as though its salty breeze soothes her. "Exactly one month ago today, Sal went in for his surgery. His last words to me were: *I'll be seeing you, Ma.*" She gives Jason a sad smile. "I'll be grieving for Sal for a very long time."

"And Maris often assures me, when I'm missing Neil, that

grieving is okay—because grieving comes from love. And she's made me realize that it's the love that gives us the strength to go on without somebody."

"You're blessed to have Maris in your life, Jason. She's got a tender soul, like her mother did. My sweet sister, June." Elsa reaches across the table and squeezes Jason's hand. "So the other day ... Water under the bridge?"

Jason raises his coffee cup to hers, knowing Elsa's doing what she can to keep the peace, too. "We'll see you tomorrow night at the gala, then?" he asks.

"Absolutely. Now where exactly is this banquet hall? Close by?"

"Hartford. Downtown Hartford. About an hour away. You're not driving alone?"

"No. Cliff is bringing me. And we're thrilled. What an honor!"

"Except that I haven't won yet," Jason reminds her.

"You will." Elsa nods while taking another bite of her sandwich, cupping her hand beneath it to catch any crumbs.

As Jason lifts his egg sandwich, his cell phone dings. A quick look and he sees it's a text message from Kyle. *Dockside Diner looks amazing*, Kyle writes. *I owe you, big time.*

One thing Jason knows is that if he doesn't respond now, he'll never get to it—his day is that overbooked. *Brew later at Sand Bar?* While typing the words, he throws Elsa a glance and tells her he needs to beg a favor.

"Of course," Elsa answers, raising her sunglasses to the top of her head. Behind her, ornamental beach grasses sway golden in the October sunlight.

"You'll be around today?" Jason asks.

"All day. I'm doing my fall weeding this morning, then I'm

going through a few boxes of Sal's things. Items that Michael brought from my son's New York apartment."

Jason's phone dings with another text. He reads Kyle's message about grabbing a beer later—*Can't tonight. Busy. Anyway, not sure you're welcome at the bar, bro.*

So Jason clicks off and looks over at Elsa. "Can you dog-sit this morning?" He nods to the German shepherd now lying beside him. "Minor emergency at work," he lies, slipping his cell phone into his pocket.

Elsa leans to the side and eyes the dog. "You want me to watch Maddy?"

"She'll be no problem. I brought a toy, some food."

"Well, I don't know now." Elsa snaps her fingers and the dog walks to her, tail swinging wide. "Will she listen to me?"

Jason wipes his face with his napkin and stuffs his sandwich wrappings into the white bag. "If you steal her heart."

"And how would I do that?"

"Wait right here."

He hurries to his SUV, all the while wondering about Kyle's last text. Not welcome at The Sand Bar? "Shit," he whispers, knowing full well it's because of that stinkin' brawl with Micelli. He grabs Maddy's care-tote from the front seat and hurries back to Elsa.

"Ha, look at us! We're good friends already," she says as the dog rests her muzzle on Elsa's lap, obviously delighted with an ear-scratch from her.

"There's a stick of driftwood in there," Jason says while setting the jam-packed tote on the bistro table. "You can play fetch on the beach, or even right here in your yard. Toss the stick for her and she'll be a friend for life."

Elsa pulls the dog's tote closer and takes a look inside,

lifting out a leather leash, a bowl. "I can try, I suppose. If it'll help you out."

"Fantastic." Jason begins backing away. What is it Maris once told him? Something about animals being the best therapy. So why not have Maddy be a part of Operation Make Elsa Smile today? "Listen, I'm late. But I'll call you and be back by lunch. Behave now, Maddy."

With a wave goodbye, Jason rounds the corner of Elsa's cottage before stopping to look back. Just as he'd hoped, Elsa's holding that driftwood, but seeming uncertain. Still she persists, and with the dog at her heels, walks cautiously to the grass near the secret sandy path. When she tosses the stick across the lawn, Maddy retrieves it instantly, runs back to her and drops the driftwood at Elsa's feet. Promptly, the German shepherd sits tall, her big dog ears straight up like radar, her head inquisitively tipped.

Which accomplishes exactly what Jason needed the dog-sitting to do—it elicits a big laugh from Elsa.

So he lifts his cell phone to photograph that wide smile on Elsa's face, an uninhibited one that she apparently only allows when no one is around to see.

⁓

"Clifton Raines."

Cliff, standing at his countertop in front of a dual-burner hot plate, jumps. By the voice alone, he knows exactly who is standing in the doorway of his trailer's back room. And it's the last person he needs watching him in his half-apron, scrambling eggs to beat the band.

"You must be violating every God damn rule in that new

handbook you're putting together." Jason Barlow steps into Cliff's as-of-now hidden studio apartment in the rear of the Stony Point Beach Association trailer. "What the hell *is* all this?"

First, because he's not about to ruin a perfectly good breakfast, Cliff shuts off his hot plate so the eggs don't burn. But not before quickly mixing diced tomato into the warm eggs, the same way Elsa does. Then he gives the pan a shimmy. Okay, and he knows it's all a ruse; a way to buy himself thinking time. Finally he turns around, spatula still in hand.

As he suspected, Jason stands there—clearly days-unshaven, wearing dark jeans and a button-down plaid shirt loose beneath an olive military jacket. But it's the disbelief in his eyes—a look Cliff doesn't want to cross—that gets him talking.

"Jason. Okay, so I'm not going to lie. Heck, you'll see right through it." Cliff scans his apartment, a space made more cozy since he had Elsa over for dinner a few weeks ago. Now, every so often, he adds a trinket or decoration to his shabby trailer décor: a set of anchor-patterned nautical chair pads, or a trivet to set a hot dish on, or a pale gray pillow for his club chair. He eyes the room, seeing it how Jason must: as some clandestine bachelor pad, well camouflaged by his cluttered work office. "Yes, I live here, okay? Temporarily." After glaring at Jason and his intrusive gaze around the room, Cliff gets back to his hot plate, turns it on and lifts the edges of his scrambled eggs.

Jason walks further into the space. "Holy crap. Is that a *bed?*"

"A futon, to be exact."

Behind Cliff, Jason walks to a round table, sits on a folding café chair with its anchor chair pad, then instantly stands and lifts two plates from the open shelving over the countertop. He also quietly takes two napkins, finds the flatware drawer and proceeds to arrange two place settings at the table.

When Cliff looks back at him, Jason isn't done. He goes to the mini-fridge, pulls out a carton of orange juice and pours two glasses.

"Guess I've got company," Cliff mutters as he cracks open two more eggs, grabs his whisk and readies them for scrambling. They cook up quickly, sizzling on the hot plate until Cliff adds more tomato into the mix and, okay, sneaks a glance at Jason—who's gone silent. Of course, it's because he's tucked his napkin into his shirt collar and holds a fork in his hand, waiting for this breakfast.

So Cliff generously sprinkles shredded cheddar cheese over the food and monitors the cooking. When the cheese is melted, he lifts his apron hem and uses it as a potholder to carry the hot pan to the table. And he can't miss it, the way Jason gives a double take at the apron while Cliff delivers the scrambled eggs onto his plate.

"Crazy day today, Commissioner. I only have thirty minutes free," Jason finally says while shaking salt and pepper on his eggs, "and three questions for you. I just saw Elsa, who happens to have a strong offer on her cottage. But as you know, since Operation Make Elsa Smile was your idea—and not a bad one—we're all working to keep her here." He forks off a hunk of his cheesy scrambled egg and holds it aloft while talking. "And to better know where you stand with things, I need you to answer my questions that you so conveniently evaded a few weeks back. On our Friday night fishing outing?"

"That's because those answers are my business." With his apron still wrapped around the pan handle, Cliff dumps the rest of the eggs on his dish and returns the frying pan to the hot plate, drops the makeshift apron-potholder and grabs two pieces of bread that just popped up in the toaster. The last thing he planned on doing today was sharing a tell-all with Jason Barlow. Cliff sits at the table, distributes the toast, sips his orange juice and shifts uncomfortably in his chair. It would certainly help his case in defending this trailer-man-cave if he wasn't still wearing a half-apron. So with no other choice, he goes for it—standing his ground and untying the apron before looping it over a wall hook. "Your fishing-night interrogation veered into my private life. Personal business which, if I might add, does not concern you," Cliff says when he settles in his seat and lifts his fork.

"Personal business," Jason repeats while buttering his toast, "that you'll now *make* my business." His knife scrapes across the toasted bread. "Because I see enough violations here—shit, every fire code in the book must be broken with that hot plate and microwave—to turn you in, otherwise."

Cliff twists around and points his fork at the countertop hot plate. "Those are non-slip rubber feet on that unit! It's very secure and won't be setting the place on fire."

"Hogwash. I can report you to our resident state trooper, Matt Gallagher." Jason folds half the piece of toast into his mouth. "Unless you talk and answer my questions."

There's a silence between them as Cliff straightens in his chair and scoops up a mouthful of egg. Behind Jason, a blanket lays rumpled on his futon. At the very least, Cliff wishes he'd closed up that bed before he started cooking. Now it's all tawdry evidence to be used against him. "You've got me," he finally says around the food. "A little coercion was involved, but you did it. Happy?"

Jason waves him off while forking egg onto his other half-slice of toast. "Three questions, then I'm out of here." He holds up the toast folded around egg. "One. What's the deal with your wife?"

"My wife." Cliff spreads a slab of butter on his toast. "She had a very difficult pregnancy, years ago, with Denny. Our son. There were lots of risks involved, which she accepted. Problem was, everything that could go wrong, did. She died shortly after childbirth."

More silence as Jason barely nods while devouring his makeshift egg sandwich. "I'm sorry to hear that, Raines. Really."

"Next question."

"Okay. Where is this son of yours?"

"He's around. In his thirties, about your age. Lives in Addison. Isn't that where Celia is? Anyway, I raised him myself. We're close enough, get together on the holidays."

"And three. What are your intentions with Maris' aunt?"

"Whoa." Cliff pushes back his chair. "You're like a helicopter parent hovering over some teenage girl."

"Elsa means that much to everyone here, especially to my wife." Jason gets his cell phone from his pocket, flicks through a few screens and turns the phone toward Cliff. "I snapped this fifteen minutes ago, when I stopped at Elsa's with egg sandwiches. My contribution to Operation Make Elsa Smile. Left Maddy with her to dog-sit, too, and that's Elsa," he says, nodding to the phone, "playing with the dog."

"Wait." Cliff glances up from the stunning photograph of a smiling Elsa. Her sunglasses are perched on top of her head, her hair blows in the sea breeze, and her eyes twinkle like those ocean stars she loves. "You just *had* an egg sandwich?"

Jason shrugs and slides his fork beneath the last of his

scrambled eggs. "That salt air … You know, it gives you an appetite."

"Dagnabbit. You're eating me out of house and home."

"Still waiting for your third answer," Jason replies before lifting his overloaded fork to his mouth.

His intentions with Elsa. Damn if Cliff's old judge's heart doesn't have a special place sequestered just for her. A little private spot kept apart from everything else, hidden away from everyone. He looks at Jason's photograph again, seeing Elsa's rare wide smile and happy eyes, all brought on by a dog at rapt attention at her feet. "Good job, Jason," Cliff says. He reaches across the small table and pats Jason's shoulder.

"We need to see more of that, you hear? Before Elsa goes and signs away her cottage—the original Foley's store and hangout—Stony Point history!"

"I've tried. Brought her flowers the other day. Mums for the fall. Wrote chalk messages on her *inn*-spiration walkway."

"Nope. Not enough," Jason tells him as he reaches for his phone and drops it in a jacket pocket. "Do more."

"Like what?"

"You know." After an uncomfortable second, Jason waggles his hand.

And yes, he does something else. Cliff can't miss it beneath the shadows and scruff on his face. Jason clearly raises an eyebrow at him.

"Oh, man," Cliff whispers as he sits back in his chair. He gets it. But something about the visual suggestion is still hard to believe, coming from Jason. "Mr. Barlow," Cliff persists. "Are you suggesting that I … *woo* Elsa?"

Jason dabs the napkin at his mouth and pushes away his empty dish. His eyes look from Cliff, to the hot plate and mini-fridge, and finally to the futon as he stands and pulls his keys from his pocket. "If you want your secret digs here to *remain* a secret," he says, leaning close over the table, "then that is *exactly* what I'm suggesting."

eight

"DAMN IT," KYLE WHISPERS FRIDAY afternoon. He leans over the sink in—well, after hearing real estate agents describe tiny half-bathrooms in all the Stony Point cottages he's toured—his *en suite*. Looking in the mirror, he touches his shaving-cream-covered cheek and eyes another fresh nick. A sharp razor blade would help, so he gives the vanity's sticking drawer a tug and brushes through the bandages and extra toothbrushes and moisturizers there. Nothing.

"Am I really out of blades?" he yells to Lauren in the bedroom.

"Hang on, Kyle. I'm finishing my makeup."

So with the bath towel wrapped around his waist and his newly cut hair spiked and his face covered with sensitive-skin shaving cream, he leans on the doorjamb and watches. Hailey sits on their bed, watching too, as her mother applies lipstick, then puckers and pouts.

"Come here, sweetie," Lauren says while turning to their six-year-old daughter. "Want some?" When she holds up a mauve lipstick, Hailey moves to the end of the bed, dangles her feet over the edge and turns up her face. Lauren, with a feather touch, dabs the lipstick on Hailey's lips while murmuring, "Look how pretty you are!"

"Want to show Grandma," Hailey insists while sliding off the bed.

"Wait!" Lauren brushes her hand through a cluttered mess on her dresser top. "Come back!" When Hailey does, Lauren drops a gold costume-jewelry necklace over her head. "There. Now scoot. Go find your brother," she tells Hailey while patting her bottom, "and ask Grandma to take a picture of you both."

"Can I use your razor?" Kyle asks before Hailey's even out the door. He touches one of three toilet-tissue pieces stuck on his bloody shaving nicks.

"Kyle! You're all cut up." Lauren looks over from the bureau where her jewelry is spread out. "Why didn't you just go scruffed tonight?" she asks, leaning close to the dresser mirror and putting a diamond stud in her ear.

"Are you kidding? It's a big night out on the town."

"But look at Jason lately. When's the last time *he* shaved?"

"Believe me. He will, tonight. Maris will have him all spit-shined." Kyle pats his forehead with his arm just as Lauren glances over while putting the back on her earring.

"What's the matter?" she asks.

"I feel tense."

Lauren rushes around the bed to the nightstand, where she picks up Kyle's Italian pocket translation book. "Kyle," she says while flipping through the pages, dragging her finger along each one. "*Sii forte*. That's what Sal would tell you. Be strong!"

"I'm trying, but I'm still stressed."

"Why? You're not giving a speech."

"Nervous for Jason. The last time *he* gave a speech, at Sal's eulogy a month ago, he ended up hitting the road, leaving his wife and everything behind."

"This is so different, and you know it. Your best friend's being honored tonight."

Kyle steps back into his tiny *en-suite* bathroom. "Do we have any mouthwash?"

"Mouthwash? Are you seriously worried about bad breath?"

"No." Kyle peels one tissue piece off a nick, rinses his razor beneath the hot stream of water and carefully drags the blade down his cheek. "Mouthwash is a good germ-killer, and I've heard it'll help these darn nicks. Back in the first world war, it was actually used as a surgical antiseptic, and right now? My face feels like it just came out of surgery."

"Oh, hon." Lauren walks closer, eyeing his partially unshaven, foamed-and-tissued face. "Just *relax*," she whispers.

Kyle watches her looking perfectly beautiful, dressed to the nines in a plum sheath, her blonde hair freshly brushed, her jewelry all sterling. "Man, I am so out of my league."

But she won't let him believe it, not with the way she presses her manicured hand on his bare chest and stands on tiptoe to leave a light kiss on his lips before saying, "Hurry up. It's a long ride to Hartford, and it's almost time to go."

⁓

Elsa keeps her look understated. She's still in mourning, after all, and wouldn't even be going out tonight if it wasn't Jason being honored. Her fitted jewel-neck dress is the same mahogany brown as her hair. The dress' long, slim sleeves leave just enough room for a single bracelet. After trying on nearly every bracelet she owns and deciding against each, she

THE BEACH INN

reluctantly picks up the only one left—and the only one appropriate for this special night.

It's gold, of course. A heavy gold rope bracelet from Italy. The problem is that the last time it hung on her wrist, she'd never been sadder. It was the day of Sal's funeral, and after burying her son, she thought she'd never be able to wear the bracelet again.

But here she is, draping it over her wrist and looking at her reflection. Her hair is pulled back in a chignon, her makeup slight. She wears her inscribed gold star pendant, the same one her nieces have, and now scrutinizes the bracelet. When she lightly touches it, she knows. If Sal were here, it's the bracelet he would insist she wear tonight. To look her finest for Jason's significant gala and award.

Outside her cottage window, the beach grasses sway in an evening breeze lifting off the sea. *Solamente il meglio*, she hears in their whispers. Only the best. So after blinking back sudden tears, she clasps the ropy bracelet.

At quiet times like this—moments when she misses Sal the most—it feels like he is still with her. What he wouldn't have given to be able to attend Jason's gala tonight. In a way, it feels like she's going more for Sal, than for Jason.

Silently, Elsa lowers the lid of her small jewelry box, lets her fingertips linger there, then walks to the open window. After straightening a white starfish leaning on one of the panes, she looks toward the street wondering if Cliff is on his way yet.

⁓

If it's true, if everybody falls in love at some time—like Dean Martin sings on the record player, the scratchy old album spinning beneath the needle—then Cliff will do whatever he can to make Elsa's time be soon.

So while Cliff polishes his shoes and splashes on aftershave, the crooner's warbling voice snakes through his trailer-apartment, giving Cliff a much-needed lesson in love. Lord knows, it's been years since he's had time for the subtle dance of romance. Because the past decades found him presiding as a judge over domestic trials, all while raising his son, solo.

Until life finally went and deposited Cliff here: alone in an industrial trailer, starting over and wondering when *his* sometime might happen. And if, as Dino instructs with a melodic low vibrato, everybody finds love some place, well, this is as good a place as any for Cliff's sometime to occur.

If it already hasn't, he thinks while slipping his arms into his suit jacket. Because when he recalls that one image of Elsa smiling at Maddy—Elsa's dark eyes twinkling in a moment of delight—it feels like the time and place are slowly aligning. If he could only get Jason to email him a copy of that picture, he'd frame it and put it right on the nightstand beside his futon.

Cliff walks to that futon while tugging his shirt cuff straight beneath his jacket sleeve. Okay, and while putting a little Dean Martin swagger in his step, too. Seeing Elsa's picture beside his pillow every day would remind him exactly what this wooing is all about, in one simple image. That smile.

After buttoning his suit jacket, he hurries across his bedroom space to the kitchen countertop and picks up a small box. A second passes before he opens it and looks at Elsa's corsage: a single burnt-orange rosebud set on autumn leaves and gold berries, nestled in a brown organza ribbon.

Now *that's* amore.

"Oh, Mr. Barlow," Maris says while knotting Jason's tie. She stands very close, her body nearly touching his as she murmurs, "You do clean up nice."

Jason looks down at her tie work, steps to his dresser mirror and discreetly adjusts the tie to his liking.

"Nervous?" Maris asks.

"Little bit." He studies her reflection in the mirror. Her black lace cocktail dress is new, and fitted in all the right places—from the narrow V-neckline to the lace three-quarter sleeves. The scattering of sequins gives it a shimmer that catches any light. A gold cuff loops around Maris' wrist, and her gold star pendant hangs around her neck. As she sits on the bed and slips on stiletto booties, it's obvious she plans to dance with him tonight.

"Don't worry," she assures him. "You'll do fine at the podium."

"*If* I win. But I'm not a fan of being in the spotlight."

"Do you have your notes?" Maris asks while bending to adjust a shoe.

Jason pats his jacket pocket. He has notes, but isn't really sure they'll do the trick. There's something about this night that's bigger than him and it doesn't feel like jotted notes can capture it. "I have a few things written down."

Maris straightens, tugs the fabric of her dress and walks over to him. She takes his hands in hers. "Ready? It's time to go."

"Why don't you feed the dog?" He touches her brown hair; tonight she wears it perfectly straight, with a side part. His fingers toy with it for a second. "I'll be down in a couple of minutes."

There's no hiding his distress, no matter how he might try;

might look away; might get busy with his cufflinks. Maris sees right through it all. "You okay?" she asks.

He scarcely nods, gives her a kiss and watches her leave the room. Once she's downstairs, he walks over to Neil's manuscript—which lately seems to always be wherever they are. Now, it's on Maris' dresser. He reads the opening lines of an early chapter, then sets the page in the manuscript box before walking to his own dresser, scooping up his father's dog tags and walking to the bathroom off the hallway. There, he stands in front of the porthole mirror and simply looks at his reflection. He shaved for this event, but didn't find the time for a haircut so his dark hair reaches his jacket collar.

A month has passed.

Four brief weeks since he packed his duffel, got in his SUV and drove away.

Thirty or so days since he's heard his brother's voice.

Jason knows this as he drops the chain over his neck and tucks his father's Vietnam War dog tags beneath his shirt collar. The only sound he hears is the rustle of his own clothes as he adjusts his tie and leather belt, shirt cuffs and black suit jacket.

Finally, he walks to the bathroom window and looks out at the dusky evening before closing the window, shutting off the light switch and going down the dark staircase to where Maris waits.

nine

IN HARTFORD, EVERY TABLE IN the grand ballroom is filled to capacity, and conversation buzzes like an undercurrent. Not one detail of the room's configuration—its own form of architecture—escapes Jason. The round tables are covered in formal black tablecloths with silver linen napkins, fine china and sparkling crystal glasses. In the center of each table, candles flickering in sculpted-glass hurricane vases cast the guests in soft illumination. A crystal chandelier hangs in the center of the room, its lighting dim, allowing for a continuous slideshow to run on a large movie screen on the stage. Each nominated architect's one project that earned them finalist status flashes on that screen. The houses range from modern new designs to renovations to preservations; shingles to glass to stone; rural barns to urban dwellings to coastal cottages.

As the emcee takes the stage to welcome the architects and their guests, Maris leans into Jason. Her hand runs up and down his arm before she whispers, "This is it."

Jason watches the emcee, but turns when Kyle gets his attention, bending over the table.

"Good luck, man," his friend says while raising his crystal glass.

Suddenly each person sitting with him—Lauren; Matt and Eva; Cliff and Elsa; his sister and brother-in-law, Paige and Vinny; Nick; Maris—silently does the same. Every glass is held aloft until Jason gives in and raises his own, then sips the wine.

Several awards are announced before Best Coastal Architect, allowing Jason to get the hang of the routine. He watches as other category finalists are named and asked to stand at their tables. At that point, the award is presented by the owner of the property that the winning architect renovated. From the podium, the homeowner gives a brief speech, including some history involved in the design, before announcing the winning architect.

So Jason and everyone at his table know that if he wins, it will be Ted Sullivan who walks onto that stage—the man who effectively changed the course of Jason's life. There are three finalists in the coastal architect category, and Jason recognizes the names of the other two nominees. He turns to find them in the room and gives a small salute as they stand when called upon. His own name is called last, prompting him to stand briefly, then take his seat and wait to hear the winner announced.

There's a long moment before someone holding the trophy walks onstage. Jason didn't think it would happen, but he is actually taken aback upon seeing that it *is* Ted Sullivan. Maris, who had been holding Jason's hand, squeezes it tighter now. And in the silence that settles on the room, he knows: No one else recognizes the thin, silver-haired man in his seventies, walking front and center.

Ted, dressed in a dark gray suit, sets his hands on the

The Beach Inn

podium and looks out at the sea of faces. As he introduces himself, the slideshow stops on a photograph of his stately, shingled cottage at Sea Spray Beach. Jason knows every inch of the place: from those new cedar shingles the color of golden honey, to the wide white trim, to the large deck facing the sea, to the enclosed upper loft—with its statement stained glass egret window.

"Nine years ago," Ted says into the microphone, "I had a heart attack at the wheel of my car. It was absolutely terrifying when it happened, and caused a horrific accident in which two innocent people suffered. Two brothers. Two brothers out for an easy weekend ride on a motorcycle."

In his pause, Maris leans close into Jason, while Kyle reaches across the table and briefly clasps Jason's arm.

"One of those young men lost his life that summer day," Ted continues. "And the other brother, well, he picked up the pieces of a life strewn across that pavement and has gone on to make significant achievements in the architecture of the Connecticut shoreline. Including my own home." Ted motions to its image on the screen behind him. "But more importantly," he says, his voice dropping as he visibly chokes up, "this man has gone on to become what I hope to call my friend."

A whistle cuts through the darkened ballroom, and a few voices call out unrestrained cheers. But Jason is motionless, his eyes on Ted. Beneath the stage lighting, the deep wrinkles lining Ted's face show his anxiety, and his eyes fill with moisture as he nods to the support already rising from the crowd.

Ted adjusts the podium's microphone, tipping it slightly lower. "Though *my* heart's been broken since that tragic day nine years ago, the one thing I've learned since then is this: Tonight's Connecticut Coastal Architect of the Year has the *biggest* heart you'll ever find."

Again, more sharp whistles and random clapping stir the crowd. Jason glances at his table when some of that racket comes from his own crew. Kyle, Nick and Vinny are grinning and punching the air.

"Ladies and gentlemen," Ted Sullivan says, his voice breaking, "Mr. Jason Barlow."

Once the thunderous applause and whistles subside, Maris is able to blink away her bittersweet tears and watch her husband walk through the crowd. Though nearly imperceptible, his nerves have him favor his prosthetic left leg as he takes the stage. In his tailored black suit, he stands at the podium, head slightly bowed until the room goes silent. Not a whisper is uttered as every guest waits to hear Jason's words. Elsa, sitting beside Maris, gives her a tender embrace in the momentary silence.

Finally, alone in the spotlight, Jason adjusts the microphone. It's enough for Maris to lean forward, to watch him intently. She couldn't be more proud. And she's not surprised, not really, when he begins talking without pulling any notecards from his pocket. Off the cuff and from the heart is Jason's way.

"My father was a Vietnam veteran," he begins. "That one fact is what most moved me to choose a life of architecture, particularly coastal architecture. Because the first thing my father did after the war was to purchase a year-round home at

Stony Point, on the Connecticut shoreline. He wanted that salt-air tonic to rid from his lungs the jungle scent of damp earth and animals and defoliants. To let the sound of the surf drown out the sound of artillery fire and whipping helicopter blades and endless insects of 'Nam."

Jason pauses, looking down as he seems to collect his thoughts before continuing. "So I focused on cottage architecture for that reason: The sea offers not necessarily peace, but a respite to those seeking it. Like my father did. And I make great efforts to ensure my coastal designs do the same."

When a sharp whistle breaks through the dark banquet room, Jason stops again, gives a slight nod, then continues. "Growing up, my brother, sister and I listened to all my father's war stories. Dad didn't hold back, didn't keep his memories to himself. Those stories became our life lessons, ones that my brother and I would live out in our childhood. For us, Stony Point's soaring seagulls became incoming artillery fire. And we sought cover, pretending to be comrades digging foxholes on the beach. Comrades paddling our rowboat through the lagoon, which transformed into the swamps of 'Nam. Rocks thrown into the sea were our hand grenades; blue crabs became toe-poppers; dragonflies and monarch butterflies were the dreaded insects of the jungle."

Maris drinks in every word, every breath Jason takes. He's putting his life beneath the spotlight, something he's never done before.

"Since the day of the accident, one war story in particular nagged at me. You see, being on that Harley-Davidson with my brother that August day, it soon felt like we were on some violent battlefield. And the car-collision's sudden detonation separated us. My brother landed on the hot, gritty road, while

I was thrown into the scrubby, dry grass off to the side. And I wasn't physically able to help him, leaving him to die alone on the pavement. Which for years was a *serious* problem for me ... tied in with this one, certain war story. Because my father always told us that in 'Nam, you *never* left a comrade, a pal, a friend, on the field. Never, under any circumstances. Every soldier fought with at least this assurance, if nothing else. You would never be left behind if you were injured, or killed. Somehow, the guys in your unit *would* bring you off that field to get you home, risking their own lives against artillery, snipers, booby traps and mines to do so."

Jason takes a long breath, and his gaze moves across the room at the same time his hand reaches to his neck. Maris knows exactly what he's doing: touching his father's dog-tag chain.

"I used to work side by side with Neil Barlow," Jason continues, shifting his stance at the podium then. "Neil was my kid brother, my carpenter, a historian and a bit of a writer. Before he died, he'd accumulated a wealth of seaside research and beach history. So in my work, *every* day, I reference the library of journals and scrapbooks he filled with facts and observations of the sea, and the sky over it. Of the salt air, and the bungalows and shanties and cottages he'd photographed. Mining Neil's penned thoughts is as close as I can bring him to my architecture now," Jason says, pausing to keep his emotion in check. Beneath the solo spotlight, he lightly places his hand on the microphone and turns a little sideways. "It's my way of keeping Neil alive, in the cottage designs he loved."

Again, pockets of applause break out around the room. Maris, touching her face, is surprised at the tears running along her skin. She blots her cheek with a napkin, waiting for the line every person in the room knows is coming.

Jason shifts again, standing center stage and facing his audience. "Doing this, bringing Neil's vision to my work, is the only way I know—every single day—to not leave my brother behind in that one dark moment. To get Neil off the field."

That line silences the room then, as Jason tugs his chain from beneath his shirt collar. He holds the gray dog tags up to the spotlight, gives the tags a shake, then looks back at the audience. "Thank you."

As he walks off the stage, the room erupts in a standing ovation, one bringing him to tears. Maris sees it; sees how he controlled his emotion when he was in the familiar territory of his father's war stories. But this deafening applause unhinges him. He winds through the room amidst endless congratulations before reaching his own table, where he finally sits beside Maris. As Jason brushes tears from his face, he also slips an arm around her. Among friends, and safe.

And so the evening goes, just as Jason had hoped. Flickering candles, champagne toasts, extraordinary food, crystal glassware, friends and colleagues. The spotlight is off of him, and he finally, for the first time all night, relaxes.

Shortly afterward, the band starts playing and people take to the dance floor. It doesn't escape his notice that Nick—yes, Nick—actually asks Elsa for a dance. She hesitates, but does oblige and joins Nick for a simple waltz. But in a couple of minutes, Jason figures that's enough of that. He leans over the table and looks at Cliff off to the side. In no uncertain terms, Jason nods in the direction of Nick, whose arm is around Elsa as they turn and sway.

"What's going on?" Maris asks, watching with a smile as Cliff walks to the dance floor. "Is Cliff trying to romance my aunt?"

"I think the term is *wooing*," Jason answers, just as Cliff taps Nick's shoulder and motions for him to scram. Which is precisely when Kyle and Lauren, as well as Paige and Vinny, head to the dance floor, too. So Jason stands and takes Maris' hand. "May I?" he asks.

Pressing close to his side, Maris walks with him through the crowded room. Jason notices that all night, she touches him in some way, never leaving him alone. But as they near the other dancers, someone else grabs his arm.

"Mr. Barlow," a voice interrupts.

Jason and Maris stop and look back at the person standing behind them.

"Your speech brought down the house," the stranger says. "It was amazing."

Jason nods. "Thank you."

"You are exactly what I'm looking for," the stranger continues, stepping closer and shaking Jason's hand while nodding to Maris. "Ever consider doing TV?"

To which Jason can only laugh as he starts to turn away. "Not my gig, guy. I work alone, in a barn studio my father built behind my house."

"Even better," the man insists, keeping up with Jason and walking beside him now. "We need to talk."

Jason eyes him closely. "If you'll excuse me, right now I owe my beautiful wife a dance." Again, he tries to make it to the dance floor with Maris on his arm.

"Of course, of course." The anxious stranger desperately pats down his pockets until he finds a business card, which he puts into Jason's hand. "I'll be in touch. For just a talk. Maybe fifteen minutes of your time."

Jason holds the card, wanting only to give it back, or toss it and get on with the night. Instead he slips it into his jacket pocket. "You do that. Give me a call," he says, leaving the man behind as he leads Maris to the dance floor, where he takes her close in his arms.

"Who was that?" Maris asks, her soft voice at his ear. "Do you know him?"

Jason steps back and pulls out the business card. "Looks like he's with CT-TV, the local public television station. Name's Trent. Probably wants a profile, or interview." He slips the card in his pocket again and resumes holding his wife close against him. "You know the bit."

"A profile?" Maris asks. "That'd be nice, Jason."

"I don't want to talk right now, sweetheart." Jason spins her beneath his raised hand, and her sequined lace dress sparkles like starlight as she twirls back to his arms. "All I really want is to dance with you."

As he says it, the music suddenly slows. And feeling Maris move with him, seeing the way her dress shimmers in the low light, hearing her voice whisper against his ear, he touches her silky hair and knows.

A month ago, he drove away from Stony Point never wanting to look up at the stars again. This woman is why he turned back. This woman, alone.

ten

LATER THAT NIGHT, THE WANING moon throws a swath of light onto Long Island Sound. But outside of that one swath, the night is dark. Only the water directly in the moonlight's path is illuminated. At the far end of Stony Point Beach, one lamp shines in an upstairs room of the lone cottage on the sand. It gives Jason a bearing in the darkness, as he walks the packed sand of the high tide line.

"Where the hell are you?" he asks, trying to summon his brother's spirit.

A wave breaks, sloshing along the beach in a quiet hiss. When it does, he stops. But the hood of his heavy sweatshirt blows up in a wind off the water, so he turns into the sea breeze—hands in his pockets, shoulders hunched against the cold—and keeps walking.

"What a night, Neil. We did it, you and me."

Again, he stops as he nears the far end of the beach. Here, the lagoon is close by. Its heavy grasses subtly sway in the breeze, whispering softly.

"Jesus, you needed to be there, bro. It wasn't easy, standing alone on that stage, telling Dad's war stories. Hell, telling *our* story." Jason picks up a stone, turns and joggles it while heading back across the beach. The cottages on the far hill are dark at this hour, so he can't even make out the gaping absence of the Woods place.

"Good food, and drink. And the celebrating? Neil, what a party." As he walks, Jason drags his hand through his hair and glances, only briefly, at the stars above. But he shifts his gaze, catching sight of the Gull Island Lighthouse beam sweeping across the Sound.

"Okay, I'm getting sick of this now, waiting for you to talk. So I'm through," he says, stopping and looking at the moonlight dropping on the water. Small waves ripple and sparkle beneath it. "I'm done chasing you down."

With that, Jason heaves the stone he still holds, throwing it far out into the illuminated sea and watching until it hits the water with a small splash. Watches and *listens*, though he's loath to admit it. Listens while the ripples expand from where the rock hit, the ripples growing wider, and fainter, as they do.

Jason didn't take the dog on his night walk, and she's done nothing but fidget while he's been gone. Madison has run up the stairs, rested her muzzle on the bed mattress, then went back downstairs. Twice. There, Maris can hear her collar jangle as she surveys the rooms and occasionally whimpers. The dog clearly has picked up on Jason's distress.

Maris has, too. She hasn't slept a wink, and when she hears Jason return home to their cottage on the bluff, she throws back the blanket, puts on her robe and goes to him.

"Jason?" she asks from the bottom of the stairs. He's sitting in his chair beneath a dim light. Madison rests beside the chair, practically leaning against it. "It's really late."

"I'll be up soon."

She can see that he still has on his dress shirt, over jeans now. And his sweatshirt is tossed on the sofa. So she walks closer. "What are you doing, sitting alone like this?"

In a moment, his low voice comes to her. "Just thinking."

By now, she's right in front of him, so she crouches and sets a hand on his leg. "Something on your mind? Because you're awfully quiet, and it was such a perfect night!" When he doesn't say anything, she squints at him in the dim lighting. "Everything okay? The gala was beautiful, babe. Everyone was so happy for you."

"Just tired."

"What's wrong?"

"Nothing, sweetheart."

"No, no, no, no." Maris leans closer and strokes his jaw. "Don't you give me that runaround."

"It was a rough night, actually."

"Jason." Maris stands and walks to the mantel. She lifts their framed wedding photograph and lightly touches the glass. "I don't mean what's wrong *tonight*. I mean for the past few weeks. Since that night you left here, after Sal's funeral." She sets down the picture frame and turns to him. "I see you walled off like this a lot. Alone."

She waits there, at the mantel, but he doesn't answer. Instead, he turns his face toward the dark window, then seems to lean back and close his eyes.

"You have to let me in," Maris insists while walking to the couch. She sits on the end cushion, near him. Sits and waits him out.

"I don't hear him anymore," Jason finally says.

"Hear who?"

"My brother."

"Neil?"

"That's right. So many times, it felt like his presence was close by. Like he was within reach, guiding me."

"Oh, Jason," Maris whispers, leaning over and taking his hand in hers.

"Maybe when I used to hear his voice, like a whisper in the wind, or in the breaking waves," Jason tells her in the shadowed room, "it was only memories I was hearing. Or hell, maybe it was my own thoughts playing tricks on me in the sea breeze. You know, when I walked the beach at night *wishing* he was around." He looks over to Maris now. "But since Sal died? It's all stopped. All of it. Nothing in the rustle of the leaves, or carried on the sea spray on the bluff." He reaches then for the Scotch she hadn't noticed on the end table. After pouring a splash into a glass, he takes a long sip. "It's like Neil's spirit is gone somehow, too."

eleven

"HMM, WHERE SHOULD YOU GO?" Elsa asks while perusing the living room on Sunday morning. She sets a stuffed black cat on a shelf, then plucks at its orange plaid bow. "No, not here."

When there's a loud knock, she scoops up the stuffed animal and hurries to the front entranceway, where she sweeps open the door.

"Oh," Cliff says, tipping his head. "I see you got a cat?"

"This?" Elsa looks at the fluffy animal and preens its fake fur. "My nieces took me to a fall fair yesterday. I think I'll sit it on the hearth. Now if I could only find a faux pumpkin to put beside it. Maybe that shop in Westcreek, I think it is?" Elsa motions for Cliff to follow her in, then walks down the hallway. "If only Celia were here. She'd come with me."

"Why decorate? I thought you're selling the place."

"What?" Elsa asks over her shoulder. "It's just that, well, I've countered that last offer from the retirees, but no word back yet. And another very fine offer came in, too, just last night. But even so, I haven't moved *yet*, Cliff." She stops and turns to him, noticing that dimple on his silver-whiskered

The Beach Inn

cheek. "Are you trying to get rid of me?"

"Absolutely not. I'm surprised to see you decorating instead of packing, that's all."

Elsa wraps her arm around the stuffed cat and holds it closer. "Is there something you wanted today?"

"Dust rags."

"Dust rags?"

"Yes. Dust rags. You're always cleaning something or other here. Thought you might have a few extra."

Elsa pushes the cat into his hands and opens a hallway closet. She reaches into a box on the high shelf and pulls out a handful of threadbare pillowcases and torn tees. "Will these do? I usually cut them up for rags."

"Perfect." Cliff quickly swaps the stuffed animal for dust rags, turns and walks toward the front door. "Thanks."

"Well, I'll be," Elsa whispers before returning to the living room, but not without looking toward the front door wondering what *that* was all about. "Whatever." She shrugs while walking to the fireplace hearth. The vintage buoys hung alongside it make her miss Celia a little more as Elsa remembers hanging the buoys early in the summer. *To bring the idea of the sea inside*, Celia had told her while looping the buoy rope over a hook.

There's a window open, across the room. Elsa wanted to air out the cottage stuffiness, but now a funny noise is coming from outside. It sounds like ripping fabric. Still holding the plush cat, she looks out to see Cliff standing at his golf cart. The sea breeze ruffles his salt-and-pepper hair as he leans over the driver's seat. So she pushes the window up further and pokes her head out.

"Clifton? What's all that ruckus?"

"Ruckus?" He looks at his handful of rag remnants. "I have a problem ... with my golf cart. Yes, with the ... cargo box, on back! It's loose. Come out and give me a hand, would you? And put on a sweater. It's chilly."

"Well, all right." After belting a sweater over her tunic and leggings, Elsa adds her slip-on sneakers, wraps a thick, ombré scarf around her neck and dons her cat-eye sunglasses. Once outside, she walks to Cliff—where he stands at the golf cart. The rags are laid out on the front seat now, and he's tying strips together into one long piece.

"You're going to secure the cargo box with *rags*?" she asks while peering over his shoulder at his handiwork.

"Just get in."

"Get in?" Elsa walks around the front of the cart and climbs in the passenger side.

Meanwhile, Cliff shoves a pile of rags into the back and gets in the driver's side. "You all settled?"

She loosens her scarf before clasping the side armrest. "I am now."

No sooner is her hand holding on than Cliff suddenly spins off in the golf cart, making Elsa lurch to the side.

"Commissioner Raines! You practically gave me whiplash! What are you doing?"

"Elsa DeLuca? You've just been kidnapped."

"What? Stop this cart," she insists. "I have things to do today."

"I'll stop." But he doesn't. He speeds—yes, *speeds*—along the sandy road. "As soon as we get there."

"Get where? The beach?"

"That's right. To fly my kite." As he says it, he pulls a tattered-rag kite tail from his jacket pocket.

The Beach Inn

"A *kite*? Oh, I see how it is. It's all a ruse, *again*! You people and your shenanigans. I'm onto you—and your golf cart, too—and know *exactly* what's going on here."

"And what's that?" Cliff asks while throwing her a glance.

Wait. Was there a twinkle in those blue eyes? Oh, it annoys her even more. These folks plumb don't give up. Elsa brushes back a blowing strand of her hair as the golf cart speeds and bumps along. "Yesterday, my nieces dragged me to the fair. The day before at the gala, it was you and your corsage! Jason has me dog-sitting, Kyle delivers me gift baskets. For goodness' sake, even Nick is in on it, bringing me a slice of apple pie with whipped cream from the convenience store past the trestle. Do you know what he told me when he dropped it off?" Elsa shifts in her seat to glare at Cliff directly. "He brought it because I'm the *apple* of everybody's eye!"

"Something wrong with that?" Cliff asks while skidding his golf cart to a stop in the beach parking lot and hurrying out with that rag-tail. As he attaches it to the back of a black bat-shaped kite with two large red-and-yellow eyes, Elsa walks to where he works at the rear of the cart. Side by side, they cross the parking lot toward the beach as Elsa continues complaining.

"It's just that I see what you're doing," she says while lifting her scarf higher around her neck. "You're all keeping me company since Sal died, thinking I'm lonely and will fall apart by myself. But I won't, Clifton, and you can tell everyone that for me. I'm holding things together."

"And hold this, too." Cliff hands her a hefty reel of kite string as they walk onto the sandy beach. "Let it spin out while I run with the kite."

"What?" Elsa asks, looking from the string to Cliff as he

97

trots ahead of her, then turns and runs backward. "Wait!" she insists.

But he doesn't, instead running faster and raising the bat kite over his head. So she does it, she grasps each spool handle, though the string barely unwinds in her tight-fisted hold while the kite swoops and struggles to rise.

"Let it out, let out more string!"

"How?" Elsa asks into the sharp wind while raising her hands gripping the spool. "I've never done this before."

Cliff walks closer. "You made it to your fifties without flying a kite?"

"That's right."

"Well, you are now!" Cliff looks up at the soaring bat.

Elsa suddenly laughs in the October sunshine, breathing in the salt air and seeing the sparkling water glimmer on the crisp fall morning. *Ocean stars.* When she raises the string spool higher, Cliff moves behind her and puts his arms over hers. She stops for a moment, until one of his hands covers hers on the spool and he guides her—with only his touch—to let the spool handles spin beneath her fingers, all while not letting go.

Together they hold the spool, and the kite soars higher and higher against the crystal-blue sky, the bat-kite dipping and bobbing in the air currents. To keep the kite closer and more in control, Cliff puts some pressure on her hands to pull back a little.

Elsa does, while watching the flying bat carefully. When she then looks over her shoulder at Cliff, his arms still over hers, he leans around and kisses her. And it's the perfect kiss, beneath golden sunlight and a brisk sea breeze, the waves breaking nearby, a seagull cawing as it soars with the kite—the moment filled with happy life, pure and simple.

Cliff rests one of his hands on her face while kissing her, then pulls back and touches her ear, gently, and nods to the kite. So Elsa turns her attention to it again with an idea. She lets even more string unspool until the black bat is but a tiny speck in the sky, nearly to the clouds.

"Maybe Sal can see it," she says as Cliff stands alongside her, awed by the kite's altitude. "Soaring to the heavens," she exclaims with unbridled joy.

"That's the most fun I've had, well … since the summer." Elsa lifts her sunglasses to the top of her head later and unloops her scarf at her front door. "Come in, we'll have a coffee in the kitchen. I left the pot on."

Cliff agrees as he hangs his sherpa-lined denim jacket on a chair, drags a hand through his windblown hair and settles at her kitchen table. He also can't help but notice her beloved herb pots on the sunny windowsill, all of them withering and drying up. This month hasn't been easy for her.

"I'm glad you had fun," Cliff says. "Haven't seen you this chipper in a long time, Elsa." He pours cream into his steaming mug of coffee. "It's nice."

"Except there's another reason I'm happy. I've been keeping it secret, but I did get some wonderful news late yesterday." She sits beside him and drops her voice. "Remember that new offer on my cottage I mentioned earlier?"

Something about the way she says it, as though this could be the one, gets Cliff to sputter on his coffee. He bends forward and slaps a napkin to his mouth as he coughs. "So you're not chipper because we flew a kite on a blue-sky beach day? And had an October kiss, some autumn bliss?"

"Well," Elsa answers while smiling demurely behind her raised coffee cup, "that, too. But look at this strong offer." She hurries to the counter and grabs up a few realty papers, which she sets in front of him. "It's not quite full price, but here's the thing." She pulls her chair in close and points out the second sheet of paper. "The interested couple even added a personal letter. And Cliff? It just warmed my heart."

Cliff looks up from the papers, to Elsa, who is pulling her chair even closer so that she's practically leaning into him as she directs his gaze to the letter.

"They intend to slowly restore this beautiful seaside structure. In my *other* offers, one hinted at razing the cottage, and that retired couple wants to give the inn a more modern look, changing the aesthetics. But these folks, Cliff, well they love the history of this cottage. Lucas even says he used to be a bagger in the original Foley's market, way back in the day. And if I sell to them, they plan to keep the inn small, open just during the summer months." She taps the letter. "Lucas and Mackenzie, they're in their thirties and have a little girl! Zoe. So they're a family who would fit in with all the gang here. You see for yourself. Read the letter and you'll understand why, if I'm going to sell this old place, it *will* be to these people."

So Cliff does. He reads Lucas and Mackenzie's plea for this home: *Our lives are most at ease when we can feel the ocean's breeze.* He scans their hopeful words about raising their daughter seaside, and their desire for a simple life of family, friends and the beach.

And Cliff does one more thing.

He wastes no time getting out of Elsa's cottage, on a serious mission now. Because there's only one way left to halt that verifiably imminent inn sale: with a Meet and Eat. That's right, ever since their pact in Kyle's diner a month ago, the emergency Meet and Eats haven't stopped. It was all Eva's idea—dinners together every week or two, when the gang regularly checks up on each other. It's the only way to keep rash decisions under control. The food, wine and commiserating have been flowing ever since.

So twenty minutes later, Cliff is in his trailer calling Jason.

"Bad news," he says before Jason gets a word in. "Need to schedule an emergency Meet and Eat, tonight!"

"At your place?" Jason asks, as though still shocked that an industrial trailer is home to Cliff. "Are you *kidding* me?"

"No, not here. Except for you and Elsa, no one even knows I live here. How about your place? Five o'clock."

In Jason's pause, Maris' voice gets closer. *What's up, babe?* she asks Jason. *Who's that on the phone?*

"It's Cliff. Emergency Meet and Eat tonight. Here, I guess," Jason tells Maris.

When Cliff hears Jason's words, he takes it as a confirmation—whether Jason likes it or not. "Get as many people there as you can, Barlow. I've got serious news."

twelve

By late afternoon, everything's done, each dinner detail tended to.

"This is nice," Maris says as she sets down the last of the forks and knives. Beneath the glow of their lantern-chandelier, the dining room table looks casually chic with its antique blue-and-white china plates, anchored by crystal goblets and slightly tarnished silverware. Every vintage piece has been in Jason's family for decades. "It's like an old-fashioned Sunday dinner, with everyone coming by."

"Right," Jason agrees from the kitchen doorway. "Like the Sunday dinners Elsa *planned* on hosting at her inn."

But when the smoke alarm blasts a shrill warning, Maris brushes past him to the stove, where tendrils of smoke escape from the oven door. The moment she opens the oven, those tendrils become a billowing gray cloud.

"Oh, shoot!" She stamps her foot, bends low for a better look and shoos away a curious Maddy before slamming the door shut. "Jason! I'll never learn how to cook on your ancient appliances! I'll need a new kitchen if we ever want to *seriously* entertain here." She rushes around the dog to grab potholders, opens the oven door again, squints through the smoke, then closes the oven and runs toward the beeping smoke alarm mounted on the ceiling.

"Can you salvage the food?" Jason yells over the noise as he still stands in the doorway.

"Don't know." Maris swishes her potholders through the air beneath the trilling alarm, trying to clear away the smoke as Maddy paces and sniffs at the oven door.

When Jason walks toward the stove, he first veers to the kitchen window overlooking their driveway. "Kyle and Lauren are here," he says, glancing down the length of the driveway. "Cliff, too." At which point he heads to the front door. Maddy—collar jangling, tail wagging—follows at his side.

Maris watches them go, then hurries to the stove to shut off the oven and stop the timer. Which is when she does a double take. The timer that hasn't *budged* from its original setting.

"Swell," she mutters. "The timer's broken. How did you ever cook here?" she asks no one, because the room is conveniently empty. So she brushes aside keys and mail and a box of dog biscuits on the counter to find her cell phone. "I'm calling my sister," she shouts while dialing. Maris counts the rings and stands in front of the still-smoking oven door. "Oh, thank God I caught you! Eva! Do you have anything to save this disaster that Jason's old appliances just made?"

"Okay, now don't get offended, Maris," Eva tells her.

"Offended?" Maris drops into a kitchen chair and blows a wisp of hair from her face. "By what?"

"It's just that when I heard the Meet and Eat was at *your* place, well, I baked a lasagna. Before you say anything, Matt and I are on our way over."

When Maris does start to talk, she hears Eva click off, ready to rescue her. "Saved by my sister," Maris whispers while setting her cell phone on the counter again. "All I want for Christmas, Jason," she calls out while opening the slider to clear the smoke, "is a new kitchen. I cannot cook with these antiques anymore!"

A blur of motion catches her eye then. It's Lauren, in a slim cardigan and bulky scarf, rushing into the room with her maxi skirt sweeping behind her and her booties clipping on the floor.

"Hey, Maris! What did you make for dinner?" she asks.

"Oh, some pathetic chicken carcass. It's smoking up the oven."

As she sits at the table with Lauren, oy-veying about the state of her antiquated kitchen, everyone else arrives—lastly Eva, knocking at the back slider and bearing gifts of warm lasagna, Italian bread *and* ready-made salads. They set the meal platters on the dining room table, then add flickering Mason jar candles and a vase of cattails and sand-pink beach-grass plumes. As usual, the Meet and Eat gets underway amidst talking voices, clattering silverware on dishes, drinks and heaping plates of food.

Until Cliff clears his throat, taps a fork on his goblet and stands at the farm table. The room goes silent with his announcement of the latest offer to purchase Elsa's cottage. Particularly when he mentions that Elsa really connected with the couple and their young daughter.

"Elsa seemed to genuinely like them, this Lucas and Mackenzie," Cliff says.

"Do you think she's serious about accepting their offer?" Nick asks as he walks in late and takes a seat.

"All I can say is that she didn't promptly turn it down like the others," Cliff answers.

"But she's had other offers to run her place as an actual inn. So why is this one different?" Eva scoops a helping of lasagna onto Matt's plate. "From what you're saying, it sounds like she's ready to sign on the dotted line."

Cliff looks at each of them seated at the table. "This couple would still open the inn, part-time during the summer. But I think what's sealing the deal is that Elsa thought they would fit right in here. That you kids could be friends with them."

"I don't need any more friends," Jason says before sipping his wine.

"But Operation Make Elsa Smile was going so good." Lauren digs her cell phone out of her handbag and pulls up a snapshot on the screen. "Look, Elsa painted with me. *En plein air!*"

Nick slides his cell phone across the table. "Check out *my* pic. Elsa eating apple pie drenched in whipped cream." He raises his hand to his chin and slides his thumb over his goatee. "Life doesn't get much sweeter than that," he says, nodding to the picture. "If anyone's winning the Operation Make Elsa Smile blue ribbon, it's me."

Maris leans forward to see the photograph of her aunt lifting a whipped-cream-dripping hunk of pie on her fork, her eyes smiling as much as her mouth.

"Oh, oh, I have an even better one," Eva announces while setting down the salad dressing. "We got her on the rides yesterday at the fair. Look!" She slides her cell phone to Lauren, who slowly passes it around the table. "She's on the Tilt-A-Whirl with Maris. And I think *I* win for biggest laugh. Do you see it, behind her hair whipping around on that crazy ride? How about that smile!"

"I might have you beat on that smile." Cliff nods at Eva's phone, then pulls up a photograph on his own, which he flashes to the table. "Elsa, kite-flying on the beach." It's hard for him to take his eyes off the picture of Elsa, her head tipped to the blue skies, her smile genuine.

Jason nudges Maris as she reaches for Cliff's cell phone. So she passes Cliff's phone to Jason, and takes his. "What's this?" she asks. On Jason's phone is a photograph she's never seen. It's of Elsa—sunglasses perched on her head, smile wide and sparkling—with Maddy sitting at her feet.

"Your aunt, dog-sitting the other day. And in Operation Make Elsa Smile, cute puppy pictures trump all." Jason passes his phone to Matt then, who shows Eva.

"Problem is, this is *not* a photo contest, people," Cliff says, standing again and pacing around the farm table. "And we are sadly out of time. I'm pretty sure Elsa's ready to move forward with this couple, so we have one shot left before tomorrow … to save the beach inn."

"Why until tomorrow?" Kyle asks.

"Because it's too late for her to sign off on that contract today." Cliff walks past the vase of cattails and pats Kyle's shoulder. "But I wouldn't be surprised if she signs it first thing in the morning."

"How serious is it, Cliff?" Jason asks. "Really."

"Dire. Down to the wire."

"Down to the wire? Well, what does *that* mean?" Eva asks.

"I'll tell you," Kyle offers. "Back in the old days, a thin wire was strung across horserace tracks, above the finish line. In really close races, it helped the judges determine the winner at the very last second, as the horses came *down to the wire*," he explains, air-quoting the words.

"And this is the last second for us. We're definitely down to the wire," Cliff agrees. "It's the letter that did it."

"Letter?" Nick lifts a slice of warm Italian bread.

"The couple, that Lucas and Mackenzie," Cliff answers, "included a personal letter with their written offer."

"Ooh, homebuyers do that all the time now," Eva explains. "I'm seeing more of it. They try to make an emotional connection with the seller. Statistics show that over forty percent of winning offers use these now."

"Okay," Kyle says quietly while typing a note into his phone, "so I'm keeping that in mind if Lauren and I *ever* find the right house."

Lauren lightly slaps Kyle's arm. "This is about Elsa, not *us*. Stay on topic!"

"Just so you know, their personal, heartfelt letter was like a magic touch," Cliff assures everyone. "Elsa said that after reading it, it felt like she would be leaving the beach inn in good hands. She could be out by the New Year!"

"*What?*" Maris asks. She sets down her tarnished fork, all her appetite now gone. "But Cliff, you said if we did little things to make Elsa smile, she'd stay on. Because it's hard to leave a place when you're happy."

"You mean we failed?" Eva looks at her Tilt-A-Whirl picture again. "Operation Make Elsa Smile didn't work?"

Cliff slowly sits, and Maris sees the defeat in his posture. "You don't think this new offer might blow over?" she asks him.

"What I think," Cliff begins, pausing to sip his wine, "is that her decision is set in stone. I swear I saw it on her face today. If she hasn't signed Lucas and Mackenzie's contract already."

Jason slices his fork through a slab of lasagna. "Son of a bitch," he whispers.

"I guess we're done, then," Matt says while pushing away his plate.

"We all put our best foot forward, that's for sure," Kyle agrees, turning up his hands. "Or our best smile-schemes, anyway."

"But can't Elsa see all the good here?" Now there's a desperation in Eva's voice. "See Sal and the memories of his last beautiful summer?"

"Which brings me to the *one* idea I have left." When all heads turn to Cliff, he simply shrugs. "But I don't know if it can work."

"Tell us!" Maris insists, pulling her chair in close. "Anything might do the trick."

Cliff watches Maris for a long second before talking. "How about if we get Celia here?"

"Yes!" Lauren jumps up out of her seat and punches the air. "She was so close to Elsa. I mean, she was going to marry her *son*!" Lauren hits Kyle's arm as she sits again. "My parents can't babysit late, but if you go home with the kids, I'll take a ride tonight and try to convince Celia to come."

"Lauren."

All eyes look to Jason, but especially Maris'. There's something in his low tone that catches her attention.

"Don't go," Jason says as he sets down his knife and leans back in his chair. "She'll never come back."

A few groans fill the room, and when Maris glances across the table, Kyle is slowly shaking his head.

"What'd you do to scare her off, bro?" Kyle asks.

It's slight, but Maris sees it, the way Jason raises his

eyebrows with some memory—most likely from the time Celia was drunk and slept it off on their sofa. And it confirms some niggling doubt Maris has had about that night. Something happened between those two, something that got Jason mad enough to, that's right, scare Celia off. Not long afterward, she left Stony Point—for good, apparently.

"Trust me on this one, Kyle." Jason pauses as he finishes his wine, then sets his goblet down again, obviously unwilling to elaborate at the table. "She won't come back no matter what anyone says."

"Unless," Maris asserts after an uncomfortable, quiet second.

"Unless what?" Jason looks at her beside him.

At the silent table shimmering with candlelight, she reaches over and touches his whiskered cheek, sees his tired eyes. "Unless it comes from you."

⁓

So on a Sunday night in October, Jason Barlow finds himself approaching a countryside yellow bungalow in the sleepy Connecticut town of Addison. He parks at the curb and looks over at the house. Cornstalks are tied to the lamppost, pumpkins sit on the stoop, and the windows glow with lamplight. As he gets out of his SUV and walks past a picket fence, he notices the neighboring white farmhouse. What gets his attention is a wedding gown hanging from a clothesline, the lacy fabric blowing in the shadows like a wavering ghost.

He keeps walking, though, and opens the latch on the picket-fence gate, continuing across the lawn until he slowly takes the porch steps. The problem is that he's still uncertain if showing up here, unannounced, is right. The last time he saw Celia was after a night when they both crossed a sexual line with each other; when he told her there's nothing for her at Stony Point. With regret, he recalls his words:

You don't belong here, Celia … Take your guitar and go home … I don't want to see you at Stony Point ever again.

Now he rubs his knuckles across his scarred jaw and simply stops doubting himself. "Knock on the damn door already," he whispers. So he gives three sharp raps at the bungalow's door, then steps back.

Moments later, Celia opens that door. She seems shocked at seeing him and holds the door partially closed. "Jason?" she asks. "What are you doing here?"

"Celia." He steps closer to talk, and glimpses a caution in her eyes. Caution and a sadness still. Her auburn hair is in a loose ponytail, and she wears a cuffed denim shirt over black skinny jeans, with a checkered scarf looped around her neck. He clears his throat. "I'm here to let bygones be bygones. And to just about beg a favor from you."

The front door inches open a bit more. "What's wrong?" Celia asks.

Jason takes an uneasy breath, looks away, then back at Celia—who is still standing partially behind the door. "It's Elsa," he says.

"Oh my God, Jason." Celia sweeps the door open to a lantern-illuminated foyer with dark hardwood floors and a spindle-back bench set against a gold wall. "Please! Please come in."

thirteen

WHO KNEW THERE'D BE A sequel? The melodrama of her life, captured in her once-imagined film, *Celia's Summer Romance*, was enough. If her summer's love story should ever be told in movie format, Celia figures the closing credits ran a few weeks ago when she packed Sal's mementoes into a trinket box and placed it on a closet shelf. She had left beach living behind and resumed a quiet, staid life in her yellow bungalow in countryside Addison, Connecticut.

But here she is, pulling that same box off the shelf for, well, for what might be a new reel in her life—a new imagined film called ... *Beckoning Celia*. She drops the flowered box on her bed and digs out two items: her pale yellow sailor's knot bracelet and the sea-glass engagement ring from Sal. When she slips the platinum band on her finger, its diamond-edged blue stone blurs beneath tears as she twists it straight. The ring is loose, as though she's lost some weight in her weeks back home. But it's as beautiful as ever, filled with such sweet love.

As soon as Jason left an hour ago, Celia's father helped her pack some things into her car: a suitcase, an overnight bag, a few clothes on hangers and her guitar. Now, wearing the ring and bracelet, she's ready to leave. To drive back to Stony Point and visit with Elsa.

But she can't leave without that trinket box. Everything in it—from the pieces of sea glass wrapped in a silky scarf, to the summer photographs, to the ice-cream stand's menu, to the dried hydrangea blossom—was intended to fill her very first happiness jar. And maybe it all still will, if she makes a jar with Elsa. So she grabs up the flowered box, hugs her father goodbye and begins her trip seaside.

Backing out of the driveway, Celia slams on her brakes. Something's missing. She runs to the trunk, digs into her trinket box and finds just what is needed for this particular beach trip—her seashell wind chime. Over the summer, Elsa found two identical wind chimes in the old Foley's cottage, and Sal had brought one to Celia.

In the darkness now, she returns to the driver's seat. There, she hangs the strung tiny white shells from the rearview mirror and flicks her finger over the shells to get them clinking. That gentle sound alone reminds her of moments with Sal, especially the night he hung this wind chime in her cottage window, and the beach breeze brought it to life—the shells jingling and swaying. *Serenata le stelle*, he told her as he waltzed Celia across the room to the shell's music. Serenading the stars.

So as soon as she's on the road, Celia rolls down her window to let in the breeze and be serenaded by the clicking shells as she drives beneath those same stars. The miles pass quickly on the dark roads until at last, Celia exits the highway and does it automatically—breathes in deeply, seeking her first wisp of salt air. *A ring, a baby, or a broken heart*, Lauren had told her months ago, sitting on a cottage stoop on a hot summer day. *Anyone leaving Stony Point takes one of those three things with them*. Which Celia did, one sad morning a few weeks back, leaving with a ring *and* a broken heart.

Maybe somehow, with this visit, she can start healing her heart, and Elsa's too.

After the forty-five minute drive, Celia finally sees the stone railroad trestle up ahead, leading to a world unto itself. Can't she just imagine this as the opening scene in her movie sequel? A new film crew would have bright lights on set, illuminating the stone trestle to guide her in. As soon as her car headlights round the bend in the beach road, a director's assistant would step into view, raising a clapperboard indicating that this sequel—*Beckoning Celia*—is about to begin. Yes, *Scene: "Hello," Take: One* would announce the night-shoot as the clapsticks snap together and the cameras roll on the grand, arched trestle, panning to the dark, damp tunnel beneath it as she takes the gradual curve into Stony Point.

Oh, the camera dolly would follow behind her car for a bit, filming Celia maneuvering the winding, sandy roads toward Elsa's place. Many of the cottages are closed up and dark for the approaching winter season, but plenty are year-round, too. At those, potted mums replace potted geraniums; scarecrows replace garden whirligigs; pumpkins replace watering cans. And the windows still glow behind lace curtains.

All this would be captured on the film, setting the scene for Celia's return. She presses the gas pedal and speeds along the narrow roads, the beach bungalows and coastal colonials blurring now until finally she stops at Elsa's cottage.

And ... Action! the director would order on this hopeful autumn evening.

So when her car is barely turned off, Celia runs through the darkness to the cottage door. She knocks loudly, pauses and bounces in place, then opens the door and steps inside, calling out, "Elsa?"

The TV is on, its volume low. Elsa's been watching while dozing beneath a light blanket on the sofa. Falling asleep like this at night, it helps to have the television background voices keeping the cottage from being absolutely quiet. Because it's the quiet that bothers her the most. Especially after a summer of hearing Sal rattling about in these big, drafty rooms, with the paned windows open, letting birdsong and her jingling wind chime serenade those warm days. Occasionally, in the TV dramas lulling her, she hears inflections of Sal talking up his business plan, or asking her what she's cooking, or mentioning hanging out with Jason, or Kyle at the diner. Television, mixed with sleep, brings back peaceful moments.

Like now, as she drifts off and hears voices calling her. Is it Celia? They must be back from their ice-cream date. Elsa sits up, pats down her sleep-mussed hair and decides to put on a pot of decaf for Sal, just the way he likes it, with no caffeine to bother his heart.

She tosses off her blanket, and it isn't until she's half standing that the realization hits her, again, that Sal is dead. Every time, the sadness is renewed. So she sits and tugs her robe tight, thinking it all a dream.

But when her name is called again, Elsa stands once more. "Maris? Is that you?"

"Elsa?" Then clipping footsteps down the dark hallway. "It's *me*!"

Elsa turns to see Celia standing in the living room doorway, casual in black jeans, a corduroy blazer and thick scarf, wisps of auburn hair escaping her low ponytail. She holds a suitcase in one hand, her guitar case in the other. Both of which she promptly drops before rushing to Elsa and sweeping her up in an embrace that melts Elsa's heart. How she's missed her dear friend!

"I am *so* happy to be here," Celia says into her ear as she pats Elsa's back and strokes her hair. "And to see you!" she says, pulling away and wiping a tear from Elsa's face. They both laugh when Elsa wipes one from hers, too, before tucking a strand of windblown hair back over Celia's ear.

"But I'm in my pajamas!" Elsa frets. "If I'd known you were coming, I'd be dressed."

"You're dressed fine, since let's face it ... our pajama talks were the best talks!"

"Celia." Elsa can only smile. "You *are* like a dream come true. Literally! Because I was sleeping, and ..." She motions to the sofa, then looks again at Celia standing there. "How I've missed you."

"Oh, Elsa." Celia takes her hands. "Why didn't you say so? I was giving you space."

Elsa hugs her again. "Doesn't matter now. You're here! Can I make up a room for you? A bed?"

"Of course. I'll help."

"After a bite to eat." Elsa leads her into the kitchen. "It's so nice to have someone here in the house. Maris sleeps over sometimes, but ..." She stops and looks back at Celia. "Why *are* you here?"

Celia shrugs, still smiling. "Foliage? Yes. *Yes*, to do some New England leaf peeping."

"At this hour?"

"Okay." Celia walks past her to the kitchen and gets a bottle of wine from the counter. "Okay, then. Since there are no secrets at Stony Point, I'll tell you." She sets the wine and two glasses on the kitchen table. "The thing is, everybody's worried about you, Elsa. Jason came to my doorstep, just a few hours ago."

"Jason?" Elsa asks over her shoulder as she pulls biscotti from the cabinet. When Celia doesn't answer, Elsa notices her crossing the kitchen.

"Elsa! Your pots!"

"My what?"

"Your pretty little herb pots."

"Oh, yes." Elsa sits at the table and sets biscotti out on a plate.

"But they're all dead!" Celia whips around, hands on hips, and glares at Elsa.

Which gets Elsa to do it; to finally—*finally*—speak aloud her sad, silent thoughts. She looks from the withering plants to Celia. "Who was I going to sprinkle basil for? Those little herbs became just a reminder ... of all I used to have. People and family and love and commotion." Elsa glances through her tears at the cottage kitchen: at the dull teakettle and pans on the stovetop, the sad herb pots, the dusty windowsill, the soft bananas and bruised apples in a bowl. "Oh, I guess I let everything go. I let everything go in my life."

⁓

After Elsa insisted she change into her flannel pajamas and fluffy slippers, Celia walks into the dimly lit back room and straight into a memory. Seeing Elsa sitting in one of the

The Beach Inn

booths, pouring their wine and setting out napkins for the biscotti, brings her back to summer nights in this grand old cottage.

"Remember our fun little pajama parties in this room?" Elsa asks as if reading Celia's mind. A small lamp glows at the table, and Elsa raises her wineglass in a toast.

"Do I ever. Painting our nails, gossiping. And always with soft background music." Celia walks over to the jukebox and plugs it in. As the lights blink on and the silver trim glimmers, she swipes her hand over the glass dome. "Gosh, it's getting dusty." After grabbing a napkin to wipe the glass, she makes a record selection, setting the volume low, then sits in the booth.

"I thought you had to go back to your old life, Celia." As Elsa says this, she slides the plate of biscotti across the table.

"That's exactly right," Celia admits while dunking one of the biscotti into her wine. "And do you know what I discovered? It *was* old. Staging a few houses, being home in Addison again." She looks out the sliding window beside them. The window's metal frame is corroded, but the misty view is as enchanted as ever, facing the distant beach. "Don't get me wrong," Celia explains. "It was nice enough. And my father is staying at my house for now, so I had company. But," she says, pausing to take in this cherished musty room with its jukebox and pinball machine and mini-fridge and secondhand restaurant booths, "it's not like here with that sea breeze, and the cottage lights on the porches. And the summer memories," she whispers, nodding to the jukebox as it plays a slow melody. "I remember dancing with Sal to that song."

Elsa smiles sadly at her, then nudges the window open a bit. "How Sal loved that air! *Aria di mare*, he called it. Sea air. Cures what ails you?"

Celia's not so sure as she bites a hunk of her biscotti. From what she sees of the cottage, the salt air hasn't worked its wonders on the place, nor on Elsa. Both seem sad, and shadowed, somehow. "I have to tell you," Celia says around the mouthful of biscotti, "I was shocked, *shocked*, to learn the inn is for sale. I had no idea."

"I don't know if you'll understand, Celia," Elsa explains while tightening her robe. "But it would be too painful for me to go on with my dream of a beach inn. Not without Sal as my partner. There would be so many ways I'd miss him and it would bring only sadness."

Lifting her slippered feet to the booth seat and sitting sideways, Celia leans against the window. The salt air wafting in feels nice, and in the brief silences, she swears she can hear the waves splashing far off on the beach. "Sal would *never* want you to sell this place," she finally tells Elsa.

"And Sal's not here anymore, is he?"

"But I am." As she says it, Celia reaches over and squeezes Elsa's hand in the scarcely illuminated room where dust particles swirl like stardust in the light of the jukebox. Together in their pajamas, the two women sit like that—hands clasped—both tired at day's end. Celia knows that Elsa's sister, June, used to do the same thing. Squeezing Elsa's hand was June's special way of telling Elsa that she loved her. So Celia hopes beyond hope that Elsa gets the same message now, sitting in this tattered booth, a tacky table between them, but the salt air as sweet as ever. "*I'm* here, Elsa."

Elsa raises her other hand and clasps it over Celia's. "Let's just not talk about all that tonight," she whispers.

Celia gives a small smile as she slightly nods. Meanwhile, a scratchy record plays a song about moonlight, and magic, and summer nights. Outside the window, the sky over the sea is dark, the air cool. She imagines that when Elsa is alone here at night, the darkness must press close against this big, shingled cottage. And in the swaying dune grasses and breaking distant waves, it would be easy to turn your head at the whispering sounds that rise, to press back a window curtain and see happier times.

To want only, on some of those sad nights, to leave Stony Point behind.

fourteen

For the first time in two weeks, Maris had set her alarm clock so that Monday morning, she's up at the crack of dawn. Now that she has a reason, it's easy to resume her old morning routine of a fashion designer heading into the city. The only difference today is the destination. So she takes a quick shower, then—quietly, so as not to wake Jason—puts on a pair of boyfriend-style jeans, a turtleneck sweater, black blazer, star necklace and, lastly, ballet flats. With no time to waste, she slinks downstairs, plucks a doughnut from the box on the kitchen counter, pours coffee into her travel thermos and kibble into the dog bowl before jotting a note for Jason.

Finally! She hikes up a tote filled with papers and heads outside through the kitchen slider. On the deck, she stops. Out past the bluff, dawn's pastel sky turns the horizon orange. Maris watches that seaside sunrise for a long moment and takes a deep breath of the misty morning air, ready to begin.

Because for the first time in two weeks, she's also off to work.

The Beach Inn

Ever since Kyle changed the diner name back to Dockside Diner, it feels like his ship has come in. Heck, the diner itself even *looks* like a big ship again. With anchors and buoys returned to the décor, and those starfish and seashells dotting the fishing net draped along the wall, nautical is nouveau. Polishing up the old lanterns in the diner windows helped, too, because when they're illuminated at night, the silver diner truly looks like a ship out at sea.

And now ... this. In his Eastfield home, Kyle lies in bed, studying the screen on his cell phone. He squints at it, scrolling through the details. Is this too good to be true? Can *two* ships come in at once? Or will this jinx things? He read in a magazine that a second good fortune often is a jinx, coming at the expense of the first.

"Ell, wake up." He nudges Lauren's shoulder. "Wake up! This could be it."

"Kyle?" Lauren pulls the sheet to her chin. "I'm sleeping."

"No, wait." He can't stop scrolling through the details on his phone. "A new listing came up yesterday at Stony Point. Listen, and I quote. Four bedrooms, one downstairs." He manages to tear his gaze off the phone and glance over at his wife. "That could be for your art studio, no? And the house even has a water view."

"Forget it, then," Lauren mumbles through her dozing. "Taxes on a water view will kill us. We can't afford water view."

"No, you're wrong. Because the taxes are really low." He squints and brings the phone closer to his face. "I wonder why. Maybe it needs some work." He whispers the compelling real estate listing, more to himself than to Lauren: *A sand pail of potential! This diamond in the rough could be the crown jewel of Stony Point's Back Bay.*

"Well?" Lauren asks, still drowsy beside him. "Anything interesting?"

"It also has a room above the garage. And hey, get this. It's an *in-law* apartment with its own kitchenette. Everything we could possibly want."

"Later. Go back to sleep, Kyle."

"Sleep?" He flips off the comforter and steps into his slippers. "I'm on my way to work. And I don't want to lose this one."

"Let me see the pictures." Lauren extends her open hand.

"Says it's too new for photos."

"Oh, convenient. A little bait and switch going on there?"

"I don't think so." Kyle, worrying now, absentmindedly scratches his bare chest. "I'll call Jerry. He can cover for me at work and we'll look at the house."

"No way." Lauren sits right up and presses back her sleep-mussed hair. "You're swamped on Mondays. But I'm going to Elsa's cottage to see Celia. So I can do a drive-by and check it out."

"Perfect," Kyle says from his dresser, where he's jotting down the address on a piece of scrap paper. After folding it into Lauren's hand, he kisses her fingers. A little optimism to start the day is nice. Nice enough for Kyle to actually whistle a happy tune on his way to the shower.

~

As dawn breaks on Monday, lightening the bedroom window, Celia remembers Elsa's words from last night: *You're like a dream come true.* If only, she thinks now, beneath the blanket in bed. If only dreams could come true. Because the last time she slept, and dreamt sweet dreams, beneath this pale blue quilt edged in a seashell scallop, Sal was alive. Alive and sleeping down the hall. Opening his drowsy eyes and taking a breath, whispering as he often did, *La dolce aria salata.*

Oh, yes. The sweet salt air. Celia inhales it, thinking that if she could drift off to sleep for a little bit more this Monday morning, she'd dream Sal was down the hall again, here in his mother's cottage. Maybe on his way to sneaking into her room and pressing a kiss on her lips.

But one thing she's learned over the past few weeks is this: Dreams only make her sadder. Because they don't come true. No matter how long she sleeps, or how hard she prays, her hopeful dreams vaporize with the morning mist each day.

So instead, she sits up in the bed and lifts a happiness jar from her nightstand. It's the same one that was there in the summer, the Mason jar filled with sand and tiny seashells. A note beside it instructs guests to fill the jar with happy souvenirs from their stay at the Ocean Star Inn. It was a practice jar that Elsa and Celia made together; a dry run in preparation for the inn's grand opening, one day soon.

Seeing that note, and thinking of all the plans she and Elsa made for this beach inn, well, it gets Celia mad that it all came to a screeching halt. Which is why she's here—to change that. To breathe life back into this big, drafty, half-converted cottage.

To start, she jumps out of bed, puts a robe over her flannel pajamas, presses out any wrinkles in the pretty blue bedspread, takes a shower and tiptoes downstairs to the kitchen.

Something's different, and Jason knows right away what it is. Usually when he's about to get up in the morning, Maris reaches her arm around him and whispers in a drowsy voice, *Stay.* But as he shifts in bed today, nothing. So he glances over his shoulder at the empty mattress, then sits up and reaches for his forearm crutches leaning against the bedside chair.

"Maris?" he asks as he slips on the crutches and stands. When there's no answer, he goes into the bathroom and looks at his reflection in the porthole mirror there. Lately, his own face has become a shaving gauge. If his skin shows through the whiskers, that's reason enough to go another day without shaving. So he presses his hand across his cheek, wincing at the slight sting, still, from Micelli's bruise above the jaw. From the look of things, he can skip the razor today.

Instead he gets right to setting his prosthesis and pants outside the tub, pulling the left pant leg over the artificial limb in preparation. Finally he adjusts his shower chair and takes a hot shower, then puts on the prosthetic leg, dresses and goes downstairs. Maddy's tail thumps the floor, where she lies stretched out in the early morning sun shining in through the slider. He gives her head a rub and sees that the coffeepot is already on, so he pours a cup and reads the note Maris left on the counter beside his empty mug.

Jason, I'm off to work. Love you.

"Work?" he asks, setting the paper down. Well, this is new. He steps around the dog and looks across the backyard to the barn. The stained glass wave window in Maris' loft is illuminated, so she *must* be working again, which surprises him. She hasn't so much as mentioned denim design in the past two weeks, never mind actually lifting a pencil and doing it again.

Grabbing his sweatshirt from the chair back, Jason goes out

through the slider, stopping on the deck to sip his coffee. The chilly October morning is quiet; even the birds haven't started up yet. A breeze blows off the distant sea, and he takes a step in that direction, listening to the leaves rustle in the big maple tree behind the house. Their whispering sound draws him; it's a sound he's craved these past weeks, hoping to hear Neil's words in the hiss and murmur of leaves and creaking tree limbs. To feel his brother's spirit in the places he'd loved.

Jason sips his coffee for another minute, silent beside the distant sea. When he hears nothing, he goes to the barn and finds Maris bent over her worktable, lost in thought in her loft studio. Behind her, bolts of denim still line one wall; mannequins stand in varying poses behind her desk; sunlight streams through the breaking-wave stained glass window he'd given her for a wedding gift.

"What's this?" Jason asks. He stops in front of a vision board. It's covered with fashion sketches of friends in varying seaside scenes: on the boardwalk, walking the tide line, sitting on a cottage deck. "You're designing again?" he asks, turning to the papers covering her worktable. "A new line of your own, maybe?"

"No! No, Jason." Maris gives him a quick smile, looking from him to the papers. "They're actually sketches of Neil's characters. I illustrate them to keep track of their traits."

"What? What do you mean?"

"Okay, don't be mad." She sets down her pencil and turns fully to him. "I've been reading ahead, in Neil's novel. And Jason?" She steps closer, dropping her voice to a whisper. "Neil didn't finish the book."

There's a look on her face that Jason recognizes. He's seen it before, the way those dark brown eyes glaze over with excitement—whether she's ripping denim, spattering paint on fabric, or pulling together their beach wedding. Her enthusiasm shows in her eyes. "So what exactly are you saying?" he asks.

"I'm saying," she begins, pausing to take off her black blazer and drape it over her desk chair, "that I don't need to read my self-help books anymore. I *know* what I want to do." Her hand motions to the vision board, then to the manuscript pages spread on her worktable. "I want to finish writing Neil's novel."

⁓

For the first time in a month, Elsa sleeps in. She pulls the covers up, turns her alarm clock away, closes her eyes and lets herself drift ... the same way Sal would on that little rowboat of his. Something about the comfort of having someone else in the cottage lulls her this Monday. By midmorning, the scent of cooking food rises to her room, where she's just gotten dressed. First comes the aroma of warming butter, followed by a bread-like smell. Then there's the clatter of pots and pans on the stove downstairs. Standing in front of her dresser while tying her hair back in a paisley bandana, Elsa turns toward her open door. This is what it would've been like to have a daughter-in-law, if Celia had married Sal. They'd planned on it, after all, before he died. Her son and Celia agreed on a quiet justice-of-the-peace ceremony after his surgery.

And though the marriage never happened, something feels right about Celia being here at Stony Point.

Suddenly everything changes, though. The food aroma shifts to an acrid, burning smell, and it's strong enough to get Elsa rushing downstairs to investigate.

"Celia?" she calls from the stairs.

fifteen

WHEN ELSA TURNS INTO THE kitchen, Celia is lifting a watering can to the mini red herb pots on the windowsill. It's obvious she's valiantly trying to resuscitate the oregano, basil and sage there. All while wisps of smoke rise from a griddle on the stove. Elsa rushes to the pan and moves it off the flame.

"Celia!" she says, eyeing the charred food. "What are you making?"

"Pancakes. Blueberry pancakes. Plus I've been busy tending your plants." Celia, holding the dripping watering can, walks to the still-smoking stove. "Oh. I must not have been paying attention."

Grabbing a starfish-print oven mitt, Elsa lifts the griddle and dumps the singed pancakes into the trash can. While cleaning off the pan, she says, "We'll pour in your batter and make more."

Celia hovers, following Elsa back to the stove. There, Celia reaches around her and slides over a bowl. "But look. My pancake batter is kind of lumpy."

"Don't worry, dear. Lumpy's normal." Elsa scoops out a ladleful. "They'll dissolve while cooking, and just need a little love." Carefully, she pours the batter onto the warmed pan. "A gentle touch." She adds more batter until the griddle is sizzling with round pancakes.

"Now when do you flip them?" Celia asks, still hovering as she sets down the watering can.

"Wait till the bottoms are golden brown." Elsa lifts a pancake's edge. "With an unexpected situation like burnt pancakes, you have to think on your toes and keep the food cooking so the recipe prep doesn't go to waste."

"Good point. Especially if you have hungry inn guests waiting."

Okay, that does it. So the gang's already gotten to Celia; already jaded her. Elsa looks over her shoulder. Celia stands there wearing a gray pullover sweater on top of a pale blue blouse—the wide blouse cuffs folded back over the sweater sleeves—all with her black skinny jeans. What can't be missed is the wide-eyed, innocent expression—a little over the top, but there nonetheless.

"Oh, I see what you're doing." Elsa checks a simmering pancake, then glares at Celia again. "You're in on it, too."

"In on what?"

"On trying to get me involved with *inn* things, to sway me to not sell this place. I'll bet you spoiled all this food," she says while waving her arm to the burnt pancakes in the trash, "on purpose."

"Maybe?"

But it's her weak smile that gives away Celia's guilt. That and the way she sidles closer to Elsa cooking at the stove.

"It's just that, well," Celia continues, "I looked in your cupboard and you have *not* been eating right." With that, she lifts a wooden spoon and gives the bowled pancake batter a swirl.

THE BEACH INN

Elsa snatches the spoon. "Don't overmix. And we can't let this go to waste." She rushes to the refrigerator for more blueberries, which she folds into the half-cooked pancakes on the stove. "It's why I'd planned to keep the inn small, with only a few guest rooms. So it's manageable. Because you have to cook quickly. Guests don't want slow food. They won't come back then."

When Celia does not answer, Elsa looks over from her busy cooking, spatula in hand. Celia has folded her arms in front of her as she leans against the countertop, legs crossed, hazel eyes twinkling. "Won't come back?" she asks.

"Tsk, tsk. I told you yesterday," Elsa reminds her as she flips the pancakes, a little too abruptly. The scent of warmed blueberries fills the kitchen now. "I didn't want to talk about the inn's future."

"But it's not yesterday anymore. It's today."

"You people don't let up on me. Don't you understand?" Elsa lifts the edges of the pancakes and scoops them off the pan. "An inn would be too much without Sal here."

Celia still eyes her, still leans on the counter, arms still crossed. "But *I'm* here."

"Celia." Elsa taps the empty spatula on the bowl edge. "Sal was going to help me run the inn."

"*We'll* run it together. You and me." As she says this, Celia carries the plate of steaming pancakes to the table set for two. "We're strong women."

After setting the griddle on a cool back burner, Elsa slams down her starfish-print oven mitts. "You're just saying that!"

"No, I'm not."

"Yes, you are. You wouldn't have even come back here if Jason hadn't asked you to."

"But I never knew the inn was for sale. Nobody told me, and if I'd known, I'd have been here, *pronto*. I thought you needed quiet time to grieve before starting up with the inn. Maybe take six months, or a year." Her voice drops to a whisper. "I was giving you space."

Elsa fills a dishpan with soapy water and looks out her window as the tap runs. Outside, her seashell wind chime blows in a sea breeze, but she can't hear the clink and clatter because the window is closed. "All I *have* is space," she tells Celia while shutting off the running water. She turns toward the kitchen table nicely set with tall glasses, and with white, vine-edged cottage dishes left behind when she bought this place last year. Her tear-filled eyes glance around the room, to the hallway and beyond. "All these empty rooms, rooms, rooms. Rooms mocking me with shadows and sad memories, every single night."

"I'm sad, too, Elsa." Celia pulls out a chair and sits at the table. "So you're being a little selfish."

"Selfish?"

"Yes. Thinking only of yourself. You're not thinking of your nieces, of the people who love you. Not thinking of me. So, yes. Yes, you're being selfish."

"Now that's a first." Elsa drops the griddle and cooking utensils into the soapy water. "No one's ever called me selfish, I don't think, in my entire life!"

"I'm sorry, but that's the way I feel." Celia gets the orange juice from the fridge and fills two glasses at the table before sitting again.

"And you've got a lot of nerve, coming here and talking to me that way." There's no mistaking that Elsa's blood pressure is rising. Her heart pounds as she grabs a towel and dries her soapy hands. "You don't understand what I'm feeling!"

The room goes quiet. But Celia doesn't look away. She continues to watch Elsa dry her hands, and set maple syrup on the table, and open that darn kitchen window a bit. Do anything, anything to distract her from Celia's stare. But finally, with the strung seashells clattering outside the now-open window, Elsa sits across from Celia. Celia, whose eyes are brimming with tears.

In the silence, Elsa puts a napkin on her lap and picks up a fork.

When Celia talks, her voice is low, but unmistakably serious. "*I* don't understand? Why don't you just sign that damn offer on your cottage, then? Sign it and be done with it. Get rid of this place. Put an end to everyone worrying about what you'll do. If you'll stay in Connecticut. If you'll open the inn. If you'll run away to Italy!" She scrapes back her chair, slaps her own napkin on the table and stomps up the stairs.

Celia's every footfall, on every single step, practically shakes the rafters. As Elsa lifts a pancake onto her plate, and adds a tab of butter, then pours on the syrup, the banging upstairs doesn't stop. It sounds like closet doors slamming, and dresser drawers opening and closing. Elsa can only assume that Celia is packing her bags to leave. The thing is, the thought surprisingly breaks her heart, so much so that Elsa can't eat. Instead, she brings her plate to the trash can and dumps in her just-prepared pancakes.

Well. Fine, then. If Celia wants to get huffy and storm off, so be it. It won't be the first time Elsa's alone, and certainly won't be the last. She slides her dish into the soapy dishpan and begins washing the breakfast mess: mixing bowls coated with egg and flour; the griddle; utensils and spatulas. After cleaning each piece, she clatters the utensil or dish onto the dish rack.

Suddenly the thudding gets louder as Celia hurries down the stairs again. "Before you sign the realty's contract," Celia insists as she drops something heavy on the table behind Elsa, "you *look* at this. It's Sal's business plan that he worked *so* hard on."

Without turning, Elsa holds two wooden mixing spoons in the stream of tap water, her back to Celia.

"*Look at it!*" Celia insists again.

So Elsa does. She sets down the spoons, wipes off her dripping hands and first faces Celia. The sight she sees surprises her, though. She hadn't expected Celia's face to be wet with tears and shadowed with sadness. But of course it is. Though Celia didn't lose a son, she lost the very love of her life. And it's clear that now? Now she's going to fight for him.

"Sal's heart and soul are in those pages. Yes, his *soul*." Celia pushes an oversized brown leather portfolio in Elsa's direction. The leather is inscribed with Sal's monogram. Celia reaches across the table, unzips the portfolio and pulls out a thick, paper-stuffed folder. "You want to sign this beautiful old cottage over to Mackenzie and Lucas? Fine. Then give them *this*, too!" She nudges the mammoth folder closer. "See what *they* do with Salvatore's inn vision."

"Who do you think you are," Elsa says, stepping closer while still drying her hands with a towel, "telling me how to run my life when I lost my son!"

"I was almost your daughter-in-law." Celia merely shakes her head while tears flow freely. "Until *I* lost my fiancé!"

"*Basta!*" Elsa throws aside the towel. "Enough!"

A tapping noise gets them both turning at the same second. Lauren, in a cable-knit brown poncho, cuffed jeans and fringed ankle boots, stands in the kitchen doorway. She tentatively knocks on the doorframe.

"Celia?" she asks, her own eyes tearing up. "Hey! You two are fighting?"

Celia, seeming frozen in place, merely opens her arms as Lauren runs over and hugs first her, then scoops Elsa into the embrace and hugs them both together.

⁓

"*Gesù, Santa Maria*," Kyle whispers when he turns the pickup's ignition and the engine grinds. "Salvatore, man. Where are you when I need you?" He hops out of the truck and looks under the hood, hoping the battery doesn't need a jump. The oil dipstick checks out fine, and so do the fluid levels. So like Sal often did over the summer, Kyle tinkers with a few wires, gets back in the driver's seat and when he turns the ignition again, the engine purrs to life.

Okay. If there's one thing Kyle's learned, it's to not always tempt fate. So before the engine has a chance to stall, he guns it, screeching out of the diner parking lot and heading to Stony Point on a quick lunch break. Traffic moves along, and he breezes through green lights, hitting the horn only once when stuck behind someone poking while talking on their cell phone.

Finally, he turns in beneath the notorious railroad trestle, drives the narrow, winding beach streets and arrives on Bayside Road. Eva and Lauren are there already, inside and touring the rooms. That buys him a minute to check out the house as he parks, trots across the lawn and stands at the front door, where he listens through the screen before going inside.

"Oh, Eva. Kyle will love this. I called him when I was at Elsa's this morning. He's on his way now."

"You were at Elsa's? Was Celia with her?"

"Absolutely."

"Good, so she made it there last night."

"She did. But from what I saw? *Not* so good. We need another emergency Meet and Eat!"

"Again? What happened?"

"The two of them were arguing when I walked in, because it seems like Elsa's on the verge of selling to ... Lucas and Mackenzie?"

"No!"

"I think so. Celia does, too. We have to stop Elsa from signing that contract."

"Okay, another Meet and Eat, then. But Matt's bringing Tay to her student council meeting later. So how about a ladies-only edition?"

"As long as it's tonight. It has to be tonight or we'll be too late."

"I'll arrange something, don't you worry. Texting Celia and Maris preliminary messages right now."

Which is precisely when Kyle raps at the storm door. Both women spin around and what he first sees is enough. Yes, he knows by the way Lauren's gray eyes instantly illuminate—she loves the place.

"What took you so long, Kyle? I already toured the house with Eva. Twice!" Lauren hurries over, opens the door and grabs his hand. She tugs him through the living room, pointing out the picture window to the sight of the bay across the street. "And Kyle? You were right. *This is it!*"

"Wait." Suddenly Kyle feels winded, and he's not sure if it's from rushing here, or from the three words Lauren just said. *This is it.* When he drops into an overstuffed club chair, he realizes he's still wearing his chef apron from the diner. "We have to think about this, Ell."

"Kyle. Look at me." Lauren crouches in front of him. Her blonde hair is down, and she wears a poncho over her cuffed skinny jeans. "Look me in the eye. This. Is. It."

All Kyle can do is exhale. Had he really been holding his breath? He needs to fill his lungs again. "Eva," he says, turning in the chair and then quickly standing and lifting off his apron. "Is there an outdoor shower here?"

Eva drags her finger down the property's spec sheet. "As a matter of fact, yes! Why?"

"I need to splash some water on my face," he mutters.

"Honey? You look like you're going to faint." Lauren touches his damp forehead and brushes her fingers across his hair. "Relax. This isn't like ... childbirth."

"No," Kyle answers her as he pats his face with the apron he still clutches, then hurries through the kitchen toward where there *must* be a back door. "But it is life changing!"

"Kyle," Lauren yells from the living room. "What did I tell you? Just put your arms over your head."

"Guys! Guys!" Eva out-shouts them. "Calm down." She runs in the kitchen, too, and fills a glass of water at the sink. "Shh," she says, handing Kyle the glass. "Now listen, I'll wait outside so you two can take a walk-through and talk things over. Calmly," she adds while patting Kyle's arm before heading out to a rear deck.

After Kyle quaffs half the water and dabs his face again, he sets down the apron and turns around. Lauren stands in the kitchen doorway and reaches for him. "Come on," she says with a smile. "You'll *love* it. Especially upstairs," she insists while tugging him up the wide staircase.

Okay, so here's a change. Without twisting his shoulders or ducking his head, his entire six-foot-two frame easily maneuvers the staircase. Which he likes, so he lets Lauren pull him along, then nudge him into the *en-suite* bathroom, which isn't half bad.

"Would you look at the shower?" she says from behind him. "It's perfect."

Again, she nudges him, so he crosses the nicely tiled bathroom and opens the shower door.

"Try it," Lauren encourages him. "You'll fit in this one. Fit fine."

So he does, stepping into the extra wide and tall shower stall, where the shower spigot is actually mounted higher than his head.

"I think this is really it!" Lauren says with a grin that won't quit.

Kyle, still quiet, steps out of the shower, but leans back in and turns on the shower nozzle. He cups his hands beneath the spray, then splashes the cool water on his overheating face and neck.

"The house needs a few projects, but it still has potential," Lauren is saying as she grabs a towel for him to press onto his dripping face. "Maybe Jason can help on the weekends. And look," she adds while rushing back downstairs, "you have to see all this natural light from the windows."

"I don't know." Kyle slowly descends the stairs and notices the brilliant sunshine glinting off the blue bay. "This seems really rash."

"Rash?" Lauren spins around. "We've been house-hunting

all summer. *Now* you're getting cold feet?"

He is, which is funny—especially after believing that a year-round home at Stony Point was what he truly wanted. But now? He walks into the kitchen again and surveys the room. It has a vinyl floor, an old portable dishwasher and needs new countertops. Heck, it's a total gut.

"No," Lauren says, pulling him out of that room. "The kitchen is the worst room, so don't judge the whole house by it. The others are better, Kyle. Just keep an open mind, remember? And anyway, you told me that kitchens recover seventy percent of their remodel money in a resale, so a kitchen redo is an investment. Not to mention that you don't like *any* kitchen we see. It always has to be gourmet, for you."

"I have to sit down."

"Come look at the view instead." Lauren pulls him to the front window again. "See? Back Bay is across the street. I know it's not the main beach. But it's quieter, an inlet—almost like the lagoon. You can get a remote-control sailboat for Evan and sail it together. And look. Look at the porch." She finagles a loose doorknob and opens an old glass-paned door. The porch has hardwood floors and painted beadboard walls. A few pieces of wicker furniture face Back Bay's distant beach. "It's a nice place to sit, and to entertain, Kyle. And can't you see Hailey playing with her plastic farm animals on the sill, while looking out at the water? And ... and we can hang little white lights around the porch windows at Christmastime. No, *all* the time." Lauren paces the porch and snaps a cell-phone picture or two. "We can even prop starfish in the paned windows, like Elsa does at the inn."

Kyle heads back inside to the kitchen, where he holds a paper towel beneath the faucet, then presses the damp towel to his forehead.

"This could really be it!" Lauren insists while chasing after him.

"Are you sure?" Kyle lowers the cool paper towel over his eyes.

"Yes. And listen, Jason's just a few streets away."

"I might have to sleep on it."

"Really? But it even has an in-law apartment above the garage!" Lauren lifts the towel off his eyes. "Now that we found *thee* perfect place—at a good price, with low taxes and big rooms—you're bailing?"

"Maybe if we use that check Sal left us. It's a big chunk of change." Kyle pulls out his cell phone and clicks to the calculator to crunch the numbers. "It could help with the mortgage."

"No way, Kyle. That money is safely put away for your new truck and you're not touching it. It was Sal's wish, and we're buying a truck *after* we settle on a house."

Kyle glances up at Lauren before tapping at the calculator again. "I just want to review our options."

"We did! We saw every option available, all summer." Looking dejected, Lauren returns to the living room and drops into the club chair. "You have to at least admit that this house is nice, right?" she asks over her shoulder.

"Well ..." Kyle stops his calculations, crosses the living room and turns his head. "Wait. Do you hear something?" he asks while tucking his phone back into his pocket. But he keeps walking out onto the front porch, where he opens one of the windows to better decipher, precisely, that low, rumbling sound.

Lauren follows behind him, placing a hand on his back as they stand side by side, both frozen, heads tipped, listening. "What *is* that noise?" she whispers.

sixteen

KYLE BRADFORD'S LIFE HAS BEEN a series of trade-offs. Once he left the potential house on Bayside Road and drove back to work, he realized this about himself. And for the rest of the day, like a song stuck in his head, he can't stop dwelling on it. His life's been one trade-off after another: In his twenties, he'd work on lucrative union shipbuilding jobs, then get a pink slip. Later, he ultimately got the girl—Lauren—and married her, but lost his friend, Neil, in the process. When Lauren gave birth to their first-born son, Kyle would, years later, discover that it wasn't his child, but Neil's. His luck really changed, though, two summers ago when Kyle bought the original Dockside Diner. Until he changed the name, updated the menu and décor there, and the numbers slid.

And now this.

"It was a God damn train," he tells Jason, who is sitting at the diner counter that evening, after hours. Outside, the street lamps come on in the parking lot, and across the road, strung lights twinkle along the distant harbor dock. Kyle just locked the diner doors and now sets down a plate loaded with the Monday special: Mega Meatloaf. Two slabs of meatloaf, mashed potatoes and green beans. Thick curls of nicely browned onion cover the gravy-drenched meatloaf, a gravy also drizzled over the potatoes.

"Seriously?" Jason asks while picking up his fork. "Was it a cargo train? They can be really noisy."

"No, passenger. The train tracks are practically in the backyard. Do you know the street?" Kyle asks. "Take a left after the trestle, down on the bay? Probably the farthest road from Stony Point's main beach, too. Shit," he gripes while lifting the edge of his apron and wiping his forehead. "*Another* effin' trade-off."

"But you can get a golf cart to trek back and forth," Jason says around a mouthful of food.

"Maybe."

"I know the street. Seems nice enough, Kyle. I took on a new job there." Jason scoops up beans and potato together, his loaded fork pausing midair. "Real peaceful spot."

"It's the last house in the turnaround, on a small hill. With amazing water views." Kyle pours himself a cup of decaf, then one for Jason. "There's a path to the water through the dune grass across the street. And yeah, it's quiet." While leaning on the counter behind him, Kyle sips his steaming coffee and thinks of that train. "Sometimes."

"If it makes you feel any better, like I said, a family on that same street hired me for their reno. So they're investing in their cottage, apparently not bothered by the train."

Kyle pulls a fudge-frosted brownie from the countertop pastry case and takes a bite. "The house is exactly, I mean, *exactly* what we were looking for." Another bite of the brownie buys him contemplating time. "We'll see. Remember our motto, no rash decisions?"

"Sure."

"Good. Because I'm taking another poll, to be certain buying this house wouldn't be a rash decision. Give it a drive-by, would you? Have a look." After pressing the last of the brownie into his mouth, he gives Jason a slip of paper from his apron pocket. "That's the address, with two boxes next to it: buy it, or skip it. Check one and leave it outside the diner. I duct-taped a cardboard box to one of the patio table umbrellas, so you all can drop off your votes anonymously."

Jason looks from the paper, up to Kyle standing behind the counter. "Why can't we just tell you? Why do all this box shit?"

"Because, dude. Remember my other motto ... about friends? If you tell me to my face, you'll all lie and say the house is perfect." Kyle tips up his coffee cup. "It's not, and I know it's not. But I still have to make a decision, even though Lauren would buy it today if she could."

"If the house makes her happy, no poll necessary." Jason tucks his slip of paper into his wallet. "Happy wife, happy life?"

"Speaking of wives, yours letting you go scruff again?" Kyle leans forward and swipes Jason's jaw with the back of his hand. "How long's it been since you've had a decent shave?"

"I don't know." Jason slathers gravy on a torn half of his buttered roll. "Since the gala a few nights ago?"

Kyle eyes Jason's faded concert tee beneath his thermal sweatshirt. "And you went to work looking like that today?"

Jason glances down at his ratty tee and touches the fabric. "No, I knocked off early and stopped home to change."

"Into that?"

"Yeah, why?"

"Maris doesn't get on you? Keep you looking spiffy now that she's home all the time?"

"She's pretty busy, actually."

"Doing what?" Kyle picks up a messy newspaper a customer left behind on the counter. He drops it in the trash, then steps sideways to check that his cook Rob shut off the kitchen lights before he left. "She get a job?"

"Not really. She's been putting something together in the loft. We found an old manuscript of Neil's."

"A manuscript? Like, a book?"

"You bet."

"No shit. Where?"

"When Micelli came, he took me to a shack Neil fixed up back in the day. A one-room fisherman shack. Out past Little Beach. Apparently Sal and Celia came upon it in that rowboat and did some exploring. They realized it had all my brother's stuff in it. You know ... journals, scrapbooks, camping gear. And the manuscript."

"For real?" Kyle walks around the counter to the locked diner doors and flips the OPEN sign to CLOSED before grabbing a stool beside Jason. "A manuscript? That's friggin' amazing," Kyle says, to which Jason nods, then drags his last hunk of buttered roll through gravy drippings on his plate. "I always thought Neil might be the one to write the next Great American Novel. What's the story about?"

"It's a big saga, actually, about a group of beach friends trapped in a cottage during a hurricane."

"Wow." Kyle punches Jason's shoulder. "A book, bro."

"The thing is," Jason continues while slicing off another piece of meatloaf with his fork, "it's not finished. So Maris is thinking of taking it on."

"Of *writing* it?"

"She's always been a storyteller, Kyle, with her denim

designs. The way she explained it this morning, she's woven and stitched stories into *all* her fashion campaigns. Every season's sketches told a story of sorts." Jason holds up his fork while chewing. "So she's trying to parlay that into writing. To finishing Neil's book."

"Think she can get it published?"

"She's got a few connections in the city, but we're not planning that far ahead. She's just toying with the idea for now. But she can't seem to keep her hands off that manuscript. I was late to work today, listening to her plotting ideas."

"Hell, if she publishes it, I'll clear a space on the shelf and sell them here, too." Kyle swivels his stool and motions to Lauren's driftwood display. "Hey. You going back to that shack?"

"I've got some plans for it, but it's plenty tricky to get to, especially with my leg. Tides have to be high, and you have to do some wading, which isn't easy with the waters being choppy now." Using a knife, Jason pushes the last of his potatoes onto his fork, then snaps his fingers for a brownie from the domed pastry case. "Maybe someday."

Several dripping pillar candles flicker in the center of Eva's round, antique table for the ladies-only Meet and Eat. Four gray placemats are covered with dishes and silverware, anchored by crystal wineglasses. Outside the paned window at the cushioned window seat, the sun sets beyond the golden marsh, and Maris notices an egret taking flight into the twilight. Its white wings slowly beat the misty air. Oh, how Maris relishes evenings like these: dining in Eva's candlelit kitchen, after discovering only two years ago they were sisters. Sitting at this table with Eva never gets old, and that their beach friends join them? Even better.

"Psst, ladies! I have a Stony Point secret, and you can't tell anyone ... yet." Maris eyes the three women with her in Eva's kitchen, all chatty except for Celia, who is a little quiet tonight. "The secret stays at this table."

"Ooh, a secret. Spill it!" Lauren says, pulling her chair in close.

"*Promise* not to tell?" Maris squints at her with suspicion.

"Wait." Eva sets down a platter of her specialty breaded chicken cutlets beside the lit candles, then drops into a chair beside Celia. "Group pinkie swear?"

So they do, all four reaching an arm across the mahogany pedestal table and hooking fingers. In the glow of candlelight, with a whisper of a sea breeze coming in through the slightly open window, Maris meets each of their eyes. She can't help but notice how Celia looks briefly away, then at her again. Whether something ever happened between Celia and Jason a month ago, it's hard to tell. But if this is to work—Maris' beach life here with Jason, and writing a novel to redefine herself—she has to let that worry go. If something went down that one drunken night, she'll chalk it up to a desperate moment of grief between those two.

Apparently Celia will, too. At least Maris thinks so when Celia tightens her pinkie-hold on Maris' and gives her a tentative, but warm, smile. Then, and only then, does Maris reveal her secret plan to finish Neil's weathered manuscript that she and Jason had found.

"The pages are sandy, and warped from years of dampness. He apparently typed the whole thing on an old typewriter, one with those big, round, clicking keys. Some of the ink's fading on the manuscript pages, but it's fascinating to read."

"Neil wrote a *novel?*" Celia asks, tucking her auburn hair behind an ear.

"He did." Maris glances from Celia to the others. "It's about beach friends, like he was writing about *us*," she explains. "And everyone ends up unexpectedly trapped in a big cottage during a hurricane on the Connecticut shore. The friends get together, hook up," she adds with a wink, "and when the hurricane finally passes, there's a change. But here's the thing: Neil didn't finish it."

"And you will?" Eva asks.

"I'm going to try, anyway."

"Have you written before?" Celia asks.

"No, but so much about fashion design is storytelling. And I've been doing *that* for years."

"I remember Neil working on that book," Lauren whispers.

Maris, Eva and Celia silently turn to face her.

In a quiet moment, Lauren nods. Before continuing, she glances back through the doorway into the living room, where Eva's husband, Matt, and daughter, Taylor, are having their dinner on trays in front of the television. So Lauren brings her finger to her pursed lips, the seashell charms on her bracelet jingling as she does. "You found the manuscript at the shack?" she asks.

"Yes!" Maris sits back, amazed. "How did you know?"

"Oh, I get it," Eva murmurs.

"Shh. That's right. Neil and I went to that shack all the time the summer he died ... almost ten years ago now." Lauren explains. "It was a hideaway for us. I painted there, and Neil wrote most, if not all, of that manuscript at a wooden table by the little paned window—its glass coated with sea spray. He'd light a hurricane lantern and type away at, yes, an old manual typewriter. It was black, with silver keys. Between the sound of those keys clacking, and the breaking waves …" With a long breath, she briefly closes her eyes. "Those were sweet times."

"But why didn't you ever say anything about it?" Maris asks. "Even to Jason? I mean, that shack's filled, top to bottom, with his brother's things."

A sad smile fills Lauren's face at the same time her eyes fill with tears. "After the awful strain between Neil and Kyle, right before Neil died? I couldn't. When I went back to Kyle, I had to let go of all my history with Neil. My marriage wouldn't have survived otherwise." She clasps Maris' hand. "It was a terrible situation that broke my heart. I hope you're not mad, but I had to leave Neil completely behind."

"Lauren." Celia leans her elbows on the table. "Sal took me to the shack a few times. It's a very special place."

"What?" Eva asks. "You've been there, too?"

Celia shrugs. "Sal was utterly fascinated with it. It's like a secret world out there."

"Nearly *impossible* to find, though," Maris adds. "You have to wait for the high tide, and then follow that overgrown, hidden path through the dune grasses."

"This calls for a drink," Eva says, retrieving a bottle from her wine fridge and filling four glasses. "It's kind of sad, Lauren, how you could never share those memories with anyone."

"Wow," Maris agrees. "That couldn't have been easy."

"It's just the way it was," Lauren tells them. "And Lord knows, life isn't always easy." She raises her wineglass and they join her in a silent toast. "So Maris, if you ever need something clarified with Neil's writing, or have any questions, you ask me. I used to read passages he'd written, and we'd talk about them."

"Are you sure?" Because Maris isn't too sure. The last thing she wants to do is drive a wedge into Lauren and Kyle's now-healthy marriage.

"I'm sure." Lauren nods. "But privately, okay?"

"I'll keep it in mind. And remember. This is all confidential, until I know if I can pull off this writing gig. In the meantime, it's simply my secret job. Imagine?" Maris forks a chicken cutlet and drops it on her plate. "Writing a novel."

"Seems like I've got a new job, too," Celia admits. "Convincing Elsa to stay put. She's a tough cookie, once her mind is made up."

"How long will you actually be at Stony Point, Cee?" Eva asks from the stove, where she scoops steaming rice into a bowl and brings it to the table.

"At least until your aunt makes a final decision. Which I'll do my best to sway in the right direction."

Lauren leans over and uncovers the green bean casserole she'd brought to tonight's Meet and Eat. "Elsa was so distraught when I walked in on you two this morning."

"She was." Celia takes a heaping spoonful of the cheesy rice. "But I must say, I *love* the idea of Operation Make Elsa Smile that you told me about. It seems like you all made lots of breakthroughs with her."

"We did," Maris agrees, sprinkling sea salt on her chicken. "But not enough."

"Nothing's sticking," Eva says as she takes her seat again. She drops a ladleful of soupy beans and onions on her dish.

Celia drags a piece of chicken through her rice. "We talked

a lot today, Elsa and I. About Sal, and the inn's potential. She did eventually calm down and agreed to *look* at Sal's business plan, at the very least. So she was a tiny bit receptive."

"It seems like she's *afraid* to change her mind now," Maris muses. "Aunt Elsa was so set on selling, I think she came to accept *that* life. One with no inn and no emotional ties to Stony Point."

"Exactly." Celia sips her wine. "So what I'm about to share is actually good news, considering. And it's that Elsa finally compromised, and is taking this week to only think about things. She swore not to sign off on *any* offer until then."

"Oh, yes!" Lauren says.

"Hooray for that. How'd you pull it off?" Eva asks.

"Huh. It was like ... pulling *teeth*." Celia lifts a forkful of green beans. "I was pretty upset with her and I think she agreed only to placate me. So we've got to put our heads together tonight and come up with something to convince her to keep that rambling cottage, for good."

Again, Lauren raises her wineglass to the others. "We're four whip-smart women. What've you all got?"

After a moment's silence—a silence filled with only scraping forks and clinking glasses and the drone of the TV from the living room—Eva pipes in. "We've tried so many things already."

If Maris isn't mistaken, there's defeat in her sister's voice. *And* in her eyes behind her blonde-streaked auburn side bangs. So Maris tries to buoy them all. "Well, Jason did convince Cliff to woo Elsa. Not that Cliff needed convincing. He's smitten with her, a changed beach commissioner, that's for sure."

"He's so blinded by his love," Eva says, "he doesn't even notice when we break an ordinance. So, cheers to Cliff's wooing."

"*Wooing?* That's so cute!" Celia tips her glass to Eva's. "Is it working?"

"According to Jason," Maris continues while reaching for the green bean casserole dish, "Cliff's still at it. So everything's moving in the right direction, but not fast enough."

"Okay, then. Come on, let's do this!" Eva punches the air. "Shoot out ideas like a cannon. Blast them at me!" She sits back and looks at each of them sitting around the table. "Lauren? You're first, girlfriend. Give me anything. Go."

Lauren looks panicked while thinking quickly. "I can finish the inn sign. *Ocean Star Inn.* I'll get it painted and hammer it in front of her place?"

After a no-vote, Celia puts a suggestion on the table. "I know!" she says around a mouthful of food. She holds up a hand while chewing. "How about getting Elsa a kitten? My neighbor's little girl, Grace, has one. It really helped her through some difficult times."

"No," Maris says, nixing the cat. "Elsa already dog-sits Maddy, and that hasn't worked."

"We're simply running out of ideas," Eva admits. "And we *have* to get those smiles!"

"Hmm. Smiles?" Celia asks. "What about happiness jars? That was going to be the theme of her inn. Every guest would receive one to fill up. Mason jars with a little bit of sand and tiny shells would be scattered throughout the rooms, with slips of paper instructing visitors to fill a jar with happy mementoes of their stay."

"Okaay ... Go on," Lauren says, dragging her fork through what's left of her cheesy rice.

"I'll buy Mason jars, lots of them," Celia begins. "New ones, vintage ones. And I'll put them everywhere!" She pauses with a sip of wine. "Elsa can help me decorate some with sand and beach trinkets and tea-light candles. They always make her smile."

"Because they remind her of her sister, June," Eva says.

"Our mother," Maris adds, pointing to Eva and herself.

"Right," Eva continues, "and Aunt Elsa always thinks of that night they caught twinkling fireflies in Mason jars on the lagoon. With you, too, Maris, when you were only two!"

"June ... June." Maris has a feeling that won't fade. "I think I have an idea. It's starting to come together." She stands, excited that this could be it. So she walks to Eva's kitchen window seat and gazes out at the view, where the setting sun casts a glow on swaying, golden marsh grasses. Maris can easily visualize a young Elsa and June one late-summer evening so many years ago, that week June rented a cottage here at Stony Point. Tonight, Eva's twinkling white deck lights become the glimmering fireflies. And the wavering evening shadows? Elsa and June, catching fireflies in jars, their arms outstretched, faces tipped up to the stars, hopeful.

Maris looks over to the ladies at the table. "Let me mull this over and get back to you all."

"Okay," Lauren agrees while patting her napkin on her mouth. "And while you do your thinking, I seriously need to ask a favor of you guys. Take a ride down Bayside Road?"

"What's on Bayside Road?" Celia asks.

"Only my *dream* house!" As Lauren tells them about the cottage Eva showed her this morning, she pulls paper scraps out of her tote on the counter. "These are Kyle's custom-made ballots, which some of you are familiar with. You each get one," she says, handing them out. "And you'll see there are two boxes on it: buy it, or skip it. You look at the house and make your own choice about what we should do, anonymously. Then give your ballots to me. I'll put them in his special box at the diner and he can tally the votes."

"This sounds like fun," Celia tells Lauren. "I can't wait to see it!"

"I know. We'll take my golf cart," Eva says, bringing her dish to the counter. "Bundle up, gals, and we'll clean this later."

But as the others bring their dishes to the sink; as Maris snuffs the candles; as they put on sweaters and corduroy blazers and ponchos and scarves; as Eva speeds her packed golf cart down the dusty beach roads, passing a few illuminated shingled cottages looking straight out of a storybook; while Celia tells Lauren that maybe Lauren will be the next to have a golf cart—Maris cannot get one certain, perfect thought out of her mind.

Yes, this is it. She *knows* it as her hand rises to the inscribed gold star pendant from her once long-lost aunt. With the star clasped in her fingers, the golf cart hurries along and her hair blows in the wind. All while she knows it, yes. Knows it without a doubt.

This one idea will be the absolute grand finale of Operation Make Elsa Smile.

seventeen

CHAMPION ROAD RUNS BEHIND THE beach, bordered by sea grass and small sand dunes on one side, weathered cottages on the other. It's a quiet, dead-end street that leads to the edge of the lagoon—one of Jason Barlow's favorite Stony Point haunts.

So before his Tuesday morning gets into full swing, he leashes Maddy for a sunrise walk along that sandy street. Because if he walks among the October marsh grasses swaying in the lagoon as the salt water flows through its tributaries and curves, might he hear a whisper of Neil's voice? Hear anything?

Instead, there is nothing: no wind setting the grasses to motion, no birdsong, not a sound. So from the lagoon, he cuts over to the far end of the beach near his Friday night fishing spot on the rocks and heads home that way, walking the driftline.

Never expecting to have company this early in the morning. But carrying a plastic pail, Cliff Raines walks ahead of him, nearly bent in half while scouring the sand.

"Commissioner, what are you doing? The sand violating an ordinance?" Jason asks just as Maddy runs ahead to greet Cliff.

The Beach Inn

Tail wagging, she nudges his hand with her muzzle. The thing is, Cliff was so focused on scanning the shore, he hadn't even noticed them and jumps at the sound of Jason's voice.

"I could ask you the same thing," Cliff tells him as he checks his watch, then scratches the dog's head. "What are *you* doing here on a Tuesday morning? No work today?"

Jason walks closer, noticing that there's not even a breeze skimming off the water. The air is as still as a mid-July day, the sky as pale blue. Early sunlight sparkles like ocean stars on the tiny ripples of the Sound. "I set my own schedule. And as a matter of fact," Jason tells him, "my entire fall *was* booked until a certain inn renovation hit the skids." As he says it, his cell phone rings. He checks it, then returns it to his sweatshirt pocket. "What's in the pail?" he asks Cliff.

"What?" Cliff raises the sand pail, glances in it, then lowers it again. "Nothing. None of your business."

"Let me see." Jason extends his hand, then quickly whistles for his dog to turn back as she lopes across the beach with her nose to the sand.

"Fine." Cliff holds out the pail and tips it in Jason's direction.

"What's in it?" Jason asks again, raising his sunglasses to the top of his head and squinting at the pail.

"Sea stones. I've got a plan for Elsa." He gives the pail a little shake, rattling the pebbles in it. "But a man does not reveal all his secrets."

Jason takes the pail and brushes his fingers through the smooth, salt-coated stones. "I hear Elsa put off her inn decision for one week. No more, no less. From what Maris says, that was Celia's doing." While still holding the plastic pail, he studies Cliff then. His fleece jacket is unzipped in the warm sunshine, his black button-down beneath it needing an ironing. The commissioner could use a shave and haircut, too, if he's going to effectively woo Jason's aunt-through-marriage. "So I'm thinking, Cliff," Jason continues, glancing at the sea pebbles as he hands back the pail, "that maybe those aren't the stones you need. It's time to light a fire in the romance department, dude. And maybe *gem*stones would do the trick."

"Are you kidding me?" Cliff snatches the pail. "First you tell me to woo Elsa, and now you're suggesting I *propose*?"

"Just saying," Jason answers with a shrug. "Because listen, man. I saw your digs in that trailer. I mean, a futon? Behind a room divider? Let's face it, you don't have a home, and she's in that big cottage … all alone." He hits Cliff's shoulder. "Might want to do some grooming for the lady, too. You're looking a little rough around the edges."

"Me?" Cliff asks, backing up and giving Jason's just-past-collar-length dark hair a once-over.

When Jason's phone rings again, he answers. "Maris, okay, okay. I'm on my way back," he says, giving Cliff a wave and messing the beach commissioner's needs-a-trim silvery hair while moving past him. "What? You're breaking up on the beach," he tells Maris as he follows the winding line of seaweed on the sand. When the phone goes dead, he gives it a shake. "Damn it," he whispers, then shoves the phone in his pocket. Ahead of him, a piece of driftwood has washed ashore, so he picks it up and tosses it for the dog. And Jason knows. She'll carry that stick all the way home so they'll have another to add to her toppling bucket of driftwood.

With the sun rising higher now, he follows behind as the German shepherd—stick clamped in her mouth—walks through small waves lapping along the beach. Each wave breaks with a gentle hiss. On the hill at the far end, rough framing has begun on the structure replacing old Maggie Woods' hovel. It's nice to see the new timber rising from the foundation.

When another wave hisses across the sand, Jason stops walking. Instead, he picks up a stone and joggles it before throwing. After watching it skip across the Sound's ripples, he gathers a few more stones. Each one, he gives a side-handed throw, flinging the sea pebbles low so that they brush over the small waves. He knows that to anyone watching, he's leisurely skimming stones.

Anyone except Maris, who is patiently waiting for him with some news at home. But she'd know what he's really doing here. That he's listening for a whisper in the wind, or in the hiss of the waves. She'd hope he hears one, too.

Though he doesn't.

Three skimmed stones, three minutes of silence.

So Jason shoves his hands in his pockets and walks the packed sand above the driftline, nearly to the footpath leading to the street now. Wagging her tail, Maddy catches up, driftwood still in tow. He leashes her and leads her to Sea View Road, then toward his home on the bluff there. Giving only one look back toward the waves before turning off the footpath.

When Jason turns into his driveway and follows it to the deck around back, leaves and twigs snap beneath his step. A few more weeks, and all the maple leaves will be down, swirling and blowing in autumn's stiff winds. He slows when Maddy drops the driftwood, then pats her back when she retrieves it and returns to his side.

"Let's go now," he tells the dog as they round the corner to the yard. "I'm running late."

"Hey, hon!" Maris calls. She stands on the deck, waving an envelope. "Jason! This was in yesterday's mail. Didn't you see it? It's from that guy."

Jason approaches his deck. "What guy?" he asks. As he does, he unclips Maddy's leash and the dog flies up the stone stairs and circles Maris.

"Trent!" Maris opens the slider screen and lets Maddy go inside. "The guy from the gala, remember? From CT-TV?" she asks over her shoulder.

"Come on." Jason stops on the top step of the deck. "We'll open it on the bench."

"I already opened it." Maris gives him a smile and a soft kiss on his lips. "It's really good news. Read it!" Her hand holds out the envelope.

"Whatever it is, Maris, I'm really not interested. I'm too busy to get involved in any scheme he's got going on."

"Oh, just read it." Her arm remains outstretched, and she gives the envelope a shake. "Okay, fine," she says when he waves it off. "I'll read it *to* you." She sits at the deck table and pulls the letter from the envelope.

The letter is brief. Jason, arms crossed, leans against the deck railing as Maris reads the words aloud. There can't be more than two paragraphs, something about meeting in person to discuss things further and cover all the details. Details about Jason filming a pilot episode for a potential TV show, one finding old Connecticut cottages and restoring them for modern seaside living. With his esteemed reputation as a coastal architect, along with his recent award, Jason's custom-made for the part. He would do much of the architectural design before contractors took over. At which point, as the show's host, Jason would walk the viewer through the entire project, from demo to reno.

"*I'm under a time crunch with this,*" Maris reads, "*and need to talk to you and gauge your interest, right away.*" She glances at Jason, her eyes sparkling with excitement, then finishes reading. "*The network is already sold on the concept, so there are things I can do to sweeten the pot for you, if it helps. I'd really appreciate a call, Jason.*"

"Maris," Jason says, walking to the patio table and taking the letter from her. "I'm not into all that. I told him that night at the gala, TV's not my gig."

"But it *could* be. It's what you *do*, cottage restorations. And this would only be a pilot episode. You can decide after that. Can't you just call Trent and listen to what he has to say?"

Something about that idea, about listening, annoys Jason. It's all he's been doing: listening to Elsa's sorry excuses to sell the inn; listening to Maris' hopeful plans to write the rest of Neil's novel; listening to Kyle fret about a house.

Listening, listening for a month now for any whisper of Neil's voice in the beach breeze.

Jason sets the CT-TV letter on the table and pulls his keys from his pocket as his cell phone rings. A quick glance at the caller ID and he sees his contractors are up and at it already, as soon as the sun's risen. "I'm done here, Maris. I was just dropping off the dog so I can take off," he tells her while turning toward the deck stairs. "My duffel's already loaded in the truck for an appointment over at Sea Spray, the new project there."

"But Jason," Maris says, standing.

So he stops two stairs down, turns around and walks back to her. "Listen, sweetheart," he says, smiling and shaking his head as he tucks her brown hair behind an ear. "I'm late," he whispers before kissing her, then turning to leave.

∼

Maris picks up the letterhead and reads the message from Trent again as she sits at the patio table. She looks from the letter to the driveway when Jason backs out to go to work. Once he's gone, she hears only the breaking waves gently sloshing and hissing out on the bluff. The sound rises and she takes a long breath of the sweet salt air … the air that cures what ails you.

The thing is, she's been trying for weeks to cure whatever's ailing Jason's heart. Lately, he keeps himself so incredibly overbooked, it feels like he's *still* running—the same way he did the day of Sal's funeral, when Jason packed his bags and hightailed it away from Stony Point, from his grief, from his memories. He's back, but there's more than one way to run, after all.

Since then, Maris can't pin him down in his busy days. And when he rarely walks the beach at night now, he returns home agitated afterward. His sleep is fitful, too. It's how she knows he still can't connect, somehow, with Neil's spirit. No matter what she's done—dinners out, romantic candlelit dances beside the jukebox, quiet evening hours reading Neil's novel together—nothing works, and Maris is running out of ideas for her own Operation Heal Jason's Heart.

Now, watching his continued solitude as he resists Trent's offer, her own heart feels like it's breaking. She begins folding the letter into the CT-TV envelope.

Unless.

Quickly she opens the letter and reads it, yes, one more time.

Unless ...

This might be her last shot at healing her husband's heart. Because in his lingering grief, he doesn't see the opportunity in Trent's offer. So she hurries inside and glances around her kitchen: at her stove with the busted timer; at her counter cluttered with unopened mail and keys and multiple device chargers juicing up tablets and phones; at the refrigerator that needs to be freshly stocked; into the dining room, to the still unpacked wedding gifts sitting alongside the baseboard.

Then she picks up her cell phone from the counter and carefully dials the number on the letter.

"Trent!" Maris says when he answers on the second ring. "Oh, I'm so glad I caught you."

⌒

"Beach blues," Celia says as she scrutinizes the living room wall in Elsa's cottage.

"What?" Elsa looks from Sal's cherished rowboat oars they'd just hung over the fireplace, to Celia.

"Beach blues." Celia steps forward and straightens one of the knotted sailor-rope loops they finagled as oar hangers. "Sal used to say he loved that he had the blues." She smiles back at Elsa. "Beach blues. Then he'd list different things ... like the wild hydrangeas in the dunes, or the blue water of Long Island Sound, or even his cuffed blue jeans." Celia touches her engagement ring. "Sea glass," she whispers before looking at the faded blue oars on the wall. The deep navy paint is weathered and streaked with age and wear from the salty sea. "I think he'd say those oars were also part of his beach blues."

Elsa eyes the oars, too. "They look magnificent there. And they really connect with the buoys we hung on the wall."

Celia agrees as she remembers buying the vintage, weathered buoys at the beginning of the summer, before she'd even met Sal. Four months ago, she was simply house-sitting her best friend's cottage while catching her breath after her divorce. At thirty-two, Celia planned to rethink her future, beside the sea. To find her own personal happiness again, strumming her guitar and searching for sea glass. To stay as far away from love as possible, thinking love would only lead to more heartache. But then, of course, she met her first Stony Point neighbor, Elsa. And the next thing Celia knew, like a breath of salt air, she was drawn into an unforgettable circle of friends—surprising herself as she, too, became a part of the beach crew.

With all that's happened, it feels more like four years ago, rather than only four months, when she and Elsa displayed the colorful buoys beside the fireplace to bring an essence of the sea indoors.

When Celia hears a click now, she turns to see Elsa raising her cell phone and taking a picture of the hung oars. "What are you doing?"

"I want a photograph," Elsa explains, then snaps another. "For when I move. So that I can set Sal's oars up the exact same way in some new place, wherever I land after all this."

"Don't you even think of that now, Elsa! Remember, you promised not to make any decisions for one full week."

Elsa starts to answer, but a loud, panicked rapping at the

cottage front door stops her. The door suddenly swings open and Maris runs inside.

"Aunt Elsa?" Maris calls.

"Maris, in here," Elsa answers, stepping into Maris' view.

"Oh, Elsa. I'm in such a pickle."

"What's wrong?" Celia and Elsa ask at the same time.

Because it's obvious from the look of fear on Maris' face that something is dreadfully amiss. Her hair is a mess, her shoes an old pair that she likely threw on last minute, her sweatshirt—wait, if Celia's not mistaken, it's so huge, it must be Jason's.

"Is Jason okay?" Elsa takes Maris' hands in hers.

"Yes. Yes, I think so. So far, anyway, until he hears what I did. It's why I need help."

"Anything." Elsa guides Maris to a wingback chair. "Tell us what's wrong, dear."

"I'm hosting a dinner tonight," Maris admits.

"*That's* the problem?" Elsa asks.

And Celia sees it, the twinkle in Elsa's eye as she sits on the sofa.

"Oh, yes," Maris groans. "Jason's going to be so mad. And my kitchen, well …"

"Wait. You're hosting a dinner? For who?" Celia asks. "Who'll be there?"

Maris looks at Celia, then at Elsa. She squints her eyes as she contemplates something. "It's a Stony Point secret," she whispers.

Celia quickly sits beside Elsa and leans close to Maris. "Which means you're about to spill it?"

"Oh, Jason's going to kill me." The torment is apparent in Maris' furrowed brow, and in the way she spins her wedding band. "But I *really* need your help because I'm not that great of a cook. And my stove is a little wonky these days. So can you help me out with the cooking?"

"How about this ... Butternut squash is in season, and I bought some from that new Maritime Market. Would a nice autumn dish work?" Elsa asks. "Because I can make butternut-squash-sausage stuffed shells. Then you just reheat them in the oven, easy peasy."

"No, no, Elsa. That's too fancy. The meal has to be really simple, a recipe Jason will believe that even *I* could make. Otherwise, he'll know I'm up to something."

"Which you are?" Celia asks with a wink.

Maris squints at them again. "Yes. Something wicked! And if you two cook a delicious, but *easy* meal for this dinner I scheduled," she says with a quick glance toward the windows, "I'll do it. Okay, I will. You cook, and I'll tell you *everything*."

eighteen

BEACHES ARE LIKE SNOWFLAKES, NEIL used to say. *No two are alike.* And that couldn't be more apparent than here at Sea Spray Beach. Though it's only twenty miles west of Stony Point, they're worlds apart in geography. Jason likes this about the Connecticut shore. Each beach trip is a unique journey.

At Stony Point, the wind is calmer, with the crescent-moon-shaped beach protected from the elements by a patch of forest at one end and rocky outcropping at the other. But at Sea Spray, the beach hugs a straightaway length of the coast where the waters run deep, with the waves strong and the wind sharp.

After meeting with his new client later that morning, Jason walks the ragged stretch of sand. Even the salt air is more pungent here. He takes a long breath and flips his jacket collar against a breeze kicking up. It lifts his hair, tossing strands as it whistles past.

As always, Jason slows his step and turns his head. Listening, but hearing nothing more than nature in the air and sea. His leg has been acting up today and feels a little stiff. So he keeps to the packed sand above the high tide line, the only spot he's found on this earth that always soothes any ache in his gait. At the same time, his resumed habit is nagging at him—enough to get him pulling a cigarette from his pocket and cupping his hand around the lighter to block the wind and light a quick smoke.

Walking at the water, he glances across the beach to the houses on the other side of tall dune grass, where a narrow, sandy street winds along. A stately cottage with navy board-and-batten siding catches his eye. Large windows in the cottage's loft addition overlook Long Island Sound. Beside that cottage is Ted Sullivan's place. A year ago, Ted's old shingled two-story was still in the redesign stage as Jason worked up the drawings and elevations. Now? Now that very cottage won him the distinction of Best Connecticut Coastal Architect. Ted's reno also led Jason down a difficult road, leading to their hard-earned friendship.

Slowly crossing the beach, Jason walks toward the dune grasses while finishing his cigarette. Finally cutting through to the street, he approaches Ted's cottage and rings the bell.

"Jason!" Ted says, opening the door wide. Even now, in October, his face is still tanned. He must spend many hours on his newly designed deck. From the deep wrinkles lining his face, Jason suspects Ted also might walk that ragged beach to work out his own lingering demons from time to time.

Jason extends his hand for a shake. "I'm drawing up plans for one of your neighbors. Thought I'd stop by."

"Always glad to see you! Come on in."

"How about we sit on that deck of yours, Ted? Feels good to be outdoors and getting some air."

"Absolutely." Ted hitches his head to the side of the house. "Walk around and meet me there. I'll grab a jacket."

Jason does. He pulls a chair away from the teak deck table and sets it near the railing, facing the sea. While sitting there and waiting for Ted, the sound of the surf carries from the beach. The wind here is roughing up the waves. *Pay attention to the wind,* his father used to say. *Especially if it's sudden; that's when it brings change.*

When the slider opens, Ted walks out wearing sunglasses and a jacket. He pulls up a chair beside Jason. "Terrific day, no?"

"Yeah, not bad," Jason says. "Hope I didn't interrupt your morning, stopping by unannounced like this."

"Not at all. Anytime," Ted tells him while settling in his chair.

"I want to thank you, Ted. For nominating me for the Coastal Architect award this past Friday night. I was totally honored to receive it."

"I saw that, and you're very welcome. No one deserves it more than you." The two of them are quiet for a second, until Ted asks, "Something on your mind today?"

"On my mind?"

Ted only nods.

Okay, so it's that obvious that Jason didn't stop by for merely a social visit. He reads Ted's silent nod, takes the cue and begins talking. "What's on my mind ..." A deep breath, then, as he orders it all first—there's actually that much. "I've got my wife working on a novel, for starters. And my wife's *aunt* is days away from making a final decision to sell her beach inn. In which case, I'd definitely lose a huge reno project I was counting on. There's an old fishing shack on the coast that I have to somehow secure for the winter before a storm takes it down. My leg's bothering me, you know, with phantom pain and whatnot. I can't seem to give up a recent smoking habit, my phone's ringing off the damn hook, *and* I don't hear my brother anymore."

"Wait. Your brother?" Ted asks. "Neil?"

Jason stands and walks to the deck railing, then turns to face Ted. "It might sound odd, I get that. But over the years since the accident, I've sensed Neil nearby. Or his spirit, at least." Jason glances out at the distant water. "I'd maybe remember snatches of words he once said as though he was saying them to me now. Or hear his voice in the wind. Maybe it was all wishful thinking, wishing he was still alive. But regardless, it happened."

"I'm sure it did. You were very close."

"But since Salvatore DeLuca died? Nothing."

"Sal?"

"I know. What's my cousin—through marriage, anyway—got to do with it, right? But it's like when Sal—who became like a second brother to me—died, he took Neil with him."

"Well, in that case," Ted says as he stands, "it's definitely not too early to mull this over with a beer."

By the time Ted returns with two cold ones, Jason wonders if he did the right thing coming here this morning. Will Ted think he's crazy, hearing voices in the wind and whispers in the waves? But Jason takes the beer and snaps the can open.

"And there's one more thing, Ted. Go figure this one. I also received a TV show offer from a connection I made at the gala."

"No kidding, mister. Congratulations!"

"No, no. Hold on. It's only for a pilot episode, but regardless, I'm not taking the offer." Jason sits back in his chair and sips the beer. "It's one of those before-and-after house do-over programs, this one involving *cottage* renovations. You know the type ... a little too formulaic for my tastes."

"Formulaic?" Ted holds up his beer can in a toast. "This one sounds like it's right up your alley, Jason. I can just see it, you telling folks all about these seaside cottages, and their history, and how you restore them. You're a natural. I'll never forget what you said when you took on my reno here."

"What's that?"

"Every cottage tells a story. Remember? It'd be something, having the chance to tell all those cottage stories with your own show."

Jason nods. "Thanks for your vote of confidence, but I'm busy enough with what I do. Because even though the TV offer is small scale, on a local basis, it would still cut into my work routine. And my life's fine right now, you know?" He takes a swallow of his beer. "So what would be the point, Ted?"

"Well, Jason." Ted walks to the deck railing now. He stands there, then looks back at Jason in his chair and motions for him to join him. When Jason stands at the railing, facing the sea across the beach, Ted pats his shoulder and continues. "What's the point of *all* the work you do?"

Jason can't help it, the way he closes his eyes with the question. Closes his eyes to fight back the surprising tears. Because Ted went and did it, didn't he? Said what Jason was too afraid to admit to himself, or to Maris. And especially to Trent at CT-TV. Said what scares the shit out of Jason.

The waves break along the beach, and Jason turns his head, listening. There's the rolling hiss of the water, and there's that wind here. It blows the dune grasses, which sway and whisper just across the narrow street. But nothing more. No inflections, no whispers, no nudges.

"What's the point of my work?" Jason finally asks, looking at Ted directly.

"That's right, my friend."

Jason shakes his head, briefly. He looks out at the water, then back at Ted. "Neil. My brother, Neil Barlow."

Neil, who wouldn't be with him on this television venture. Because Jason can't seem to find him in his solitude, in his work, or anywhere in his life, anymore.

nineteen

AFTER LEAVING TED'S, JASON'S TUESDAY seemed like it went on for a week. Which is why the very first thing he wants to do after dropping his work duffel on the kitchen counter at the end of the day is take off his prosthesis. Today, he seriously felt it. All day long. So he heads upstairs to change into more comfortable clothes and remove the prosthetic leg. His stump, or *moncone*—as Sal kindly referred to it in Italian—feels better already. Sometimes his crutches are a blessing.

Except for the way Madison nips at them when he comes down the stairs. Wearing his forearm crutches now, Jason warns her away as he maneuvers the steps. Because whatever Maris is cooking in the kitchen, the aroma's drawing him straight there. He walks through the living room, past the illuminated jukebox alcove, into the brightly lit kitchen, where she's got dishes and silverware stacked on the counter, ready to set out.

"Let's eat in the dining room, okay?" she asks while scooping up the plates and breezing into the other room.

In another second, the black lantern-chandelier comes on, casting a glow over the painted farm table there. Jason, as he brushes through the mail on the kitchen counter, hears Maris lighting candles, too.

"What's in the oven?" he asks while lifting envelopes. "Smells amazing."

"It's not in the oven, actually," Maris says from the dining room. "Not after my chicken fiasco the other night. I'm using the slow cooker. A nice pot roast is simmering, with carrots, potatoes and lots of brown gravy, just the way you like it."

"Can't wait, I'm starved." Jason heads into the dining room and sits at the table as Maris sets out their empty plates. It feels so good to be home, and quiet—just the two of them—with a hot meal cooking. Outside the window, it's already gotten dark with October's shorter days. But inside, beneath the chandelier, Maris arranged a centerpiece of candles and scattered fall gourds, all around a small white pumpkin. The candles flicker as she places his silverware on a folded linen napkin. "This is nice," he says, giving her hand a squeeze.

"I'm glad you like it."

After she leaves a light kiss on his cheek, Maris turns to the sideboard and lifts two amber-colored goblets, then sets them on the table. As she does, Jason notices how she's straightened up the house; even the unopened wedding gifts have been somewhat cleared. He leans his elbows on the table and glances around the dimly lit room. The partially gift-wrapped boxes are stacked further in the dining room corner, not as visible as they'd been.

"Are those new?" he asks when she puts crystal salt-and-pepper shakers on the table.

Maris nods. "A wedding gift. I opened a few things today." When she turns back to the sideboard, the doorbell rings, getting Madison growling and rushing to the door. "Oh,"

Maris says while setting out a third dish and silverware. "That would be Trent."

"What?"

She gives Jason a quick smile and promptly puts a third amber goblet on the table. "Trent. He's coming for dinner."

"Are you kidding me?"

"No." Maris skims her fingers back through Jason's hair, as though to neaten it. "I called him today."

"Son of a bitch," Jason whispers while reaching for his crutches, slipping the cuffs on his arms and standing. "I'm not ready. I need to get dressed." He glances at his threadbare flannel shirt over a tee, then at his worn jeans—the pair Maris cut and hemmed just below the knee to accommodate his missing left limb.

"You're fine, don't worry." As she says it, she gives him another easy smile.

"Maris." He feels a bead of perspiration run along his face—his face that hasn't been shaved in four days. "I'm on my crutches." He looks at them again. "I need to put my leg on for this."

"No. No, you actually don't." She turns to him and brushes a speck of dust from his shirt. "You only need to be *you*."

"Come on," he says while standing with his hands leaning into the crutches' handgrips. "Tell me you didn't do this."

"But I did. I jumped through *hoops* to get this dinner arranged." She glances into the kitchen at the slow cooker on the counter, then hurries past him. "And don't forget, you owe me."

"Owe you?" Jason follows behind her, aware of the dog still growling and sniffing at the closed front door. "Owe you for what?" he asks as Maris unties her half-apron and tosses it over a kitchen chair. Now Jason notices she wears skinny black pants with a soft camel sweater and black flats. Her hair is pulled back in a loose chignon, and gold hoops glimmer on her ears. She dressed for dinner.

Maris rushes out of the room, heading down the hall toward the front door. "You owe me for when you *left* me!" she tosses at him.

"For God's sake, that was for thirty minutes," he tosses back. Catching up to her, his stride is amplified with the thumping rhythm of his crutches—which only gets Maddy's attention off the door and on to nipping at them. "I left for thirty minutes! Forty, tops. And I came right back," Jason says, feeling winded as he stands behind Maris in the dark foyer. The doorbell chimes once more.

"You did," she says softly while flicking on the outside porch light, as well as a small foyer chandelier. Then, and only then, she turns around and touches his whiskered jaw. "But you came back different. Sadder. Lonelier." Her finger drags across his cheek. "And so ..." She gives him a big smile, her eyes instantly sparkling, then turns and pulls open the door to Trent standing there. "Hello!" she says, sweeping her arm to invite him inside.

~

One thing Cliff's glad about is that it's not too cold out. Light layers are enough to keep him warm: a long-sleeved white thermal beneath his blue plaid flannel, topped with a puffy vest over his khakis does the trick. He only wishes there was more illumination as he walks through shadows around Elsa's big cottage.

The Beach Inn

Only four months ago, folks were buzzing that the original Foley's store and hangout was mid-renovation—before the Stony Point Hammer Law stopped all construction in June. Residents and summer renters alike were scoping out the place and already haggling with a certain beloved innkeeper for next year's room availability. But instead of the hammers resuming after Labor Day, that very innkeeper—Elsa—went and cancelled the rest of the remodeling upon the death of her son. Scaffolding had been taken down; safety fencing rolled up; lumber removed; pallets of roof shingles lifted onto a flatbed; rocks for a stone wall loaded into a dump truck.

Still, some debris remains. Cliff just bumped into a forgotten stepladder leaning on the side of the house, near the chimney. And he occasionally steps on shingles that had been torn off the roof on an interim patch job. So he steps lightly while holding his pebble-filled plastic bucket and looking up at the windows. The problem is figuring out which one belongs to Elsa's bedroom. Downstairs, a kitchen nightlight is glowing, bright enough to illuminate some of the paned windows with thin white starfish propped on the framework. But most of the house is dark this evening.

Maybe she's reading in bed. He squints at the upstairs windows and, yes, deciphers a dim light behind the curtains. Maybe Elsa's reading one of those inn guidebooks Kyle anonymously left for her in a gift basket.

There's only one way to find out. Cliff's fingers skim the stones in the pail and pluck out a few. He steps back, positions himself at a good angle and tosses a stone upward. But it misses its mark and hits the shingles before ricocheting directly at him, making him quickly duck. No sense in quitting, though. So he steps a little further away and puts more zip in this toss, hitting his target with a loud plunk. Which he immediately follows with another toss, that stone zinging across the glass pane, too.

Bingo! Another light comes on. Elsa must be approaching the window, so he steps to within clear view. While waiting, he gives his sand pail a little shimmy, swishing the sea stones around.

Finally the window is raised and a woman's silhouette leans out, squinting into the night. "Commissioner Raines?"

"Oh, criminy," Cliff says with a double take as he sets down his sand pail. "Celia?" he asks in a loud whisper. "That's *your* room?"

"Yes. What are you doing down there?"

"Shh." Cliff glances over his shoulder to be sure no one's hearing them, then up at Celia again. "Looking for Elsa," he says, still in a loud whisper.

"Elsa? Why?"

Okay, so the evening wasn't supposed to play out like this, with explanations and wrong windows, and … oh, heck. He rolls his eyes and takes a deep breath. "Operation Make Elsa Smile?"

"Oooh." With a sly smile of her own, Celia leans her elbows on the sill. "I get it. But now? It's late."

"I'm wooing her."

"What?" Celia yells, craning her neck to better hear.

"Shh!" He steps closer and tilts his head up. "I'm wooing her. *Woo-ing*."

Celia, still smiling, waggles her finger at him. "You're off by two windows."

When Cliff steps aside, he trips on his sea-stone bucket, then looks at the dark paned windows to the left.

"Not there!" Celia whisper-yells. "Thataway!" She points in the opposite direction.

"Okay, thanks." He scoops the fallen stones back into his

tipped-over bucket, picks it up and walks off. When he looks over his shoulder, Celia is still leaning out, watching. And smiling, he can't miss that. "Goodnight!" he insists, waving her away and walking right past the noted window. Because, seriously, a man has to regroup, and prepare. This wooing thing takes a lot more stamina than people might think. So a deep breath or two behind closed eyes, then a loosening of his flannel collar—it all leads to the inevitable.

Cliff plucks a perfectly smooth stone from his bucket and gives an underhand toss. The stone plinks against Elsa's bedroom window and falls back to the yard. Then, nothing. So this time he doubles up, throwing overhanded, two stones in a row. *Bing, bing.*

Instantly, a light comes on. So he gives one more stone a toss, for good measure. Of course, it plinks the glass right as Elsa is lifting the sash. Her reading glasses are propped on top of her pillow-mussed hair. Honey-highlighted brown hair that cascades over her V-neck, fitted tunic pajama top.

"Clifton?" Elsa slips on her glasses, then perches them atop her head again. "Cliff, is that you?"

"Come down, Elsa. It's a beautiful night."

"Are you okay?" She tucks her hair behind an ear and eyes him closely. "A beautiful night for what?"

Cliff isn't sure he's ever met a more suspicious bunch. Questions, questions: multiple choice, short answers, fill in the blank. It's like he's always being tested here. "Damn it, woman," he yells, then looks around at a dark neighboring cottage. "It's a beautiful night ... to break some ordinances, okay? Now get dressed and let's go!"

After dinner, once Trent left, Maris worked her magic. Her words asking Jason to walk with her on the beach came with just the right softness; her touch on his arm, and his neck, soothed; her hands fitting his prosthetic leg onto his stump showed only gentleness; her fingers running across his shoulders brought the lightest caress as she helped him put on his black sweatshirt.

Now, as they step up onto the boardwalk in the dark of night, her body leans into him and she loops her arm through his. Feeling her against him, it's enough to give Jason the courage to look at the stars. Because no matter what he's felt recently, in this moment on the beach, his life is good.

"See?" Maris asks. "It wasn't so bad having dinner with Trent."

Jason doesn't answer. Instead, they slowly stroll the boardwalk toward the center pavilion, where they had their seaside wedding reception a year ago. He feels the grit of sand beneath his footsteps, feels the breeze lifting off the water. Finally he presses a kiss to the side of her head. "How can I stay mad at you?" he whispers into her hair while holding her head close.

They sit on the boardwalk bench, facing the beach. The dog is with them, and Jason keeps her on the leash so that she stays close. All the while, there's a rhythm to the small breaking waves rolling onto the sand, and it has a way of stopping time. It's a sea sound that Jason can call upon anywhere: in his home, on a job site, driving to Kyle's diner for a bite to eat. There's a comfort knowing that this one sound always plays on, no matter what, no matter where. He's heard the sound of waves enough to summon it anytime.

"I saw Ted earlier," Jason tells Maris.

"You did?"

"I was at Sea Spray, so I stopped by his place. We had a beer, bullshit a little." When Maris does nothing but squeeze his hand, he knows. She wants him to tell her everything. "He felt the same way you do."

"About what?"

"When I told him about the TV pilot, his first thought was that it was an incredible way to honor my brother. To use Neil's thoughts and ideas from his journals and scrapbooks and bring them to an entirely new level." Jason is still letting the scope of that sink in. "I'm not sure, though."

"But Trent said the network will give you free rein. You can do the pilot your way. And if you don't sign his preliminary contract, he already committed to a brainstorming session to convince you!" Her hand runs along his arm for a quiet second. "So *you* can decide the shape of the show, babe."

"Yeah." But something about it all scares him still. He can't shake that feeling. "Trent had an interesting premise. I like each project being segmented into three episodes."

"First, finding historical elements in the old cottage? You could even bring in Rick from the salvage yard, to assist."

"I could."

"I, personally, love that you'd be filmed actually drawing blueprints and referencing Neil's journals and scrapbooks. In your amazing barn workspace."

"Then comes the second part, meeting with the homeowner to review the new design before demo begins. And construction."

"And finally, the finished cottage, peppered with local Connecticut lore and glimpses of the beach area. Oh, it all sounds so fun, Jason." Maris gives him a quick kiss.

"I still have reservations, though. Because I'm not cut out for television." Jason stands and paces the boardwalk, the dog anxious beside him. "I don't run a huge operation. I keep Barlow Architecture small, under my control. It's really me and my outsourced contacts. Not to mention all Neil's ideas pulled from his handwritten notes and photos."

"Which is precisely what Trent likes about you. It's you and your brother. Kind of a team, still."

"And not meant for an audience. It feels personal, Maris."

Maris stands and takes Jason's hands in hers, leather leash and all as the dog sniffs the sea air beside them. "That's what people love—that heart. That honesty." She reaches up and touches Jason's tousled hair. "Maybe this new opportunity can help, hon. You still seem so sad," she whispers.

Jason shakes his head and takes a long breath. "Signing Trent's contract means I'd have to change. The network will want me to cut my hair, shave when I don't feel like it, wear appropriate clothes."

"No, no, no. Trent wants you just the way you are now. Didn't you hear him?"

"I heard him." Jason steps off the boardwalk onto the sand. He turns to face Maris. "But I don't believe him."

"Okay, well how about this?" She sits again on the boardwalk bench. "We'll make a list, together, to put in the contract. A list of things you want. You can have your lawyer review it. And if CT-TV thinks you're a prima donna, they can walk, then."

Jason turns toward the water. The crescent moon throws little light on the sea, so the night is black. But in the distance, the Gull Island Lighthouse beam sweeps across the water, catching a slow-moving barge in its path. Jason unleashes

Maddy to let her run, then zips his sweatshirt and takes a few steps in the sand.

"Listen." Maris' voice comes from behind him. "You don't hear your brother anymore."

That gets him to turn to her. She still sits, wisps of her hair blowing in the sea breeze. Even in the dark, he can see the worry in her eyes.

"I know you sit alone at night, downstairs, Jason." She stands and walks to the edge of the boardwalk. "Maybe this opportunity is a way to bring Neil back."

"The whole thing scares me, though. Cameras, lights, film crews. Hell, an audience. It's a big change."

"You know what you need?"

"No. But I'm sure you're about to tell me."

She steps onto the sand beside him and touches his face. "You need to talk to the boys."

"The boys?"

"Kyle, Matt, Nick. You should have a boys' night out to chew on this one. They'll put it into perspective for you."

"I don't know."

"Go tomorrow, when me and the ladies are presenting our grand finale for Operation Make Elsa Smile."

"You don't need me around to help set up?"

Maris shakes her head. "I need you to hang out with the guys. To chill a little. Have some laughs."

Jason takes her hand and they head toward the water. Maybe walking the packed sand will allay his fears, calm his worry.

"Look!" Maris points to the far end of the beach, near the rocks. "Someone's having a campfire."

Jason squints into the darkness. Two shadowy figures sit

near a small fire, the flames flickering and sparking to the sky. "I'm pretty darn sure that's Cliff."

"Cliff?"

"With Elsa."

"Really? Out this late?" Maris takes a few quick steps closer. "Let's go say hello, then."

"No." He gives a short but sharp whistle to the dog. "Maddy!" he says quietly while patting his upper leg. "Over here."

The dog returns and sits at his side, her ears pointed, waiting for Jason's command.

"That *is* Elsa, isn't it?" Maris raises her hand to shield her eyes. "I wonder what they're doing."

Jason clips on Maddy's leash, takes Maris' hand again and walks in the opposite direction, away from the lovebirds on the beach. "I believe Cliff has upped his game, wooing your aunt like he means business."

―

"Mmm. The last time I had one of these, I brought them to Jason's barbecue on the Fourth." Elsa pokes a twig through a marshmallow and holds it over the fire. "Hard to believe that was only three months ago." Sitting on a washed-up driftwood log, she draws her knees up close and looks into the flames. Lazy waves lap at the nearby rocks, beyond which the patch of woods rises in dark shadow, blending with the night sky. The damp air is misty, heavy with a salty scent.

Sitting in a low sand chair across from her, Cliff turns his marshmallow, which is starting to sag on a crooked beach stick. "I used to pitch a tent in our backyard to take my son camping, right at home. We'd have a campfire and do this."

"The three of you?"

"Three?"

"Your wife, too?"

"No, just Denny and me." Cliff moves his marshmallow away from the fire. "My wife died from pregnancy complications, so I raised our son alone."

"Oh, I had *no* idea! I'm so very sorry," Elsa says, reaching over and squeezing his hand.

"It was a long time ago. But thank you, Elsa."

"You must be close to your boy, then."

"Close enough."

Elsa gazes into the flames again, thinking how love can be sad sometimes. But there's something about a campfire on the beach that's so peaceful, and it lulls her. Its warmth, and flickering light, and snapping wood, make her want to sit here beside it for hours, while listening to the waves.

"Careful now ..." Cliff says, pointing to her marshmallow.

Her soggy, hanging marshmallow—which just dropped off her stick, into the flames. "Oh, shoot," she whispers. "It was just the way I like them, browned and crispy."

Cliff extends his cooling marshmallow. "Have mine."

When Elsa looks to his face, she can't miss it. His blue eyes are twinkling, just like the sparks from the flame. And yes, she sees that darn dimple, too, as he holds out the lightly charred marshmallow. Wordlessly, she takes it and presses the whole thing into her mouth. "*Magnifico,*" she manages around it, opening her fingers to the starry sky. After poking another marshmallow onto her twig, Elsa tells Cliff, "I'd love to meet your son. Meet Denny. But I don't know how much longer I'll be around here."

Cliff looks at her, then past her to the water. Finally, he stands and moves to the driftwood log where she sits. He sits, too, then turns to face her. "Here," he says, raising a finger to her cheek. "You have some marshmallow on your lip."

Elsa moves to swipe her mouth, until Cliff stops her hand with his. "Let me," he says, brushing his fingers across her lips, then leaning in and kissing her. His hand tenderly holds her face, and when they deepen the kiss, his other hand reaches up, too. It feels nice on this cool night, beside the sea. Especially when both his hands lower and cradle her neck while they kiss longer, and the fire crackles in the darkness.

"Cliff," Elsa whispers when he stops. But she notices he doesn't move away. Instead, he takes her hand and stands, leading her to the packed sand right past the breaking waves. There's something about the moment, the night, that keeps Elsa from saying anything more.

Instead, for the first time in a month, she stops resisting, stops pushing others away and stops pulling herself away. She simply lets happen what may, beside the dark sea with a small fire burning driftwood and dried twigs, the flames casting wavering light on them.

And what happens is that Cliff takes her in his arms, hums a familiar Dean Martin tune and leads her along the deserted beach in the sweetest dance she's ever had, swaying gently with the breeze, the swishing waves serenading their every step.

twenty

"SOMEONE'S GOING TO CALL THE police, Kyle."

But as Lauren says it, Kyle notices how she turns in her seat to glimpse the house on Bayside Road—even though it's the fourth time they've driven past it.

"Because we probably look suspicious. I mean, who drives by a house this many times early on a Wednesday morning?" She rolls down the pickup truck's window and leans out, craning her head as they pass. "No one, except a thief casing out the joint."

"I'm just trying to picture us living right there. And relax, it's not *that* early. Your mom must be getting the kids on the bus right about now. But fine." Kyle turns off of Bayside and cruises the other Stony Point streets. Because he's still not convinced this cottage is *the one*. Maybe something else has come up for sale that they're not aware of. Anything to get him from committing to the bungalow on the bay. They pass Elsa's semi-renovated place and spot Celia coming out the door with a carton in her arms.

"Hey, Cee!" Lauren calls out her still-opened window. "What are you doing?"

Kyle pulls up to the curb, glad for the distraction. All this house pressure is taking its toll on him. It feels like his heart has been randomly pounding lately.

"Moving in to the guest cottage," Celia says, hitching her head to the run-down, gingerbread shanty in Elsa's backyard.

"Really?" Lauren stretches around for a look. "I thought that was Foley's shed."

"Nope. It's actually a tiny cottage, which we sort of cleaned out." Celia turns and heads in its direction, carton in arms. "So it's home sweet home. For a while, anyway."

"That's so great!"

As Lauren says it, Kyle nudges her, whispering for her to hurry up.

"I'll call you later, Cee," Lauren yells before rolling up the window.

Celia waves her off right as Elsa, carrying a vase of flowers, walks out her back door.

Before Lauren gets more involved in *this* household move, Kyle puts the truck in gear and drives away. "I'll go down Bayside *one* more time," he relents, and Lauren gently shoves him with a happy grin on her face.

But whether sneaking in this last drive-by is a mistake or a blessing, Kyle's not sure. As they approach, a couple is standing beside a parked car in front of the house that's for sale. The woman helps a little girl out of the backseat, just as another car pulls up. That woman gets out carrying a briefcase and pointing to, wait, to *their* house!

"Kyle," Lauren harshly whispers, as though the other people might hear. "Look."

"I know," he says, driving slowly. "They're checking out our house."

The Beach Inn

"Wait. Do I know them?" Lauren discreetly slides her sunglasses down her nose and peers over the frames. "Yes! Yes, it's that *Mackenzie*. Mackenzie and, and, Lucas! They're the ones who put in an offer on Elsa's."

"How do you know?"

"I read their personal letter the other day when I went to see Celia. They're *very* thorough and included a *family photograph*. Yes, that's their girl. Zoe!" Lauren raises her sunglasses again. "Keep going, so they don't get suspicious."

Kyle drives past the house, but has to turn around at the end of the dead-end street. As he does, he rolls down his window and sneaks a deep gasp of cool, salty air.

"They must be keeping their options open," Lauren says, slapping Kyle's arm, "since Elsa hasn't responded to their offer yet. Looks like they're *very* set on living here at Stony Point."

"I can't believe they're touring our house," Kyle says, just as the couple walks through the front door. Oh, he can imagine their reaction to the natural light spilling in; to the perfect view of the bay; to the porch with its multipaned windows that Lauren wants to set a-twinkling every night of the year. "What are we going to do?"

"Well, you've been such a wreck and that's not helping! We seriously need to put in an offer. Right away!"

"But they might, too. And what if it turns into a bidding war?"

"No. It won't." Lauren sits straight and motions for Kyle to hurry past the house. "Because here's what we'll do." She looks at Kyle directly as he drives. "We're going to submit a personal letter with our offer, and it has to be *better* than theirs. You have to write it, today."

"*Me?*"

"Yes, you. I'm busy all day, getting things ready for Maris' Operation Make Elsa Smile event tonight. So I can't." She looks over her shoulder at the house. "But you can. Make it all sentimental, and talk about Hailey and Evan, and … and how special it would be to raise our children overlooking the bay."

"I hate writing things like that. Jason's best man speech nearly did me in last year."

"You were great." Lauren actually unbuckles her seatbelt to twist around and watch the house diminish behind them. "I have an idea. Aren't you going out with the guys tonight?"

"Just for a beer and bullshit."

She clasps his arm while he drives. "They can help you write it."

"The guys?"

"Yes, Kyle." She grabs a napkin from the console and swipes his sweating forehead. "We'll never get this house with you coming undone like this. So get it together. You have to *man up*!"

At first, Jason thinks he's hearing the waves breaking out on the bluff. Maybe the bedroom window is open a little. But, no. The sound is getting louder, like a dark whirlpool coming up behind him. Now he recognizes it. It's the sound of a roaring car engine, fully opened up, the pedal pressed flat. The noise affects his breathing, his pulse, warning him to flee it. But they're stopped at a traffic light, sitting on the idling motorcycle. Every bit of his energy struggles—his legs kicking, his arms pushing. As he does, he knows what's coming next. It'll be his brother pointing to the reflection of Ted Sullivan's speeding car in the Harley-Davidson's mirror. *Jay. Hey, Jay*, Neil will say just before the crash.

But Jason's wrong. *Andiamo!* Sal orders instead, his voice smooth, but urgent. *Let's go!*

And though Jason tries, the sunlight suddenly turns glaring white at the same time that he feels a pressure on his back.

That's the turning point. Because now any sound can't keep up with the motion swirling all around him: the motorcycle spinning incessantly; his jeans hooked onto the bike and twisting up his leg; his brother flung haphazardly through the air before hitting the pavement. Until finally, there is no noise. Just a soundless ripping, burning through his leg as he thrashes about until there is the sound of nothing but silence. And wait ... a whisper, too. Yes, whenever his father wanted to make a point with his war stories, didn't his voice drop so low—to nearly a whisper Jason and Neil strained to hear.

Fear, Jason deciphers now. He instantly tries to recall the story, the event his father endured that led him to these whispered words. *Once that chopper lifted off, bringing my injured comrade to a medevac unit, silence dropped like a bomb on those left behind. That whirring, chop-chop of the propeller faded, and then? Nothing. The world went mute. And in that silence was one thing. Fear. Fear I'd never get out of that hellhole. That I'd die in the jungle. And that fear kept me alive, made me find ways to keep living so that one day it could be me leaving the nightmare behind and going home again.*

With a sudden gasp, Jason lurches up in bed, his body coated in perspiration, his half leg tangled up in the twisted sheet. He looks at his hands, expecting to see the dirty grit of pavement coating them. But they're clean, and his eyes drop closed with relief as he falls back onto his pillow, thankful that Maris is already up and not witnessing this nightmare.

For several long moments, though, he grapples with his breathing—sucking in air as though he can't get enough. He drops an arm across his closed eyes and waits for everything to slow, especially the powerful memories of three important men talking to him: Neil, Sal, and his father.

Jason waits, too, for his pulse to slow, and his breath. But his panicked thoughts still swirl like the sheer chaos of the motorcycle accident: Maris writing a novel; Jason giving Sal's eulogy before driving away and *leaving* this life—his wife, his house on the bluff—behind; Trent, nipping at his heels like the dog, wanting television cameras brought, essentially, into Jason's private world.

He slowly turns on his side and looks toward the open window. Even in his sleep, there's no escape.

Later in his barn studio, Jason lowers the swing lamp at his drafting table and pulls a partially finished rolled design from the bin beside it. Choosing the right pencil, he sets his arm on the table to begin but finds himself pausing, mid-sketch, with an eerie feeling of being watched. So he looks up toward the loft, where Maris stands frozen at the railing, studying him.

"Okay, okay, I confess," she says with an easy shrug.

"To what?" he calls up to her.

"To being worried about you."

Which is precisely when Jason realizes that though he relishes having his wife around, he does not relish her scrutiny. Small beach towns and thin cottage walls, not to mention both his and her self-employment, it all means there is no safe place to hide here. It's not the first time he's caught Maris checking up on him—no doubt gauging to see if he ever might get in his SUV again with a packed duffel bag ... and simply drive away.

"Come on down," he says, resuming his sketching and calculating.

"No, you're working on a new design. I don't want to interrupt."

"Sweetheart ..." But he doesn't look up. Doesn't give her the chance to glimpse the circles beneath his eyes, the fatigue on his face, the effects of the nightmare on his mind.

"Now that my handsome husband's my coworker," she adds, still standing at the upper railing, her clasped hands leaning over the edge, "we should probably wall-off this open loft space. Less distractions for the employees."

When he motions for her to join him, she grabs some of Neil's manuscript pages and walks down the stairs, patting the mounted moose head as she passes it.

"I want you to read this paragraph," she says, pointing to a dusty page she sets on top of his drawing.

He does, reading Neil's words about a character unsure of where to go when he's caught in the driving rain of the approaching storm. "This is good," Jason says, dragging his finger along a line of text. "As though Neil had been writing all his life."

"I thought so, too." Maris thumbs through more pages beside him, her body bent low, her brown hair falling alongside her face.

So this is something Jason never saw coming: the two of them collaborating on a creative project. He sits back, watching how intent she's become with the novel. "Have you thought about what's next? If you'll actually publish this book?"

"I have," she says, then looks around for a stool, which she wheels over and sits on beside him. "And I'm really unsure about what to do."

"What's the matter? Don't you know some people in the publishing business?"

She nods. "That's why I'm apprehensive. There's a literary agent I met. We sat on the train together a few times. She's nice enough, you'd think. But wow, does she like to gossip."

"About what?"

"The book industry. Especially her clients. The things she's told me make me reluctant to put Neil's beautiful work into *professional*, if you'd call it that, hands."

Jason picks up a sheet of the manuscript, flips it over to read Neil's jotted notes, then looks to Maris. "Why? Wouldn't they know best what to do with this?"

"Not from what I've heard." Maris wheels her stool closer and straightens Neil's pages. Sunshine spills in through the skylights above her, the golden rays lighting on the wall of bookshelves, the barnwood floor. "The agent signed one of her authors with a publishing house. The editor there is Sam Gorman, you might've heard of her."

"I have actually. Didn't she snag that megaseller last year?" Jason asks. "The tear-jerker everybody was reading on the beach?"

"Yes!"

"I think they're making a movie from it now, because Kyle wants to do a double-date night when it comes out."

"That's the one. So anyway, the agent told me that her author—*not* the megaseller, by the way—had a problem working with that publishing house. Apparently when Sam Gorman edited her manuscripts, whenever she'd read any of the sex scenes, they were so badly written that all Sam could do was write *Yuuuck!!!* across the margins. And the agent was sure to tell me, with some amusement, that the word was all capitalized and included several exclamation points to show the editor's disgust. Finally the author couldn't take it anymore and begged the agent to tell Gorman to stop doing that."

"The sensitive type, maybe?"

"That's what I thought, so I asked. Turns out it's more an insecurity hang-up. According to her agent, the author knows she's not all that, so always needs her hand held. But when I innocently asked if her writing warranted that type of seemingly callous editorial response, her agent could only nod. *Slowly* nod, which said it all."

"This was all divulged to you?"

"And more."

"Shouldn't that be confidential information, between agent and author?"

"You'd think. I'm sure the author doesn't have a clue her agent gossips about her. I still get her random emails once or twice a year. As a literary agent, she likes to keep in touch, dish a little dirt, see what I'm up to. Says the door's always open if I ever get the writing itch. Anyway, I'll tell you more of her stories later."

Jason rolls his stool back, knuckle to his scarred jaw. "So publishing's nothing but a catty business, then. I guess I'm not really surprised. And you don't want any of that bullshit put on Neil's work …"

"Absolutely not." Maris reaches over and draws her fingers down Jason's cheek. "Your brother's novel deserves the finest treatment."

"And no less. I also know *you*, and I know you'll somehow

get it published—on your terms. We'll just have to research our options."

"Exactly. Let me get the book finished first." Maris scoops up the papers and heads across the wood-planked floor to her loft. "Oh, and Jason?" she asks, turning back and taking a few steps closer again. "Did you sleep okay? You look tired."

"Eh. I tossed and turned." He rolls up the architectural plan on his drafting table and drops it in a rack of tubes. "Lots on my mind."

"Trent?"

"Partly that, partly a packed schedule." He gets up, raises his hand to her neck and kisses her. "I'm stopping at the Woods site this morning."

"Aren't they framing the new cottage now?"

"They are. And I'm project manager on this one. The foreman has some issues with the old cottage footprint, which we're adjusting. This way, the new structure will actually face the water. So I'm meeting with him to discuss, and really have to run, sweetheart." He gives her another light kiss. "Don't you have to set up on the beach for the Elsa thing you've got planned tonight?"

"Yes! Lauren's coming over to help me."

"Okay. It's supposed to be a warm evening, so it'll be nice. Indian summer, feels like. And I'm off now, to do my part, too."

"Your part? Of what?"

"Figure we might as well lay it on thick today, making Elsa smile. I'll swing by there on my way to the Woods place. Because nothing lights up your aunt's face more than a convenience store coffee and greasy egg sandwich."

THE BEACH INN

Elsa sets the take-out coffees and paper-wrapped egg sandwiches pronto on her kitchen table. A bandana holds back her hair, and she wears a knotted blouse over her jeans. "It's so good to see you, Jason," she says, pausing to hug him, then resuming setting knives and forks beside their plates.

"To see *me*?" Jason asks while unwrapping his sandwich. "Or see my stash of goods here?"

"Ah, yes." Elsa sits across from him and lifts the top of her warm croissant roll. The way she can't take her eyes off of it, there's no doubt she's smitten with the illicit food. "You know me well."

"Yeah, because I'm your partner in crime." Jason tears open the ketchup packet with his teeth and swirls the ketchup all over his steaming egg. Toasted hash browns spill from a paper bag between them.

In no time, Elsa is digging into her sandwich, cupping her hand beneath the gooey cheese dripping from it. "Oh! This food is the best. And I *am* starving. I just moved Celia into the guest cottage."

"Is that right?" Jason glances around the kitchen for any sign of Celia, and instead sees the reviving herbs, their red pots freshly watered around the sink.

"This way," Elsa says between sandwich bites, "she'll have her own bathroom, her own kitchen. A little more privacy." Elsa adds a dash of salt to her croissant-egg concoction before taking another double bite. "One or two nights here in my cottage is okay," she says around the food. "But Celia seems to have planted herself."

Jason sips his coffee. "So she's sticking around?"

"For now, I guess. Until I move. My neighbor in Milan, Concetta, is holding a room for me to visit, which will hopefully be soon. Because I have such a wonderful offer from that lovely couple, Lucas and Mackenzie, I'm sure I'll be able to close in no time." Elsa points to the multipage contract on her kitchen counter. "But I promised Celia I'd take this week to think about it, before signing the paperwork. And while she waits for my decision, Celia's been a great help, staging this place to help negotiate *any* sale that might come up."

That's when Jason realizes what he's seeing in Elsa's cottage. It's obvious, now, that Celia's not staging for a sale. She's staging the cottage simply to sway Elsa's heart. Reviving her beloved mini-potted herbs, setting more thin white starfish in the windows, hanging Sal's rowboat oars over the fireplace, cozying up the place with soft throws and plump pillows. She's transforming the original Foley's joint into Elsa's *home*. But he also notices a suitcase set in the hallway, and wonders if Elsa's leaving for Italy soon.

"Celia was in love with my son," Elsa is explaining, "so it's nice having her around." As she says it, Elsa gets a small bowl of raspberries and blueberries from the refrigerator, then sprinkles the fruit on Jason's plate, beside his half-eaten sandwich. "We talk about Sal. What I can't get over is how, all his life, I knew about his health ailments … the heart complications from a bad bout of rheumatic fever he suffered as a boy. Back then, the doctors said he was living on borrowed time. So I'd always been waiting, waiting, for the shoe to drop. But as the years went by, and he worked, and lived, well, I got a false sense of security. Maybe the doctors were wrong. *Because look*, I'd think. *Look at him living!*" She stops then, lifts a fork and moves around the berries on her plate without eating any. "You figure you're prepared for the worst, but there is no preparation for losing a child. So yes, I'm glad Celia is here.

The Beach Inn

Because some days are good, some not."

Jason forks a couple of his raspberries. "If there's anything Maris and I can do ... We all try to help, Elsa."

"Oh, you people!" she says with a wink. "I'm onto you and your shenanigans. Did you know that Cliff threw pebbles at my window last night?"

"Cliff? Our curmudgeonly beach commissioner?"

"Yes, that's the one. He took me to a campfire he made on the beach and we roasted marshmallows."

"Another favorite food of yours, if I'm not mistaken."

"Sure, but I saw what he was *really* doing. He was trying to sweet-talk me into staying here."

"Did it work?"

"Let's just say it made me forget things, for a little while."

"Forget." Jason motions over his shoulder to the suitcase. "So are you packing for a *visit* to Milan? Or are you running to Italy to do just that ... to forget?"

Elsa's voice drops. "I'm not sure."

"You don't want to forget, Elsa. Not even for a little while. I did, after Neil died. Got busy with a corporate job in Hartford. Tried commercial work, drove a long commute to the city, lived in a sterile condominium. Made myself too busy to remember him. And do you know what happened when I *forgot* Neil?" he asks, air-quoting the word.

"No, I don't."

"My memories of him hid behind corners and chased me down. Coming upon them unexpectedly in quiet times, they became *more* painful. More painful and difficult to get through. Because memories don't want to be forgotten, Elsa, and they eventually soften when you stay with them. So believe me, Sal's memories *will* chase you down ... if you run from them."

"But maybe I'm not running. I just don't want to face those memories right now."

"Right. But if you think that by moving—back to Milan, or anywhere—that you'll accomplish this, you won't. Because those memories will still find you, nonetheless. Except this time, they'll take you by surprise." Jason lifts the last of his egg sandwich and stuffs it into his mouth, then grabs a napkin and wipes his face. "Not to mention, you'll miss this good grub here."

"Okay, point taken," Elsa says while waving him off and simply picking at her food for a few moments, no doubt mulling over his words. Finally, she dots ketchup on a remaining scrap of her sandwich. "Now tell me about your TV show."

"My what?"

"Come on. You know that there are no secrets at this little beach!"

"But, how …"

"Who do you think cooked that delicious pot roast for—Trent, is it? Your wife made a deal with me and Celia. The full story for a ready-made meal to serve."

With a slow grin, Jason shakes his head. He never even suspected the pot roast wasn't Maris'. So while standing and bringing his dish and silverware to the sink, he quickly tells Elsa about Trent's meeting. "For now, CT-TV just wants to film a pilot episode, to gauge viewer interest. And sure, it's a way to grow my architecture business. *And* a way to push myself. But something about it feels like an intrusion, too, the way I'd be broadcasting Neil into each renovated cottage."

"You do that anyway, no? Bring your brother's ideas to your designs?"

"Yes. But privately, not in front of cameras."

Elsa sits back and folds her napkin on the table. "Well, Jason," she eventually says, quietly. "Wouldn't this TV program be a nice way to get your brother out from the hidden corners, so that memories can't really haunt you anymore?"

"Okay, I see what you're doing, twisting up my own words to trap me," Jason answers while pushing in his chair. "This is different, but nice try. My life's complicated enough as it is. There's just no way I'm ready to sign any television contracts."

As he lifts his olive military jacket from the chair back and slips it on, Elsa raises an eyebrow at him. "Jason, we're never ready for change. Sometimes you just have to dive in," she says. "So what exactly *would* it take for you to sign those papers to have your own incredible cottage-renovation TV show?"

Jason zips his jacket and glances around the kitchen. He walks to the counter and lifts the multipage real estate contract from Lucas and Mackenzie, scans the money figures, the personal letter, the photograph, then sets it all on the table.

"I don't get it," Elsa says, looking up at him standing there.

"What would it take for me to sign my contract?" Jason raises his eyebrow right back at her before giving her an answer. "You ripping up yours."

twenty-one

WHEN JASON PULLS INTO THE Sand Bar's parking lot later that Wednesday evening, he knows Maris was right. All it takes is one look at the low, dark building to realize he needed this night with the guys. While sitting in his SUV, his blood pressure lowers, his breathing comes easier, and his muscles loosen. The night is so warm, apparently the patio's been reopened. At its black mesh tables, the umbrellas are all up, their spokes wrapped in twinkly lights. Jason can make out shadows of customers enjoying the evening there.

When he gets out and walks across the parking lot, he can already hear some bluesy tune playing on the jukebox. It's no wonder; someone propped the entrance door open, letting the sultry air mix with the nostalgic summer songs. Jason glances at the sky. It could be a steamy July night as easily as October.

A sharp whistle cuts through the air and gets him to turn then. Kyle just pulled in and is getting out of his pickup. "Yo, man. Wait up!" he calls while crossing the parking lot and finagling on a denim jacket over his gray jeans. Jason waits at the bottom of the stairs and shakes Kyle's hand when he catches up. "What a sweet night," Kyle says. "Indian summer has officially arrived."

"Feels good. Maybe we'll take a pitcher out to the patio." Jason turns to the stairs. "Come on. *Andiamo.*"

"Hang on." Kyle raises his hand, which Jason now notices is cupped around a burning cigarette, thus the jacket finagling. "Let me grab a few drags."

"Seriously? I thought you quit."

"Quit?" Kyle answers through an exhaled cloud of smoke. "I've been trying to mentally control myself. You know, use willpower. They say it's the most effective way to give these up, permanently."

"No luck?"

"No. You got me friggin' hooked again after Sal's funeral, remember? Give up *your* smokes yet?"

Jason shakes his head. "Working on it. Just had half of one, driving here. Maris is really getting on my case about it."

"Nice having your old lady around, isn't it?" As Kyle asks, he stamps out his cigarette butt and gives Jason a shove. "Okay, I'm good. And ready for a brew."

They climb the few stairs to the open door and walk into the dimly lit bar. The jukebox glows near the entrance, and orange lights are strung around the top of the bar.

"Keeping things very seasonal," Kyle says from behind Jason.

Glancing at the autumn lights, Jason wonders where the hell summer went. But then the magic of The Sand Bar casts its spell. It *always* feels like a summer night in this joint—with its low lighting and easy banter; its cool drinks and familiar tunes on the jukebox. He veers off to a booth until someone calls out, "Stop right there, Barlow."

When he does just that—stops and turns toward where the

voice came from—Kyle nearly walks right into him.

The bartender, Patrick, leans an elbow on the bar and points to the doorway. "Turn around and get your sorry ass out of here."

"Me?" Jason steps slowly closer, squinting through the misty lighting to see Patrick's face.

"That's right. You've been nothing but trouble here lately. First with that dame with the guitar."

"Dame? Are you kidding me?" Kyle asks while grabbing Jason's arm from behind him. "What the hell happened with you and Celia, anyway?"

Jason shakes Kyle off and keeps heading toward Patrick.

"And then having the balls to take a swing at that police officer?" Patrick reminds him. "One of New York's finest, I might add."

"Patrick ..." Jason begins.

"Out." Patrick stands straight and crosses his arms in front of him as he hitches his head toward the open door. "Maybe we'll see you after the New Year, when you make some resolutions."

"Hey, Patrick, my man." Kyle catches up to Jason and swings an arm across his shoulders. "Come on, cut him some slack. It's been a rough few weeks."

"No shit." Patrick glares at Kyle then. "And I've got the broken chairs and tables left over from your friend's brawl to prove it. Not to mention the lost business. So keep it up, and *your* ass is outta here, too."

Jason sits at a barstool. "Let's talk, guy. Because I came here fully intending to make restitution."

"Right, give him a chance," Kyle adds as he settles on a stool beside Jason. "Can't you work this out?" he asks Patrick.

"No. And as for you, Barlow," Patrick says, leaning close and lowering his voice. "You're not to return here unless you have your *wife* on your arm. Maris. *She'll* get you to behave."

"Listen," Jason continues. "I understand you're mad."

"Mad? That's too kind a term."

"Fair enough. And what I did *was* uncalled for. But like my friend here says," he adds, nodding to Kyle, "it's been a rough few weeks. I'm good now, though."

"And no worries, Patrick. I'll keep him in line, too." As if to prove it, Kyle stands and towers behind Jason, first. Then he lifts one of his sizable arms, wraps it around Jason's neck and gives a faux chokehold.

"Cut it out, man," Jason tells him, shoving his shoulder back into Kyle. As he does, he notices Matt and Cliff walking in and heading straight toward them. "Listen, bro," Jason tells Kyle. "Grab a seat with those two and let me square things here with this guy."

"You okay with that, Patrick?" Kyle asks, backing toward Matt and Cliff while waiting for an answer. When Patrick gives a nod, Kyle slaps Jason's shoulder, then reaches past him to snag a basket of pretzels from the bar before spinning around and heading to a large booth with the others.

"So what gives?" Patrick asks Jason. "You've been a wreck lately."

"Yeah." Jason takes a long breath. "Seriously, man. Some shit really did go down and it threw me."

"When DeLuca died?"

"Absolutely. One of a kind, Salvatore was. He'll be missed in these parts for a long time to come."

"Your wife okay with the stunts you pulled?"

"Not at all." Jason eyes Patrick, who's warily watching him

right back. All the while, a warm October breeze comes through the open door and brings piecemeal sounds of passing traffic into the bar. There's a murmur of voices and laughs behind him, and someone in the back is shooting pool. All of it—every sound, every sight in this dive—holds some of Jason's fondest memories because it's one of the few places where he leaves his worries at that propped-open door.

"I'm busy, guy," Patrick warns him. "You need to be straight with me, and quick, or out you go. For real."

"Maris is the only reason I'm here, Patrick. Not *here*, at your bar. That I'm in Stony Point at all. I hit the road leaving this all behind last month, and she reeled me back." Jason drags a hand over his face. "Hell, Maris is my world. You know that."

"Yeah, I do. I was at your wedding last year. That's why I figured it had to be some stupid shit with the other dame. The singer."

"Celia. And it *was* stupid. But in her defense, the lady's all right. She was engaged to Sal, you know, and lost the guy she loved. So if anybody should be cut some slack, it's her." Jason clasps his hands on the bar and looks at the liquor bottles lining the shelves behind Patrick. The autumn-orange lights above cast a golden glow on them. "If she should ever show up here again, you just pin that night on me."

Patrick does nothing more than raise an eyebrow, which Jason takes as his cue. The talking is done, except for the talking that money does. He pulls his checkbook from an inside jacket pocket and motions to Patrick for a pen. "What do I owe you, for damages and reparations?"

"Nah, put it away." Patrick extends a hand. "Give me a shake, man. It's worth your weight in gold."

After a silent standoff second, Jason obliges, clasping

Patrick's hand, then standing and clapping his arm. "Thanks, man. Appreciate it."

"Oh, I'm not letting you off that easy. You're on probation, Barlow. All I'm serving you here is Coke on the rocks. For the foreseeable future."

Jason turns up his hands, not really believing him.

"Take it or leave it," Patrick says.

Jason looks over his shoulder to see that Nick arrived in the meantime and is foolishly arm wrestling Kyle at their booth. "I'll take it. Anytime." He shakes Patrick's hand again. "And really. I'm sorry about what went down the other nights here."

"The next time you walk through those doors, you bring that wonderful wife of yours." As Patrick moves toward a customer calling him from the end of the bar, he hitches his head to a crowded booth off to the side. "For now, go join those clowns, would you?"

⁓

Celia's been waiting, and pulls the door open just as her friends are about to knock. "Hey, guys!" she says, backing up and letting them come in, which they do—spilling through the doorway like a cresting wave.

"Shh!" Eva warns, a finger to her lips as they huddle inside Celia's guest cottage. Their jackets are open and loose on this warm evening, and Eva holds a rolled-up blanket beneath her arm. "We want to surprise Elsa."

"Oh, it's such a perfect night," Maris says. "What is it Sal would say?"

"How beautiful." Celia gives a sad smile, then kisses her

fingertips and sweeps them toward the starlit sky beyond the door. *"Che bello!"*

Lauren throws a glance back at the dark cottage across the yard. "You don't think Elsa saw us sneak by, do you?"

Maris looks, too. "No. She'd be putting on lights and coming outside if she did." She shifts several bags in her arms. "You ready for the big event?"

"Absolutely." Celia takes one of Maris' bags and peeks inside. "Oh, how sweet!" she says while lifting out a fluffy slipper-bootie. "This is so much fun!"

"I hope Elsa thinks so, too." Maris reaches into the bags, digging through each one carefully. "It's getting late, ladies. Let's do this!"

And wouldn't the cameras start rolling on them after they all change into their fleecy pajamas and fuzzy socks and furry slippers, adding light scarves and jackets, too. Yes, it's the perfect mid-movie scene for her imagined film, *Beckoning Celia*. Because wasn't she called here for this? Beckoned to help Elsa, and to save the beach inn—Stony Point style? Celia watches her friends chatter and fuss with their jammies; watches them laugh and whisper plans for their sneak attack on Elsa as they all head to the door and out into the night.

Celia follows behind, hearing the director's words in her mind: *And ... Action!*

~

After a quick stop outside to lock up his checkbook in the SUV, and to sneak another half cigarette, Jason walks into The Sand Bar just as a roar erupts. On the wall-mounted TV over the bar, some lucky at-bat dude hit a home run in the pennant race. Jason walks past the guys watching, slapping a familiar few on the shoulder as he does, high-fiving the game with them. When he finally sits beside Cliff in the booth, the gang at the table goes quiet.

"What's up?" Jason asks.

Kyle is pulling scraps of paper from his denim jacket pocket. One by one, he unfolds each piece, then sets them down for everyone to see.

"Shit," Kyle says. "It's unanimous."

Jason slides over a ballot to see for himself. "What's this? Your house poll?"

"Yup. Not even a close call that I could argue, or contemplate."

"That's great, right?" Nick reads a ballot, too. "So you're in?"

"Unless I can find a way out." As he says it, Kyle scoops together the paper ballots.

"What's the problem?" Matt looks across the table at Kyle. "I thought you wanted this."

"Yeah. Me, too." Kyle stuffs the ballots back in his pocket, then takes off his jacket and hangs it on a coat hook behind their booth. "It's just that commitment thing. You know," he says, sitting again. "Houses, women. Whatever."

When everyone's done groaning and tipping their beer glasses to his, Matt asks, "And it looks like the women have something up their sleeve for Elsa tonight?"

Jason heard some worry in Maris' voice when she talked about Elsa earlier. The last thing Maris wants is to lose touch with her aunt again. "Operation Make Elsa Smile was a great idea, Cliff. I'll give you that. But my wife says that after this final plan she's hatched, she's out of options. You getting anywhere with Elsa?"

"What?" Nick asks, tossing a handful of pretzels in his mouth. "Sounds kinda risqué, boss. *Getting* anywhere?"

Jason raises an eyebrow at Cliff and motions for him to elaborate.

"We had a little campfire on the beach last night."

"Niiice." Kyle gives Cliff a thumbs-up. "A sexy seaside romance?"

"*Campfire?* I believe that violates an ordinance, Commissioner," Nick warns.

Jason brushes off Nick. "Desperate times call for desperate measures."

"And Maris convinced me to pull the Parks and Rec projector out of storage for tonight. After I nicely packed it up till next summer," Cliff tells them.

"So, what are the women cooking up, boss?" Nick asks.

"Don't know, Nicholas. Maris wouldn't say. Flew into my office with her request, took the projector and hightailed it out of there. She say anything to you?" Cliff asks Jason.

"It's movie night, on the beach."

"Movie night?" Nick asks.

"Home movies," Jason explains.

"According to Lauren," Kyle adds, "it's all sentimental stuff to tug at Elsa's heartstrings."

"I'm headed there, after here," Jason lets on as the waitress sets down his iced glass.

"What's your poison, man?" Matt nods to the drink.

"Soda."

"What?" Nick leans forward. "You going wussie on us, guy?"

"Pipe down, pipsqueak." Jason sips the cold beverage. "You're just a pup, and wouldn't get it."

"Get what?"

Kyle reaches over and gives Nick's scruffy goatee a rub. "Life, man. Shit happens, sometimes."

"Get off of me," Nick says, shoving Kyle aside.

"Hey, badass timepiece." Kyle grabs Nick's arm and scrutinizes a rad wristwatch, then lets out a low whistle.

"Easy with the merchandise." Nick pulls back and straightens the heavy silver watch. "It's from Salvatore."

"No shit." Jason reaches across the table for Nick's arm.

"Check it out, dude," Nick tells him. "Subdials, date windows, and look at that tachymeter. When Sal rode shotgun in my security car, he was fascinated with how I timed my route."

"A shame time wasn't on that man's side," Matt says.

"Micelli delivered this to me, couple weeks ago." Nick raises his glass in a toast. "To Sal."

"To Sal," they all answer, clinking glasses over the table. "*Salute.*"

"Well fellas, we ready to order? I'm starved." Cliff picks up a pile of menus from the end of the booth and passes them out.

In a few minutes, the waitress makes her way to their table again. "Let me guess," she says. "Deluxe burgers all around. Loaded, with all the extras."

"Keep going," Matt says, setting down his menu.

"Okay." She puts her pencil to her chin and eyes them. "A few orders of onion rings. Steak fries. Slaw. Ketchup. The works?"

"Extra pickles," Kyle adds.

"Sounds good," Jason tells her while handing her the menus. But he nearly gags on his soda with what Kyle spills next.

"Hey, man. You are *thee* talk of the Stony Point town, dude." Kyle reaches across the table and slaps Jason's shoulder. "A TV star, practically famous already."

"You kidding me?" Jason asks after sputtering for a second. "How the *hell'd* you know?"

"Cheers to you." Cliff tips his beer glass to Jason's soda. "That's big news—and everyone knows."

"Knows what?" Nick sits back and turns up his hands.

"Jeez Louise, you really *are* out of the loop." Cliff grabs a handful of pretzels from the plastic basket on the table. "A television scout is after Jason to host a show."

"No shit." Nick reaches his hand across the table.

"It's nothing." Jason extends his hand for a shake, then turns it away at the last second to mess with Nick. "Just a local thing, with CT-TV. One of their reps was at the architecture gala and heard my speech. The dude thinks I'd be the right host for one of those house transformation shows. Redoing cottages on the Connecticut shore. The kind of work I already do."

"But a TV host?" Nick asks. "You don't even like people, man."

To which Kyle elbows him, sharply. "Sheesh, who let you out of the kennel tonight?"

"Shut up, Bradford." Nick reaches around Kyle and slides over the pretzels.

"Listen, Barlow," Kyle says while leaning his elbows on the table. "Your best man votes for a rash decision *exception*. This is an opportunity of a lifetime, don't you see it?"

"What a way to grow your business," Matt tells him. "You'll be raking in the dough. If I had some extra cash, I'd be buying my own RV. Something sweet to hit the road in."

"That's not bad," Kyle says. "Me? I'd buy myself a golf cart."

"Golf cart?" Cliff asks.

"To go with the house I apparently have to purchase, which is about to bust the Bradford bank. That reminds me," he says, pulling a notated index card from his shirt pocket. "You've all been assigned by my wife to help me pen the personal letter to accompany our desperate offer."

"Seriously?" Jason slides over Kyle's scrawled notes and skims them.

"Oh, yeah." Kyle grabs his card back and flattens it on the dark table. "Cutthroat tactics are the norm in house-buying these days, as evidenced by Lucas and Mackenzie making a move on Elsa's place first, and now mine."

Nick whips a pen out of a cargo pocket on his jacket. "I just wrote a persuasive essay for a class of mine. I'm on this, give me your notes."

"You really still in school?" Matt asks. "How old are you now?"

"Twenty-nine and feelin' fine. Because it's my last year. Another semester and I'll have my college degree all sewn up. Hell, then *I'm* free to make extra cash. I'd blow mine on …" He rubs his goatee and pauses. "A gym membership, since I'll have the time to go then. And hey," Nick advises Jason. "You might consider one, too. Get yourself *ripped* for the cameras."

"Hang on, hang on. No TV show will be happening anytime soon." Jason sits back and eyes them all, then motions for Nick to slide open the dusty window beside their booth. "I like my architecture business fine the way it is. Small, and under my complete control. I'm not listening to any boss or management telling me how to do my own thing."

"Isn't that what your contract is for?" Cliff lifts his beer for a sip. "To iron out those details?"

"Didn't sign the contract."

"What?" they all ask, practically in unison.

"It's just a provisional contract at this point, like a letter of intent committing to the project. But I need more time to think about it, you know. Hell, I'm busy enough as it is. My days are booked, sun-friggin'-up to sun-friggin'-down."

"*Gesù, Santa Maria.* You're killing me, Barlow." Kyle sits back in the booth and swipes his forehead. "How could you not sign?"

"You sure about passing up that TV offer?" Cliff asks. "Maybe you need a talisman, for some luck."

"A what?" Matt lifts the pitcher and tops off his glass.

"A talisman." Cliff pulls a scratched-up domino from his pocket. "You know, like a lucky charm. To bring you good fortune."

Jason takes the domino and turns it over in his hand. "This yours?"

"Sure. I found it at that new Maritime Market, in the parking lot. Picked it up and had some good luck ever since."

"From this dirty kid's toy? What kind of luck would that bring?" Kyle asks, squinting across the table with his hand outstretched.

Jason tosses Kyle the domino.

"You know," Cliff explains, reaching his open hand to Kyle, "little things. They've gone my way."

"So it's basically a good luck charm," Nick says, catching the domino when Kyle tosses it to him, ignoring Cliff's waiting hand.

"That *is* the definition of a talisman." Cliff motions for Nick to toss it his way. "A little positivity never hurt anyone," Cliff adds while snapping his fingers.

"I could use one of these," Nick says while toying with the domino. "Need some luck in my days."

"You need to *get* lucky, man," Kyle counters.

"The single stag at the table," Matt declares. "Holding on to his freedom."

"Hey, stop right there, boys." Cliff raises his beer glass. "We've got two bachelors at this table."

"Eh, you're just about spoken for," Jason says. "By a certain difficult *signora*."

Kyle nudges Matt to move so he can slide out of the booth. "Got to use the can."

"Hey," Nick calls, raising the domino over his head. "Go out for a pass."

"Bring it!" Kyle walks backward, hands raised, and catches the domino. When he brushes against a small table, he stops and apologizes to the couple sitting there.

Which gives Jason just enough time to leave the booth and head toward the jukebox, then turn and give Kyle a whistle.

Kyle veers away from the table, sidesteps and adjusts his stance. Finally he pulls his arm back over his shoulder and throws the domino, rolling it off his fingers to spin it straight across the room.

Jason sees it coming and gives a two-handed catch that snags the domino as he trots backward. When the gang erupts in a cheer, one particular voice out-yells them all.

"What'd I tell you, man?" Patrick hollers over from the bar. "Knock it off already, Barlow. No more funny business."

After giving Patrick a salute, Jason takes his seat in the booth beside Cliff and gives him his talisman. "Here you go, man. You hold on to that now, before it becomes part of our second down."

"Hey," Nick says to Jason, "passed your place the other day on my security route. Shit, that beach is dead off-season. But I waved to you, which you conveniently ignored. You miss it?"

"You can stay away from my place. Last time you were there, you got the rumor mill turning, big time. All of Stony Point thought I was having an affair."

"Nick the snitch, man," Kyle says under his breath as he returns to his seat beside him.

"Hey, I was on *your* payroll," Nick throws back at him.

Jason sees it coming before Nick does, the way Kyle shifts, then gets Nick in an arm-lock and gives him a noogie, rubbing his folded knuckles across Nick's head.

"You still owe me for that screwup, Nick." Jason leans back, eyeing him.

"Fine. Name it." Nick runs a hand through his messed hair once he pulls out of Kyle's muscle-bound grip. "Need an on-camera assistant? I'm your man."

"That's not a bad idea," Jason says, toasting his soda to Nick's beer glass.

"I'm required to do an internship last semester. Maybe that'll be it." Looking pretty damn proud of himself, Nick swigs his beer.

"But don't forget. You work for me, Nicholas," Cliff reminds him. "You're practically top guard now."

"A guy's got to keep his options open, boss," Nick muses. "On-camera assistant has a nice ring to it."

"Good one," Kyle says to Nick. "First, Jason's snitch. And now you'll be Jason's bitch."

"Hey, whatever it takes to stay in this *exclusive* club." Nick shrugs, all while air-quoting the words.

When the whole table's done laughing and busting his balls, Nick gives Kyle the last dig.

"You're just mad you didn't think of it first. See if I help you write that letter now."

"Oh, shit." Kyle grabs a paper napkin and swipes his forehead, then checks his watch, right as the waitress arrives with trays of overloaded plates. She sets them down one at a time and they disburse them—swapping dishes, grabbing sides, snagging tastes.

And around mouthfuls of dripping burgers, and between swigs of cold drinks, and while raising salted, ketchup-laden greasy fries, doesn't that letter take shape ... Oh, Jason can just imagine Lauren piecing together the lines and suggestions Kyle tries to jot down between bites.

"How about putting this in the letter?" Jason asks. "Me and my wife, Lauren, love Stony Point, especially Little Beach on hot summer nights. When no one is around, and clothing's optional."

"No, no," Nick interrupts while digging into his second burger. "Put this. I tend to sweat a lot, so it'll be nice having a sea breeze ... putting me at sweet ease."

"And don't forget your kids," Matt adds, before formally clearing his throat. "Tell them: My young'uns, Evan and Hailey, will have unforgettable summers, being raised by surrogate parents—your wonderful Parks and Rec crew."

With the warm Indian summer air drifting in, and the playoff game on the big-screen TV, and the second pitcher of beer on the table, Jason realizes that, yes, Maris knew all along. For a while anyway, as he sits with these guys with their food and drink, as they become the noisiest table in the bar with their outbursts of laughter and good cheer, for one evening, everything's right in their corner of the world.

At first, Elsa thinks she's hearing things. Maybe it's coming through her open kitchen window; the night is so warm, it feels like summer. But she swears she heard whispering, loud whispering, and someone hushing people. Then ... footsteps.

When the loud knock comes at her front door a moment later, it's definitely *not* her imagination. Sitting with a light sweater over her shoulders at the kitchen table, she leans back to get a clear view of the door down the hallway. And when Celia *opens* that door and walks inside, followed by Maris, Eva and Lauren pushing in behind her, well, Elsa knows the shenanigans are about to resume.

"Yoo-hoo, Elsa!" Maris says, sweeping into the kitchen. She raises a brown shopping bag and waves it in Elsa's direction.

"What's all this racket I've been hearing?" Elsa asks while lowering her leopard-print reading glasses on her nose and studying the women over the frame's edge. Steam rises from a cup of tea on the table.

"Noise?" Lauren asks.

"Yes. Giggling and shushing and chattering."

"Well, I guess we *can* break noise ordinances tonight," Maris tells her as she pulls out a chair and sits beside Elsa. "Because our Stony Point security force is unavailable. Aren't Nick and your boyfriend over at boys' night out at The Sand Bar?"

"My *boyfriend*?"

Celia waggles a finger at her. "Clifton Raines? Throwing pebbles at your window in the dark of night?"

"Ooh la la!" Lauren and Maris say in unison.

To which Elsa rolls her eyes, then lifts her tea for a sip.

"Is it just a fling?" Eva asks.

"Or will you go the distance?" With a mischievous grin on her face, Lauren sits across from Elsa.

"Oh, you kids!" Elsa raises her reading glasses again and pulls over the papers she'd been studying. As she does, she's fully aware of Celia inching around the table.

"Hey." Celia sets her hand on Elsa's shoulder and bends close behind her. "I recognize that folder. It's Sal's business plan. For your inn!"

"Yes. Well. You see ..." she says, glancing at Celia's face at her shoulder. "Okay, I was just moving it for now. For safekeeping."

Celia reaches her hand to the thick stack of typed pages and thumbs through the fresh, new sticky notes. The pale yellow sailor's knot bracelet Sal gave her hangs from her wrist. "Okaay," Celia says quietly.

"So that's good if you're putting it away." Maris lifts her shopping bag to the table. "Because that means you're free to hang out with us tonight."

"Hang out?" Now Elsa raises her glasses to the top of her head.

"Yes, Elsa DeLuca." Lauren walks around the table and takes Elsa's hand in hers, tugging it until Elsa stands. "Because tonight is also *ladies'* night ... on the beach."

"The beach?" Elsa glances at each of their smiling faces. Their twinkling eyes. Their ... wait. Their fleecy, fluffy fall pajamas—thermal leggings on some; tunic sleep-shirts on others; striped and plaid and cozy as can be. Not to mention their matching, furry slipper-booties, with pom-poms dangling and swinging from each pair.

"Yes, a beachside ladies' night. For a very *special* lady, actually." Maris reaches into the bag and pulls out a pair of star-and-moon flannel pajamas and brand-new booties, too. "And Aunt Elsa? *You* are the guest of honor."

twenty-two

IT ALL PLAYS OUT JUST as Maris had hoped. Wearing their warm bootie-slippers and fluffy pajamas, she and Eva each take one of Elsa's hands and walk with her up the boardwalk steps. There, the beach opens before them like a misty dream. Near the water, decorative nautical pilings are spaced across the sand. Rope is looped from one wood piling to the other, and on top of each, a candle flickers inside a Mason jar. More Mason jars—filled with sand, seashells and tea-light candles—line the edge of the boardwalk leading to the center, roofed pavilion. There, white twinkly lights are strung along the exposed beams to cast a soft glow. Eva's teenage daughter, Taylor, along with her best friend, Alison, work the Parks and Rec popcorn machine, as well as the movie projector.

Which is facing the framed, pull-down movie screen on the beach. In front of the white screen, sand chairs are neatly lined side by side. Each chair has a light blanket hung over the back, to drape across laps and legs if the sea breeze lifting off the water gets chilly. A few folding tables are set in the sand, too, to hold drinks and napkins.

Yes, all the stars are perfectly aligned tonight. Once on the boardwalk, Maris turns toward Long Island Sound. The seawater is dark beneath the dusky sky. As she looks up at the early stars faintly glimmering in the evening light, she can't help thinking of her mother, June. It feels like her mother's here, somewhere … in the twinkling Mason jars, in the stars above the sea, in the gentle breeze that touches her face as Maris steps onto the candlelit beach.

⁓

Long Island Sound's lazy breaking waves chase her back onto the sand. She watches them carefully, obviously believing they are truly after her. Upon the waves' retreat, her little legs dare to step back toward them, never to quite within their reach, while never far from her mother's reach, either. She is only a toddler, the girl in the blue-and-white ruffled bathing suit, her light brown hair falling with a salty fluff to just below her tanned shoulders. The last of an ice-cream bar clings to its stick, melting slowly and dripping on her toes.

"It's you!" Elsa whispers to Maris beside her while pointing to the movie screen. Maris simply takes Elsa's hand in hers and squeezes tightly. Together they watch the silent 8mm home movie playing seaside … to the backdrop of small waves lapping at the beach.

Now, a woman looks on from her low sand chair. Long, slender arms loosely hold her knees pulled up close while she glances from her daughter, Maris, to the sparkling expanse of salt water before her. Deep brown eyes level that gaze from beneath a wide-brimmed straw sun hat. She looks past the horizon, then closes her eyes as though thrilled that some ocean-star-wish has finally come true. Her sister, Elsa, made the journey across the sea and is here!

The Beach Inn

It suddenly feels as though Elsa is back on the beach with June again. Seeing her sister in her mid-twenties, sitting beneath that straw hat, takes Elsa's breath away and fills her eyes with stinging tears. The nostalgia of it all is almost painful. But she can't look away from the scene playing out silently, and larger than life, before her.

Beneath the September sun, June stands—casual in loosely cuffed jeans and an embroidered tunic, a brown wooden bangle on her wrist—and walks to little Maris. Ever so lightly, June's fingertips rest atop her daughter's head, moving through strands of salty hair. Life momentarily pauses in their brief seaward gazes, as though this forms the core of it.

Maris leans close and tells Elsa, "I always thought my mother was describing ocean stars to me in this scene." She points to the sparkling water on the screen. "Starlight in the daytime."

Elsa can only nod, unable to physically take her eyes off the movie on the beach. Because by watching, June is simply here again.

June nudges up her straw hat and walks ankle-deep into the water. A flash of summer sunlight flares as the camera turns into the sun, capturing her wading in the Sound.

"That was me filming your mother," Elsa tells both Maris and Eva now. "I remember holding that camera like it was yesterday. It was the September week your mother rented that cottage on the lagoon, thirty-five years ago now."

As she explains, the screen flickers between washes of light and June fading in the sunshine's glare, until a spray of dull white speckled with wavering black threads overcomes it as the scene ends.

But another begins right away as Maris' old 8mm silent home movies segue from one scene to the next. So together with her nieces, and with Celia and Lauren, Elsa watches her long-gone and dearly missed sister on the screen. While having hot buttered popcorn and drinking lemonade, they all see the Addison home where Maris grew up, and day trips to state parks and, of course, Stony Point.

It's a little surprising for Elsa, then, to see even herself on the screen—three decades younger on a long-forgotten Christmas Eve in June's Connecticut home. June and Elsa sit on a brocade sofa, their eyes shining, their heads tipped together in the telling of some delightful secret. June's auburn hair is brushed back, her wide-set eyes alive again. Maris, only a toddler and wearing a red velvet dress, sits on Elsa's lap and touches a beaded necklace hanging around Elsa's neck. Behind them, a cherry clock keeps time on the fireplace mantel, nestled in the greens of Christmas.

And it's beautiful, every moment of the lives replayed on the screen. Though the old films are silent, Elsa's thoughts fill in the talks, the laughter, the love ... as though she's right there in the scenes again. Her emotions and memories are as sweet as the beach breeze sweeping past, touching wisps of her hair; as constant as the rhythm of the tides, with their waves splashing over and over on the shore; as strong as the pungent salt air that fills Elsa's lungs when she gasps at what she sees next.

"It's Sal!" she exclaims, pointing to the screen. And the way she says it, the words filled with love and disbelief at once, gets Celia to rush to Taylor at the projector. Together they rewind the scene, then pause it.

"There?" Celia asks Elsa, coming back and kneeling behind her to watch over her shoulder.

Elsa nods at the stilled image. On the screen, people sit

around June's dining room table sparkling with crystal and silver. Each chair is filled, and more are pulled up to the table laden with food and drink. It's the celebration of Eva's christening, a celebration which Elsa, her husband and son flew to from Italy. Her husband, wearing a suit and loosened tie, sits at the table with a baby in his lap. With Salvatore, not yet even two years old; her husband, still alive then.

So Celia hugs Elsa from behind while Eva passes out tissues. Maris reaches for one, too, as they all talk of missing Sal.

But he isn't the only reason for their tears. Elsa feels it; feels the sad reality of two sisters separated once their mother, June, died. She imagines the reels of film that *never* came to be—of Maris and Eva growing up together the way that Elsa and June did. So Elsa discreetly blesses herself, ever thankful that the three of them—Maris, Eva, and herself—found each other again all these years later.

The film is eventually resumed, and just when Elsa thinks her heart can't burst any more than it has, it suddenly does. All while sitting beneath a star-sprinkled October sky and breathing the salt air that cures what ails you. The same salt air rustling the dune grasses off to the side. The dune grasses leading to the one mysterious and magical fairy-tale place of this special beach ... the lagoon.

The very same place the home movie takes her now.

―

Jason sits on the far end of the boardwalk. He and Cliff arrived here from The Sand Bar in time to watch the last two home movie scenes play on.

"Never seen anything like it," Cliff tells him. He sits beside Jason, seeming quieted by the candlelit beach before them. "Elsa will be very moved, I'm sure."

"No doubt. Especially seeing her sister, June, on the screen like that." Jason nods toward the dining room christening scene. "She's been gone for over thirty years now."

"There's no sound on the movies?"

"No. They're Maris' old silent 8mm films, which she had copied to DVD. The films ended up a little out of sequence in the transfer, but she loves them just the same." The two of them watch from a distance as the scene fades out. "It's funny how you can practically *hear* the voices anyway, can't you? Somehow."

When Maris stands and heads across the beach to the projector, Cliff gets up, too, and taps Jason's shoulder. "Listen, I'll grab us some of that popcorn now that they stopped the film." He walks down the boardwalk toward the pavilion, where the twinkly lights casting a glow on the popcorn machine apparently proved too much a temptation for him.

Alone now, and leaning his elbows on his knees as Maris pauses the movie for a brief intermission, Jason looks beyond the sand to the dark sea. How many scenes of his own did he live out with Neil in this very place … from crabbing on the rocks, and taking their little Boston Whaler out around the bends of the coast, and swimming to the big rock. To reenacting their father's Vietnam war stories—heaving their rock-grenades into the waves; hiding behind sandy foxholes; maneuvering the jungle-path to Little Beach as they fought off imagined snakes and insidious insects. To hanging out with the gang, filling empty summer hours together beneath the sun and stars as they all came of age.

He sees now what it does, watching real life on the screen. And he wonders if this was Maris' intent, too. To show him how our personal stories can move people in sentimental ways.

To convince him to say yes to Trent.

His gaze shifts to the stars over Long Island Sound. *The darker the night, the brighter the stars*, his father said of the skies of 'Nam. Jason drags the Vietnam War dog tags along the chain around his neck. If his father were still alive, what would he make of the twists and turns of Jason's life? Would his father tell him to take that TV offer? Or encourage him to live out his days quietly … a staid life, comfortable home, beautiful wife.

Fiddling with his chain, Jason keeps his gaze upward. Water and sky are the same midnight blue now, but the sky is alive tonight, with stars. Stars Jason couldn't look at just a month ago. Those stars mocked him with their hope, on a night when he *lost* all hope and shunned every memory as he drove away from this place. Tonight, he lets himself look at those stars, look long, before turning to the movie screen when the film resumes rolling.

"Check it out," Jason says to Cliff sitting beside him on the boardwalk again. While reaching over for a handful of buttered popcorn, he nods to the movie screen on the beach. "The movie's starting."

The scene opens with a twilight shot of the lagoon. And though the scene was filmed over three decades ago, time has a way of standing still here. And that's the magic—or the curse, depending—of Stony Point. If it wasn't for the tiny dark flecks and spots moving across the filmed silent scene, Jason could think the marsh images were from this past summer, when he rowed through the lagoon with Sal. Or from twenty-five years ago, and he'd half expect to see a moppy-haired Neil traipsing the marsh banks during childhood summers.

So this place frozen in time has the ability to evoke happiness at the same time it breaks his heart. Watching the home movie premiering on the beach big-screen, he's sure it's doing the same for Elsa.

In front of a lavender sunset on the screen, tall marsh grasses gently bend and sway. They silently move in such a way, you can practically hear them whisper. The calm lagoon waters wind and curl through the grasses, and the 8mm movie camera pans to shingled bungalows nearby. The paned windows are lamplit while the evening settles on the misty salt marsh.

And Jason knows exactly what's coming when soft glimmers stir in the tall marsh grasses. They flicker and rise to the dusky sky.

"What is that, in the grass?" Cliff asks.

"Fireflies."

As Jason says it, the camera focuses on a woman, her brown hair pulled back in a bandana, her hands holding an open Mason jar, her arms stretched to the sky as she slowly spins in the shadowy evening. If the sight of a young, carefree Elsa filling her very first happiness jar with fireflies brings tears to *his* eyes, Jason can only imagine what it's doing to Elsa right now. On the screen, she captures several fireflies in her jar, then turns and bends low. The smile on her face is tender as she shows the magical jar to the very little girl slowly approaching.

Jason looks from the screen to the beach his wife decorated today by placing simple Mason jar candles and tiny strung lights beside the sea. Maris sits close to Elsa, her head resting on Elsa's shoulder as they watch the home movie together from their sand chairs. Beyond them, the waves continue to break along the shore.

Seeing all this, seeing what Maris pulled off tonight, he falls in love with his wife all over again.

When Jason finally looks to the screen once more, he is taken far back in time. And what is playing out is the love Elsa had for Maris before June's tragic death separated them for over three decades. In this scene, Elsa steps closer to the child utterly enchanted by the twinkling firefly lights within the glass jar; her inquisitive eyes are riveted to it when Elsa crouches down in front of her. The twilight sky behind them is deep violet, the grasses lush and green and illuminated with more flickering fireflies. In that moment, Elsa places what looks like a jar of stars into the girl's hands.

Into Maris' hands.

twenty-three

As THE MOVIES ENDED THE night before, a silver mist rolled off the sea and hovered over the sand. To Maris, it was a magical moment—especially after watching old films of her mother on the screen. The very idea of her mother's essence here at Stony Point feels gentle, and reassuring, and she always feels that same gentleness in the sea mist.

Thursday morning, that magic continues when Maris sips her coffee while standing at the slider to the backyard. Outside, again, a faint mist floats above the grass. The gentle feeling inspires her, now more than ever, to finish Neil's novel. To not leave undone what is left behind. It's a good day for it. The house is quiet; Jason beat her out the door with some ridiculously early, and important, project on his agenda. He was so rushed, he didn't even have time to tell her about it.

But Maris lingers alone in the kitchen. Still no word from Elsa on whether she's been swayed to stay in Stony Point. Maris' secret hope is that Elsa felt such an emotional connection to this cherished beach last night—seeing faded movies of her sister strolling it, wading in the waves, catching fireflies—that she'll change her mind and stay here; stay with

The Beach Inn

all that love. Maris touches her watch, deciding to check in with Elsa later. Right now, it's time to immerse herself in Neil's manuscript.

So after tying back her hair and slipping a fisherman sweater on over her jeans, she hurries across that dewy lawn. It feels so spiritual to walk right through the mist that she bends down to sweep her fingers into the silvery haze, then raises her fingers to her lips while glancing up at the morning sun on her way to the barn studio.

Her first stop there? Jason's special bookshelf holding Neil's salty journals they rescued from the shack. She scoops all of them into her arms, rushes up the stairs while managing a clumsy pat of the mounted moose head, then spreads the journals across the grooved wood of the worktable Jason made for her. Aged tree knots and plenty of her own sewing nicks from hours of denim designing cover the table's surface. For luck, she runs her fingers over the *J + M* initials carved into the corner.

Next, she drags her inspiration board to within clear working-view. It's crammed with all the unfinished novel's character sketches, posed in various seaside scenes: hanging out on the boardwalk; strolling the beach; talking on cottage porches; painting a dinosaur boulder-mural at Little Beach; sitting on benches beside dune grasses swaying in hurricane-force winds. Visuals help bring details to her words.

Third on her itinerary? Stack Neil's manuscript pages neatly in front of her for a second read-through. Beside them, she opens a blank leather journal of her own, one in which to write notes and tap into Neil's voice. Finally, she settles beneath her blue-wave stained glass window and turns to the very first manuscript page.

"Maris! Come here, quick," Jason suddenly calls from down below.

Surprised that he's home, Maris spins around and sees him standing in the barn doorway. "I *just* sat down to work," she says as she turns back to the manuscript.

"You can work later. Because you've *got* to see this. Hurry up and come down!"

When she turns again, Jason's gone. And that worries her. There was an urgency to his words, and now Maris is afraid something's awfully wrong.

With one last look—okay, a look filled with longing—at the manuscript, Maris hurries down the stairs while slipping on a jacket and patting the moose head, too.

⁓

The last memorable boat Jason spotted from this vantage point on his father's stone bench was Sal's. Sal's little wooden rowboat, drifting in the dark of night. When Jason pictures it, the thought breaks his heart.

But now? Now, this.

"Do you see it?" Jason asks Maris beside him on the bluff. He points to where he wants her to look. The early morning fog has burned off and the day is crystal clear with bright sunshine and blue skies.

From the bench, Maris squints out at Long Island Sound in the distance. "What am I looking for? Where?"

"Here. Use these binoculars." He hands her a black pair.

"Where'd you get these?"

"Swiped them from old Maggie Woods' place before it went down." He leans over and helps Maris adjust the focus.

The Beach Inn

"First time they've been put to honest use."

Maris presses the binoculars to her eyes. She's silent for a long second, but a smile forms on her lips. "Jason Barlow." She glances at him, then through the binoculars again. "You *didn't*."

As she says it, he can start to make out the slow-moving tugboat pulling a barge. On the barge is Neil's dilapidated, silver-shingled seaside shack. It's strapped and roped and glimmering beneath those morning rays of sunshine.

"What better place for you to finish writing my brother's novel than in his buoy-strewn fishing shack?" he asks.

"But ... How did you ever?" The binoculars follow the tugboat moving across the water.

"Connections, darling. My contractor took care of it all. His crew emptied the shack and prepped it for the journey a couple days ago, bracing the walls, stabilizing the structure. Then they actually excavated around it to insert steel beams underneath, for support. After jacking it up, they moved it onto the barge and secured it yesterday, at high tide, of course. Now they're bringing it to their marina. It'll stay on a flatbed in their construction yard until I get a foundation poured, here." Jason looks out at the slow-moving barge getting closer and closer every minute. "That shack never would have survived the winter."

"Why didn't you tell me, babe?"

"Remember yesterday, when you asked me if everything was okay? That I looked tired?"

Maris nods, still riveted to the barge.

"This was part of it. I *knew* the shack was being prepped, and I didn't want to say anything in case it didn't work out." Jason looks at that little shack floating on the Sound and swipes away a tear. "But it did."

"My God ..." Maris rests the binoculars in her lap and turns to him. "It's like you're bringing Neil home."

Jason looks from her, out to the blue waters buoying up his brother's secret shingled shack after all these years. He may not feel Neil's presence anymore, or hear his voice in the wind, or breaking waves. But at least he'll have this hideaway shanty that his brother so apparently loved. As it floats beneath the sun, he sees the deep wood grain of the silver shingles, and the faded white wood-planked door, and the four-paned window with its curls of weatherworn paint peeling off.

His hand reaches to the dog tags hanging around his neck. Maris might call it bringing Neil home. But Jason? He'd call it something else.

Still holding the Vietnam dog tags, he looks up at the blue sky. It's all he can do to not break down and cry, thinking of his father's war stories. Leaving Neil's shack deserted on that ragged beach felt too much like leaving a wounded, or dead, comrade behind.

Finally, yes, Jason's doing what his father would have done. He's getting his brother off the field.

―

"They accepted your offer." Eva motions Kyle and Lauren into her front-porch office early that afternoon.

"What?" Kyle asks while opening the door. Before Eva can answer, he drops into a wicker chair.

"The sellers accepted your offer, including covering the closing costs."

"Are you kidding?" Lauren asks. "But you just presented

the offer this morning!"

"First thing, *with* your personal letter. Which is what I truly believe clinched it."

With sudden tears streaming down her face, Lauren spins around to Kyle. "You did it," she whispers. "Hallelujah! You nailed it with that letter."

He nods, feeling unexpectedly calm now that their house-hunt is over. Calm enough to stand and give his wife a hug without feeling woozy. He kisses the side of her head, saying into her ear, "We'll have to sell our house in Eastfield, fast."

Lauren pulls back, holding his hands now. "Maybe Celia can help stage it for a quick sale."

It's funny how when Lauren turns to Eva and hugs her, too, Kyle pulls it all together. He's surprising even himself with the way he's ordering his thoughts. But it's hard to get a word in edgewise, with Lauren and Eva getting carried away already. "We'll need to get measurements and photos of the new house," Kyle interrupts. "Inside shots, to plan reno projects with Jason."

"Yes," Lauren agrees. "And I talked to my mom."

"Already?" Kyle asks.

"This morning. She said that if it all went through, we could live with her and Dad so the kids can finish out the school year in Eastfield. You know, when *our* house sells. Because we don't need to juggle two mortgages, on top of everything else. And that gives us time to tackle some of the remodeling before moving in here."

"Guys," Eva says from her desk, where she finally sat. "Yoo-hoo!" she calls out, waving the signed contract. "Chill … One thing at a time."

Lauren walks to an old trunk Eva had stenciled starfish on,

and picks up a piece of painted driftwood from the windowsill above it. "I can't believe you still have this. It was my *first* driftwood scene," she tells Eva. "I was a teenager, sitting on a boulder at Little Beach and painting an old rowboat I saw abandoned in the beach grasses."

"It's beautiful, Lauren."

With a sob, Lauren drops into a chair. She holds the painted driftwood in her lap. "It's just hitting me, how much of my life has happened right here, over the years."

Kyle steps behind her and squeezes her shoulder. "Let's take a drive-by, Ell. Okay?"

She sets the boat-art down. "You take good care of that, Eva."

"Oh, I will. And congratulations again! I'll be in touch with more details soon."

"Speaking of details," Kyle says while sidling up to her desk. "Any chance you can slip us the house key? Just for today, so we can sneak in for another look around?"

"Kyle!" Lauren scolds with a light slap. "She'll get in trouble." Lauren throws a glance at her watch. "Plus I'd have to call my mom to get the kids off the bus, then."

"I don't know." Eva eyes them. "If you get caught, or do any damage, I'd lose my license."

"Seriously?" Kyle asks Eva now. "You're worried, after breaking into Foley's two summers ago and throwing the illegal party of the decade?"

"Okay, fine. But keep it under your hat." Eva pulls a key ring out of her desk drawer. "The house is empty, so I don't think the owners will mind. Just make it a quick visit, you guys."

She hands the key ring to Kyle, who tosses it in the air and turns to leave. Opening the door, he waits for Lauren to go ahead of him. When she grabs her tote and does, she obviously can't contain her joy and gives him a quick kiss. But it's when Kyle finally steps outside and the door closes behind him that Eva calls out from her desk.

"Bye, *neighbors!*"

Which brings instant perspiration to his face as his calmness evaporates and the harsh reality of the moment hits.

He and Lauren did it. They bought a Stony Point house and are on their way to see it, right now. He breathes in a long breath of that salt-air-that-cures-what-ails-you and hopes it does, fast.

Because the panic is all sweeping back like a wave—a tidal wave, to be exact—the pounding heart, the sweats, the feeling winded. Mortgage, commitment, home improvements, money, money, money.

"And you bring that key back by tomorrow," Eva calls out the door. "Lickety-split!"

twenty-four

THAT AFTERNOON, ELSA AND CELIA sit in a window booth at the newly renamed Dockside Diner. Outside, the sun sparkles on the harbor water further down the street. Elsa manages to glimpse the masts of a few large sailboats bobbing in the water there. Right across the street, twinkly lights and autumn-leaf garlands are strung across the quaint shop windows. Some of the storefront doors are propped open to the Indian summer day. One boutique has a sign in its window: *Prices are falling, so you can rake in the savings!*

"Maybe we can stop in and find a bargain," Elsa tells Celia right as their sandwiches are delivered.

"Personal service today," Jerry says as he sets their lunch plates down. "Any friend of Kyle's gets the very best here."

"Why thank you, Jerry," Elsa tells him. "And where is Kyle? I'd love to say hello."

"Rob and I are covering the kitchen. Kyle took the afternoon off, something to do with house-hunting."

"Ooh," Celia muses while taking off her embroidered denim blazer and eyeing the plates of food. "I wonder if they got the one on Bayside Road."

"Elsa," Jerry says, pulling a chair up to their booth and sitting there wearing his chef apron. "I was so sorry to hear about your son. Sal." He reaches over and clasps her arm. "I never got a chance to tell you that he was a wonderful person, and we really enjoyed it when he pitched in here. That guy always got a smile out of everyone."

"Thank you, Jerry. Thank you so much."

He gives her arm another pat. "Just know, he's very much missed by all of us here."

"By me, too," Elsa whispers with a nod. As Jerry walks back to the kitchen, she can picture her Wall Street son wearing his waitstaff apron while weaving between tables, nodding to one customer, winking at another, saving his smile for a third. Sal would tell her about things like the driftwood paintings Lauren displayed, and he even brought Elsa a new diner T-shirt—which she often wears while gardening.

"The food looks amazing," Celia is saying in the meantime. She lifts the top of her turkey club and adds a sprinkle of salt, then pulls her side of potato salad closer.

"Yes." Elsa pats the top of her chicken salad roll. "And I'm starved! Exciting news always whets my appetite."

"I'm famished, too. Being back in this salt air, lately I simply *cannot* stop eating." Celia bites into her sandwich and reaches for one of Elsa's French fries at the same time. "Wait a second. Wait." She squints at Elsa while lifting her ketchup-laden fry. "News, you said? You have news, Mrs. DeLuca?"

"Mm-hmm. Let me explain," Elsa says before tasting her chicken sandwich. "I knew when that first frame hit the movie screen on the beach last night."

"Knew? Knew what? And Elsa," Celia adds while leaning close, "I do hope it's what I'm thinking."

Elsa sets down her sandwich and sips her iced water. Celia's had a difficult time with Sal's death; it shows on her gentle face. Even now, as Celia tucks her auburn hair back behind her ear, Elsa notices shadows beneath her eyes. It also can't be missed that Celia still wears Sal's sea-glass engagement ring on her finger. So this feels right, sharing her private thoughts with her almost-daughter-in-law today. "When I saw those old home movies of my sister, it felt like she was alive again, walking the beach, sitting on the boardwalk with me and pointing out the fallen stars twinkling on the morning sea. And I imagined what June might tell me to do with my life, if she were here. Especially if she saw us all together on the beach last night, beneath those stars."

Celia squeezes Elsa's hand. "I think she did. Because her daughters, Maris and Eva, have beautiful souls. What an incredible evening they put together for you."

Elsa is nodding, unable to contain her words. "I *felt* June there, felt her hand brush mine. And I know she wants this." She sits back in the booth and smiles at Celia across from her.

"Wants what?"

"This ... After a night of many tears, Celia, and so much love, my decision is definite and final. As of this spectacular Thursday morning, my beach inn *will* open next year, as planned."

"Elsa! I am *so* thrilled!" Celia jumps out of her booth seat, rushes around the table and wraps Elsa in a long hug before sitting again. "But are you absolutely sure?"

"Never been more certain. I've already asked the real estate agency to remove the For Sale sign. Now, I need to reinstate the Ocean Star Inn's dream team, and pronto! My architect, Jason. Artist Lauren to paint the inn's sign, as well as complete

The Beach Inn

several driftwood centerpieces. And of course ..." Elsa pauses, her eyes tearing up. "You," she whispers.

"Me?" Celia asks around a mouthful of sandwich.

"Yes, you. Way back when, you agreed to use your home-staging skills as my inn's interior decorator. We'll need to bring in furnishings and accessories after Jason's renovations. But first we'll need to fine-tune the inn's room themes, as well as make lots of happiness jars for the guests to fill." Elsa adds more ketchup to her fries. "I understand if you have to go back and forth to Addison to stage homes before the holidays, and to check on your own house there."

"Oh, my house is fine." Celia scoops up an overloaded forkful of potato salad. "My dad planted himself there. He'd been living in a condo, so he loves having a yard again."

"Then I should be asking you the same question. You're *absolutely sure* you can stay on?"

Celia considers Elsa, then sets down her fork. A waitress carrying an overloaded tray scoots past on her way to a nearby booth. "Yes. But with stipulations," Celia says.

"Such as?"

"I'll help you decorate your beach inn on two conditions. A, you are *not* to rent out the guest cottage as part of the inn, as it will be my permanent residence now. With some updates from your architect."

"Wait. Permanent?"

"Yes. Which leads me to B." She pauses as another waitress breezes to their table carrying a pitcher of iced water to top off their glasses. Finally, Celia continues. "I've given this some thought, and even reread Sal's business plan. It is too much to run a beach inn alone. To run *anything* alone. And your son wanted your inn to be *thee* finest bed-and-breakfast on the

Connecticut shoreline. Which is not going to happen, Elsa, not all by your lonesome."

When Celia pauses, Elsa sees something in her hazel eyes. A change. A confidence. Maybe it comes from being back here. From sitting on the beach last night and breathing that sweet salt air. From feeling right at home in this coastal diner with its walls draped with seashell-dotted fishing net, with its nautical lanterns glowing in each window.

Maybe it comes from being right where she needs to be.

"So," Celia continues, "I want you to hire me—not *only* as your decorator, but as assistant innkeeper, too." She pauses again, then extends her hand firmly across the table. "Deal?"

Elsa squints at Celia. "Assistant innkeeper? But you don't have experience."

"I don't, Elsa. I know." Celia slowly withdraws her waiting hand. "But neither do you, to speak of."

"That's only partly true. You see, in Milan, I owned my own clothing boutique. I was a businesswoman and worked for years with my customers, not only in selling, but with hospitality. Because yes, there were times when I actually served coffee and snacks in my shop, too."

"And you could teach me everything, Elsa. I'll learn quick, I promise."

Elsa glances outside at the small boutiques here, across the street. Businesses on the sea—they make it feel like hers is meant to be. Yet all the while, her mind dwells now on something Celia mentioned. It *would* be difficult to run an inn alone, even a small one. In Milan, her husband often helped out before he suddenly died a few years back. So she looks at Celia across the table. It's obvious by her now-worried eyes that she doubts Elsa will accept her proposition.

The Beach Inn

"Well, I'm not sure ..." Elsa reasons.

"But you know you can count on me. And we've worked together already, starting to decorate your inn. The buoys alongside the fireplace, for one? The summer parties we arranged?"

"But taking on innkeeping responsibility is huge, and sounds like it might be one of those rash decisions, no?"

Celia wastes no time; her nod begins before Elsa finishes her thought. "Oh, it is a rash decision, Elsa. It *is*, and I don't care!" With tear-filled eyes, she continues. "We're two strong women, and heck, life's for living," she insists. "If anyone ever taught me that, it was Sal."

"But what about your *life* in Addison? Your friends. And your home and job there?"

Celia's smile is genuine, with some sadness, too. "My home feels *here*, now," she whispers. "Because ever since I fell in love with your son, my *heart* belongs to Stony Point Beach."

"Assistant innkeeper, you say?" Elsa tips her head to the side and eyes Celia, then extends her hand. "Sometimes rash decisions are meant to be!" She stands and leans over the table to turn the business handshake into a long hug filled with love, excitement, and lingering grief, too. Because they both sense who else was supposed to be shaking on this business deal. Sal is gone, but Elsa knows he'd want only Celia working alongside her. When they finally sit, both women give each other napkins to wipe the tears from their faces.

"Oh, they're such happy tears, Elsa."

"Sal would be so happy, too, knowing that we'll be working together." Elsa looks outside toward the distant harbor water again, hearing the words he'd surely say: *Sorridi, Ma. Sorridi.* Smile. And so she does. When she turns back to Celia, their partnership begins. "It's official, then. First order of business?"

"Wait, I call dibs on that one." Celia motions for their waitress to get her attention. "Cupcakes, here! Two, with lots of chocolate frosting! And a candle in each, if possible."

"Okay," Elsa relents. "So, second order of business?" she asks while pulling her cell phone from her handbag. "Here, help me word this carefully. I have to go into New York next week to meet with Sal's lawyers about his estate. So this will have to happen before I go."

"What will have to happen?"

Just then, their waitress sets down two cupcakes, each sparkling with a tiny, lit candle, which they promptly wish upon and blow out together.

"Now, back to business," Elsa says as she slides her phone close, and as Celia sinks her teeth into her sweet cupcake. "We'll make the formal announcement of our partnership at a grand beach party this weekend," Elsa says as she taps the phone screen. "Oh, will everyone be surprised!"

So together, huddled over their very first business lunch, an invitation is group-texted from a window-side booth in the Dockside Diner:

> Please Come: The Inn-Is-Not-For-Sale Party!
> Hosted by: Elsa DeLuca
> When: Saturday, October 10 at 7 PM
> Where: Ocean Star Inn, main dining room
> Attire: Casual
> Attitude: Happiness

twenty-five

To KEEP EVA OUT OF trouble, Kyle and Lauren are extra careful when they quietly close the pickup's doors and tiptoe across the front lawn later that afternoon. The empty house on Bayside Road rises before them, the windows dark, the street quiet. Beyond the dune grass across the street, silvery waves of the bay lap along the narrow beach.

Kyle jumps, though, when the peace is disrupted by both their cell phones dinging at the same time. He pulls his from his back pocket and scrolls the text message.

"Group text, Ell. You're going to like this one. It's a party."

"For who?" she asks while digging deep into her overstuffed tote where her own phone must be buried.

"More like *from* who. Elsa."

"Really?" Lauren comes up behind him, grabs his hand holding *his* phone and pulls it closer. "Is this what I think it is?" She takes Kyle's phone and reads the message. "For real?" she asks while tucking a loose strand of blonde hair back into her topknot. "It worked, our movie night worked! Elsa's keeping the beach inn! Oh my God, I don't believe it." After more quiet moments when she instantly RSVPs to the party invitation, she says, "I have to get her inn sign finished. She'll be needing it soon."

"Don't worry. Plenty of time for that." Kyle takes his phone and returns it to his pocket. "Let's get inside here and see what we got ourselves into. And we can't be long, Ell. Eva's antsy to have the key back."

At the front step, Kyle jangles the key ring while Lauren stands close behind him, fidgeting and bouncing on her feet. He feels her pressing against him, slipping her arms around his waist as he slowly opens the door. But he stops suddenly then, and hesitates.

"What's the matter?" Lauren whispers.

Kyle turns around to her standing there in her poncho over torn skinny jeans, her thick blonde hair looped in that high bun, her gray eyes spilling with happiness. It's clear how badly she's wanted this—a year-round house at the beach. And so he does it, just for her. He bends and scoops her up into his arms, then gives a joggle to shift her into a comfortable position. After a quick kiss, he turns again and carries her over the threshold.

"Whoa! Whoa, Kyle!" she says with a wide grin while swinging her ankle-booted feet.

Lauren deserves this. Kyle recalls that carrying someone over the threshold is a way to ward off evil spirits as you move from one life to another. Doorways are a portal for those spirits, so keeping your feet off the floor prevents this from happening. And Lord knows, he and Lauren have plenty of haunting spirits following behind them.

If there's one other thing Kyle knows, it's this: Starting right now, he's leaving all their past troubles on the *other* side of that door.

"Shh, Ell," he warns, keeping his spirit-thoughts to himself so as not to ruin the moment. Still holding her in his arms, he bends and kisses her once more, deeper this time, because this time he means it, as he silently kicks the door shut behind them.

⁓

By the time Celia and Elsa left the diner and shopped for things they'd need for the inn-is-not-for-sale party, it happened. Celia convinced Elsa to make her *second* major decision of the day: to drop by Cliff's trailer and tell him the inn is back on.

"I want you to wear that cropped jacket you told me about. It'll look good over the denim blouse," Celia says later in Elsa's bedroom. She stands behind her at the dresser mirror and runs a brush through Elsa's thick hair. "It's good you freshened your highlights. That color is so pretty."

"You think so?" Elsa lifts some strands and scrutinizes the caramel streaks.

"I do." Celia sets down the hairbrush and turns to a rack of scarves. She picks a silky tan one and wraps it around Elsa's neck, right at the collar of her fitted denim shirt. "Tuck it in to where your top buttons are opened."

Elsa fusses with her scarf as Celia runs out of the room knowing precisely what the outfit needs. She returns minutes later holding a pair of shoes. "These are mine, but we're close in size. And they're *exactly* your style." She drops the zebra-print ballet flats on the floor. "Your boyfriend will love them, they're very sexy."

"Boyfriend?" Elsa asks as she lifts the cuff of her black pants and sets a foot into one of the shoes, then turns it for a better look. "I wouldn't call Clifton Raines my boyfriend."

"I would. Cliff's been trying so hard to get you to stay in Stony Point. I told you this whole Operation Make Elsa Smile was all his idea." She nudges her second shoe closer to Elsa. "Cliff may be gruff around the edges, but he's a softie. I see it. He melts when he looks at you."

"All right, so I'll go see him and tell him my mind's made up. I'm staying put. But how do I do this? Just show up at his, well, at his *trailer*?"

Celia briskly nods. "Put on some lipstick, first." She hands Elsa a pale shade. "Just a little. And remember ... the way to a man's heart is through his stomach. So come with me," she says when Elsa's done with her lipstick. "I have just the thing." Celia takes her hand and leads her through the rambling old cottage. They continue on, straight out back to the porch stoop of the gingerbread guesthouse that is now Celia's. The sun is going down, and the sky above the distant beach has a pink hue.

"Wait right here," Celia warns her as she rushes through the living room to the quaint galley kitchen.

"Are you sure about this?" Elsa asks when Celia returns to the doorway and drops a wrapped loaf of bread in her hands.

Again Celia only nods. Well, she throws in a wink, too, as she nudges Elsa, all dolled up, straight outside and off her mini-cottage stoop.

For the first time in a long time, Elsa drives under the fifteen-mile-per-hour speed limit, instead of zipping along at her usual whooshing pace. Anything to give herself a few extra seconds to change her mind.

The Beach Inn

"I can't believe I'm doing this," she whispers while steering her golf cart into the gravel parking lot outside the white, flat-roofed trailer. "Here I am in my late fifties, going to a man's apartment?" She scoops up the wrapped loaf of bread and walks toward the four steps leading to a steel entry door. The trailer's sliding windows are glowing with lamplight, so Cliff must be inside. Must be ... home.

But Elsa hesitates as she climbs the dingy steps. After a glance at the cranberry-nut bread in her hand, followed by a look back at her golf cart, she takes a deep breath. "Well okay," she says in the evening light, "here I go."

Then, she does it. She gives three raps on the industrial gray door.

"It's not locked. Come in," Cliff's voice calls.

So she pushes the door open and steps into the reception area to see Cliff huddled over a computer at his old metal tanker desk. Celia really needs to spruce up *this* place, too, she thinks, to give it the right Stony Point beach vibe.

"Elsa?" Cliff rolls his chair back from the desk. "What are you doing here?"

"Didn't you get my text message? You didn't RSVP."

"Text message?" He reaches across the desk for his cell phone and gives it a shake. "No. Service is so fickle in this metal trailer. It blocks the signal so sometimes calls come through, sometimes not."

Elsa closes the door behind her, then turns toward Cliff. The front lobby is sparse—the reception desk, a few steel-framed chairs scattered about. A small office to the side houses a printer, which is printing and flipping pages as she stands there. "Well, how long do you plan on living in this, this ..." She points to the wall further behind his desk, where an open door leads to his temporary apartment. "It's just not a proper residence for a former judge, after all!"

"Suits me for now. And I like the look of this little trailer, with all the clean lines—a bit mid-century modern, if you ask me. Anyway, I'll get around to moving. Eventually." Cliff gives her a quick smile, then rushes to retrieve the printer papers, which he spreads out across his desk before looking at his computer screen. He wears an unbuttoned gray-marled sweater over a red flannel shirt—the flannel cuffs casually turned back.

Elsa steps closer, clutching the loaf of bread and craning her neck to see the computer screen. "Is that the latest Stony Point newsletter you're working on?" She suspects it is simply by the way he's so engrossed in reading it. He always crafts his news updates with the utmost attention to detail.

"I'm just about to finalize it at this moment," he tells her vaguely while skimming the screen, then glancing at the printed version on his desk.

"Wait!" She steps to his desk and puts down the bread, first, before finding her cell phone in her purse. "Stop the presses, would you?" she asks while pulling up her inn-is-not-for-sale text on her phone and lowering it for Cliff to read. "Because I might have news to add."

He rolls his chair closer to read her text message celebrating the return of the beach inn. "Well, I'll be damned," he softly says.

She steps back when, yes, he finally looks up at her. Okay, looks at her with a raised eyebrow, too. And that dimple! Elsa touches her hair. "It's just that I thought you should know."

"So my wooing worked?" Cliff asks, looking pleased as punch while smiling and leaning back in his office chair.

The Beach Inn

"What? *Wooing?*" Elsa snatches her phone and tosses it in her bag. "You're being a little presumptuous, Commissioner Raines, to think that my decision to keep the inn was *your* doing!"

"Well, it just seems," he says while motioning for her to sit in the chair alongside his desk, "that your staying *followed* my wooing."

Elsa slowly drops into the chair and fusses with the loaf of bread. "It's not that, not at all. It was the home movies, and the beach ... those candles, and the waves. Such a lovely night ..."

"It was, actually. Your nieces went all out." Cliff slides his chair closer and leans across the desk for the wrapped bread. "I'll slice this," he quietly says. "Stay for a nice warm piece? I have a microwave in the back."

When he stands up, taking the bread with him, Elsa stands, too. She tosses a glance behind her toward the trailer entrance, then clears her throat and follows Cliff through the accordion-style door separating his private back living quarters from the office. He sets the bread on a laminate countertop in his kitchenette, unwraps the loaf and places it on a plate before getting butter from his mini-fridge.

All the while, Elsa walks past a new four-panel room divider screening off his futon and sleeping area—which is looking all cozy, illuminated by a soft lamp. She continues past his bistro table with its two chairs, and inches closer to Cliff. "Celia baked that. It's cranberry-nut bread," she says.

Rummaging through some tiny cutlery drawer, he glances back at Elsa. "And a perfect evening snack."

By the time Cliff finds a sharp knife and cuts one slice, Elsa is beside him. "You're cutting it wrong!" She leans in front of him. "It's fresh baked, and you're slicing it too thin, making the bread all crumbly. And look," she insists, holding up a sad piece. "No berries in your slice."

What she failed to notice is how, when she inched closer and picked up the slice, Cliff backed up. Backed up holding the knife—his other hand to his scruffy chin, his blue eyes twinkling—and simply watched her. She does notice this now, every bit of it, including that darn dimple again, when she says, "Here, cut it like this," and looks back with her hand extended for the knife.

And that's where her empty hand stays, midair, hovering. Neither one of them moves as Elsa's eyes take him in, from the top of his swept-back salt-and-pepper hair to the bottom of his leather trail shoes, and then up again.

Which is precisely when she makes her *third* momentous decision of the day.

Elsa moves her already raised hand to his face, rests it on his cheek and, yes, leans over and kisses him. Deeply, too, as she steps close. After he awkwardly bends mid-kiss to set down the knife, his hands come around her waist and pull her even closer against him. Which is when she stops, though. Stops with a new thought as she brushes her hand over her hair, loosens the silky scarf at her neck and backs away.

"Hold that kiss," she whispers.

"Hey, hey! Where you going?"

Elsa walks to the open door leading to the office area, stops in front of it and turns around to face Cliff. With a small smile, she raises her foot wearing the zebra-print ballet flat and kicks the pleated door closed.

The Beach Inn

"It arrived on its trailer and is being stored at the moving company's truck yard, on a flatbed," Jason says into his desk phone in the barn studio. He can't talk enough about how Neil's dilapidated shingled shack was brought home, finally. Through the skylights above him, a few early stars glimmer in the inky sky. "You've got to see it, Rick. There's no telling how old that shack was when Neil came upon it, so it's right up your historical alley."

"Can't wait. Name the day, Barlow."

"It'll be hauled to my place once a foundation slab is poured. But the boxes of Neil's gear and furniture were delivered already. Hell, even his old manual typewriter is here—and Maris is *itching* to get her hands on that piece. You know, since she's tinkering with that manuscript I told you about." Which gets Jason to spin his desk chair around and consider several cartons stacked on the wide-planked wood floor, along the wall of immense framed photographs of his completed cottage renovations. The rest of the shack furniture—tables, chairs, loose shelving—is stored in a back room off his studio. Jason hasn't had a day this good in weeks.

"And what's going on with your CT-TV offer? Cameras ready to roll?"

"Whoa, not quite. That's a whole other animal," Jason tells Rick. "I talked with Trent again, but no meetings are scheduled unless I'm ready to sign a preliminary contract."

"If it helps your decision, I can assist with the historical aspect of any old cottage you might feature. You're here all the time—my salvage yard's filled with artifacts to place architectural details within a timeframe, or a certain era."

"Thanks, I'm just not sure yet, guy. You know, I'm not really down with putting my personal thoughts there on the screen. For the world to see."

"Or all of Connecticut, at least. Because let's keep it real … it's a local station, man. Anyway, it's your call, remember that. But only because I have a wedding to attend this weekend and can't be at Elsa's party, where I *would* do my best to wrangle you into signing that contract. That TV gig is just what you need. Get you out of your comfort zone. Not to mention, people would love the old cottage angle."

"Wait." Jason rolls his chair back to his desk, brushes loose papers off his leather planner and turns the page to October. "Party? What party?" he asks.

"Didn't you hear from Elsa?"

"No. Maris actually hides my cell phone sometimes. Thinks I work too much."

"Ah, she's got good intentions, my friend. Go easy on her."

Jason shakes his head with a glance toward the double slider and his weathered gray house across the yard. The kitchen is lit up, and a few other windows glow with lamplight.

"But it looks like the inn is on again, which Elsa will be formally announcing," Rick is saying.

"Hang on, back it up here. How do you know this before me?"

"She called the salvage yard to place an order for as many vintage Mason jars that I could find. When I asked for details, she said they'll be for her new inn. At which point she invited me to a party celebrating it all. I'll be away, but she's got some grand shindig planned."

"No shit. Elsa's beach inn is happening?" Jason reaches over to his bin of rolled inn blueprints and runs his hand over them. "Looks like my schedule just toppled, man."

"Unless you combine that reno with the TV show pilot."

"Right. That'd be something." Suddenly the slider is opening behind Jason, and he looks to see Maris in the doorway. "Later, dude," he tells Rick and disconnects the call. Then he does one of his favorite things: merely watches his beautiful wife breeze into the room, all smiles, holding up a cell phone. She wears silver-paint-speckled skinny jeans with a V-neck, camel-colored sweater over them, loosely tied white sneakers on her feet.

"We got a surprise text today!"

Jason motions her closer and she gives him his phone. When he reads the inn-is-not-for-sale party invitation, Maris reads it aloud over his shoulder.

"Attitude happiness?" she asks. "As if!"

"Well, will wonders never cease," Jason says. "Your aunt finally came around."

"So it worked." Maris brushes aside papers and bills and sits on the edge of his desk. "My movie night did the trick."

After Jason sets his phone on the desk, he reaches up and strokes Maris' hair. "I'm not surprised. Last night was unmatched, sweetheart. Everybody was moved to tears."

"Oh, this is such wonderful news! Elsa's *staying*, and is opening her Ocean Star Inn! I'm over the moon," Maris says while picking up Jason's cell phone. "Let me text our RSVP right away, because we are so going to be there."

"When is this shindig? Saturday?" he asks while glancing at his planner again.

"Yes. Saturday night. I'm sure it'll be a bash to beat all others."

"No doubt."

"Listen," Maris says when she's done texting. "I really need you for a sec. I've been working on Neil's novel in the dining room, reviewing the manuscript, and I have a question for you. Do you have a minute?"

"For you?" Jason stands and gives her a kiss. "Always."

They close up the barn studio and cross the backyard toward the house. The air's cooler tonight, and fallen leaves and twigs snap beneath their feet. Inside, Maris takes his hand and sits him at the dining room table, beneath the black lantern-chandelier. He notices how she'd lit several candles around the manuscript, too, to set an evocative atmosphere for her workspace.

"Read this," Maris says as she hands him one of the manuscript pages.

Jason takes it, and feels that the paper is slightly warped from years spent in that seaside shack. He reads the page, then glances over at Maris sitting beside him. "Looks like a love scene."

"It is." She turns sideways on her chair and leans her elbows on her knees. "Let me explain where the storyline's at. The friends are stranded in a cottage during a hurricane. And this love scene starts to unfold, with different characters pairing up."

"Okaay." He raises an eyebrow and looks back to the typed page. "But a love scene … in a *closet*?"

"Exactly." Maris nods, her eyes twinkling, too. "And Jason, when I write these scenes, I really need them to be authentic. Especially if I'm to be taken seriously as an author. So is having sex even *possible*, do you think, in those tight quarters?"

He shrugs and turns up his hands.

"Well," she continues while tucking her hair behind an ear, "that's the scene I'm jotting notes on because it's one of the unfinished passages I need to complete."

"And you have to make it realistic," Jason repeats.

Again, Maris nods. But this time, she does more. She first slips off her white sneakers, then takes Jason's hand. "So I need a favor," she says as they both stand and she leads him to a small closet in the paneled hallway, near the jukebox alcove. "Will you help me?" she whispers, nodding toward the closet. "See if it can be done?"

Jason opens the closet door and turns on the overhead light.

"No!" she quickly says. "In the hurricane, the power's out. No lights!"

"No lights?" he asks with a glance back.

She shakes her head, smiles, and steps beside him.

So he switches off the light while still watching her. Her brown hair hangs loose, and her casual sweater is actually cut pretty low. The lacy edge of her black bra shows in the edges of the deep V-neckline.

"Okay," Maris tells him, setting her hands lightly on his chest. "Now back in a little. And ... and we have to be *real* quiet, because in the novel, other people are trapped in the cottage, too. In nearby rooms."

Now if anyone ever told Jason Barlow this morning that he'd end his day making love to his wife in a cramped closet, he'd have told them they're crazy. But from the look of things, that's precisely what's about to happen.

Because as Maris stands barefoot in the closet doorway, she easily lifts that loose camel-colored sweater off over her head and tosses it out to the hall. After a moment, she stands on her toes and kisses Jason's whiskered cheek, then works her way along his jaw and to his neck as he leans into a rack of soft coats hanging behind him. When her mouth finds his, he deepens the kiss while his hands slide up the soft bare skin of her sides, over the curve of her breasts, then move to her back to unclip her black bra.

"Wait," Maris says, backing up a step and pressing a finger to his lips. The closet door is open behind her and light from the living room makes its way into the stuffy, crowded space. She stands there, simply breathing in the tiny, warm closet, her breasts spilling from that lacy bra. In a moment, she takes his hand and brings it to her jeans, so he unbuttons and unzips them, first, slipping his hands beneath the denim fabric and feeling her silk panties—right before she looks back at the open closet door, reaches for the knob and shuts out all light as she very slowly pulls the door closed behind her.

twenty-six

SATURDAY NIGHT, ELSA SITS AT her dining room table, pauses, and takes in the sight. Gold-glittered pinecones and tiny white pumpkins are casually placed around flickering lanterns atop her long, wood-planked table. Every one of her distressed navy French country chairs is occupied, with a few extra chairs pulled up, too. Many of her mismatched china pieces have been moved from her chipped-paint cupboard and set on the table. Still on her cupboard, though, are white pitchers filled with dried lagoon grasses and cattails. Above, the chandelier is dimmed as candles glimmer on the server, on the cupboard, along the table, everywhere around the room: tall pillars, tea lights, tapers in silver candlesticks.

And in the dining room windows, thin decorative starfish lean on several squares of the multipaned windows, the white color of the starfish contrasting against the dark night outside.

It's a moment she'd never seen coming only a month ago, in the days following her son's death. A moment when everyone she loves is gathered around her—with smiles, rather than stifling sadness—plates nearly emptied, silverware clinking, wineglasses refilled, chairs pushed back. Because though the meal is over, the talk doesn't stop, and neither does the happy laughter.

Except for this moment when she's paused, looking at each of her beloved guests—Maris and Jason; Eva, Matt and Taylor; Kyle and Lauren; Nick; Cliff; Jason's sister, Paige, and her husband, Vinny. And, of course, Celia sitting beside her. It's when Celia reaches over and clasps Elsa's hand that Elsa continues telling the story that's enraptured the table.

"We'd sit on the boardwalk like this all the time," Elsa says while lightly touching a framed photograph. In the image, she and her sister, June, sit on the very edge of the Stony Point boardwalk. They were teenagers—their blue jeans faded, their tank tops fitted, their bare feet set in the sand. Long Island Sound shimmered across the beach, an egret rose from the distant misty lagoon. Yes, life was as peaceful as their surroundings. Elsa passes the picture around the table.

"The sun was brilliant that morning, sparkling on the little ripples of the Sound. It gave the illusion of thousands of twinkling stars," Elsa explains. "They're stars that fell from the sky overnight, June told me. In awe, I remember watching them glimmer atop the gentle waves. Ocean stars, she called them. They float on top of the sea, twinkling until they regain their strength and rise back up to the sky later in the day."

At that point, Cliff hands back her framed photograph, which Elsa stands beside a silver candlestick on the table. "June told me that ocean stars are just as magical as night stars," she continues, looking at everyone listening. "So before we move to the back room for a little dessert and dancing, I want you all to make a wish—like you would on a star. A secret wish! Right now, in honor of my sister ... for whom my Ocean Star Inn is named."

The Beach Inn

"Auntie Elsa," Taylor says. "Do we say our wish out loud?"

"No, dear. Would you mind getting me that pretty Mason jar on the server? The one with mini starfish scattered inside, another type of beach star."

When Taylor gives her the jar, Elsa lifts off the lid and pulls out slips of paper, rolled and tied with twine. As she distributes a piece to everyone gathered at her dining room table, she explains. "Happiness jars will be at the heart of my inn's décor, and tonight we'll fill its first official jar with our secret wishes. And here's the thing," she says while sitting again. "A year from now, we'll all gather here and reopen this special happiness jar—a wish capsule of sorts. To see if our wishes came true."

Elsa picks up a pen and jots down her private wish. It's a simple one. All she hopes for is smooth sailing in the year ahead as her inn undergoes renovations. Smooth sailing for all of them. After the tumultuous, stormy days since Sal's death, they all need that type of easy peace.

By the glow of candlelight, the room hushes as her guests put wishes to paper. The jar slowly fills, one sealed wish at a time. Matt first, then Celia. She watches the attention some bestow on their wishes: Lauren kisses her rolled paper before dropping it into the jar, Maris and Eva toast their twined pieces as they nestle their wishes together with the mini starfish. Finally, only Jason is left writing. It's his wish that Elsa wonders most about as he rolls his paper, ties it up in twine, drops the wish in and closes up the happiness jar.

"And now," she declares while standing and raising her crystal goblet, "mark your calendars. Or write it in the sand! The Ocean Star Inn *will* be open for business by the summer, now that my dream team is back." Raising her glass of prosecco, she toasts everyone at the table, lastly Celia beside her. "And I'm so honored," Elsa adds, "to announce my new assistant innkeeper, Celia Gray." She bends down and hugs Celia. "Celia, the floor is yours."

The applause is instant and raucous. It seems the beach crew is thrilled that they're all together again, and that life is getting back on track at Stony Point.

Celia stands, a tear running down her face. "Oh, Elsa," she says while lifting a napkin and pressing it to her crying eyes. "Wait," she whispers, looking more sad than happy. "I'll be right back." Her words are soft as she inches away from the table. "There's something I want to do for you, but I need my guitar."

Before Elsa can say a word, Celia is a mere flash of color: her auburn hair flying behind her cropped black top; her gold chain necklaces jangling; her burgundy maxi skirt fluttering in a blur of motion.

The room quiets, noticeably so, as the candles and tabletop lanterns flicker all around them. It's Lauren who stands first. Stands, excuses herself and quickly leaves the table.

"Hang on, Celia!" she calls out while rushing toward the front door.

⁓

"Celia, wait up!"

As Celia pulls her squeaky wood-framed screen door open, she hears Lauren approaching behind her.

"What's wrong?" Lauren is asking as she catches up to her at the little guest cottage. "You should be happy."

Celia steps inside. "Oh, I am," she says without looking back. She had left on a lamp in the living room, so the lamplight casts a golden glow on the white board-and-batten walls. Elsa gave her pillows and a throw to put on the sofa, and Celia added a seashell-encrusted vase and mini wire lobster trap to the end table beside it. "I'm happy," she insists as the tears stream down her face.

"Oh my God!" Lauren takes Celia's arm and turns her around. "You're so *not* happy. You just burst into tears!"

"I'm kind of happy." When Celia brushes away a tear, she adds, "And kind of not."

"What happened, Cee? You seem ... just devastated. And I'm not leaving here until you tell me." So Lauren sits on the sofa and waits.

Which gives Celia a chance to turn away again and retrieve her guitar case from where it leans in the corner. She picks it up and holds it close. "Remember how you said that when you leave Stony Point, you drive beneath that train trestle and leave with one of three things?"

"Sure. And it's true. A ring, a baby, or a broken heart. It's happened to all of us here."

"Well, Lauren. I may be the first person ever in Stony Point history who left with all three things." She sets down her guitar case and drops onto the sofa beside Lauren.

"Three?" Lauren stops, instantly, for just a second. "Wait. A ring ... a *baby*?"

Celia only nods, because if she speaks, she'll sob. Okay, so she tries to explain anyway. "It's either the most beautiful thing that's happened to me," she says before the first sob comes, "or the most cruel."

Lauren grabs her hands. "You're *pregnant*?"

Celia nods again, because that one word brings a fresh round of tears.

"With Sal's baby? That is amazing!" She jumps up and looks first at Celia, then to her stomach, then at her face again. "Oh my God, what does Elsa say?"

"She doesn't know."

"What?" Lauren slowly sits back down on the couch.

"I haven't told her yet."

"Is that why you came back? Because you're pregnant?"

"No." Celia takes a long breath and walks to the paned window. One of the first things she did when moving into this little guest cottage behind Elsa's place was hang the seashell wind chime Sal had given her this past summer. Months ago, he placed it in front of a window in her cottage living room, and the beach breeze instantly brought it to life, the shells jingling and swaying. "*Serenata le stelle*," Celia whispers now, her hand over her stomach as she thinks of Sal telling her how the clinking shells serenaded the stars. Now they'll serenade his child.

"I only came back to talk to Elsa, to convince her to not sell the old cottage. That she belongs here." Celia touches the strung white shells and turns to Lauren. "I had no idea I was pregnant until today. This very morning. My period was late, but I figured my cycle was a mess this past month—just like my state of mind. So I didn't give it much thought. Until suddenly I realized way too many days had passed, and nothing. When I suspected that I might actually be pregnant, because Sal and I *had* slept together a few days before his surgery, well, I bought a home pregnancy test." She swipes a lingering tear from her face while whispering, "I'm really afraid, Lauren."

So Lauren bolts from the sofa and takes her up in a hug. "Oh no, hon. No, no," she says while slightly rocking Celia.

The Beach Inn

Then she backs off, smiling at her. "Don't be afraid! You can always call upon your new neighbor here at Stony Point—*me!* I'll help you through this." She presses aside a strand of Celia's hair. "A baby! I'm so happy for you! It's like everything with you and Sal was meant to be. But you *have* to tell Elsa. She'll be ecstatic."

"I know, and I will. Just not tonight with everyone there. Please, please don't say anything."

"Okay. I won't." Lauren gives her another long hug, saying into her ear, "I promise. And that's a *real* promise, don't you worry. Not a Stony Point promise that gets broken immediately."

Promises. Vows of loyalty. Of love. Sal promised he'd love Celia always. And now, well, now she'll see that love in the eyes of his very child. As Lauren hugs her, Celia looks outside through the screen door.

And can't she just hear it. *Roll camera*, the director of the latest imagined rom-com film of her life would say now. That's right, *Beckoning Celia*, a romantic comedy. Because isn't the laugh on her this time? A baby! But seeing the crew mesmerized by this turn of the script, the director would issue the order quietly. And the camera, to set the atmosphere, wouldn't it open the scene directly on that misty crescent moon hanging low in the dark October sky, the moon seemingly looking down on her sad happiness.

Tonight, that crescent moon—the same shape as the stretch of beach Sal loved to paddle his rowboat along—somehow assures her as she knows the waves of Long Island Sound lap in its glow. And the camera would pan down then and bring into soft focus Elsa's rambling cottage across the yard. Nearly every paned window is illuminated in the old shingled place—a cottage chock-full of love and sentimental stories, including Celia's now, too. While the camera zooms in, the beach friends would move onto the deck outside the infamous back room, drinks in hand, talk and laughter flowing easily.

As Celia picks up her guitar case and walks outside, closing the screen door behind her and Lauren, that camera would swing around. From a distance, it would stay focused only on her, a silhouette in her long skirt and cropped top, as she walks beneath the twinkling stars toward the anticipated beach inn. A foghorn's low call drifts over the distant sea, and a salty breeze gently touches her face.

twenty-seven

THE HANGOUT ROOM DRAWS THE others like a mystical magnet, and Elsa follows behind them. While walking through the dark hallway off the dining room, she listens to their voices and laughter. What an extraordinary building she bought a year ago, one with deep roots as a cottage and small market for the locals. She's sure that when old man Foley tacked on this sparse back room for his teenaged grandson decades ago, he never envisioned this: a grand gathering beneath twinkly lights, with warm toasts made with fine Italian wine, all while being serenaded by a vintage jukebox.

Because tonight, rusty sliding windows are pushed open to the hitching sea breeze; feet are stamping on the original wooden floor; dusty secondhand restaurant booths overflow with good friends and good cheer celebrating the old shingled cottage being transformed into a beach inn.

Feeling such promise, what Elsa knows is this: Her future guests will find a seaside haven here, especially in this room filled with ghosts-past from raucous beach parties, and epic card games, and sweet slow dances. Ghosts from love, and from broken hearts, and from memories swirling like stardust in the night. And once Jason's turret goes up—bringing a sense of the sea and sky inside—even better.

In the meantime, Elsa sets her finest dessert plates on the counter. Only the best for this exclusive event. It's why she dressed formal: a fitted black jumpsuit, its tailored top having a sheer lace neckline and sleeves, the look finished with her cherished star pendant hanging on a long, double-layer gold chain. Yes, *solamente il meglio*. Only the best for this evening.

Her niece Eva helps slice tiramisu and scoop chocolate gelato onto each plate, then places them at the booths.

"On the dessert menu tonight is my table-toppling tiramisu," Elsa announces to the milling beach friends. "Because in Italian, tiramisu means—"

"Wait!" Kyle interrupts. "I know this. I read it in my Italian handbook." He pulls the battered and dog-eared guide from his back pocket and thumbs through it. "Cuisine, cuisine," he mumbles under his breath while dragging a finger down the pages. "Aha! Here it is. Tiramisu means ... pick me up."

"Exactly." Elsa sets a dessert-laden plate at his booth. "And that's what we all do here at Stony Point. Pick each other up in good times and sad. Times when we need a nudge, or a reality check." She delivers a plate to a hovering Vinny, who's been dangerously eyeing the specialty pastry. "So if you're ever feeling blue, well ..."

"We're all your real-life tiramisu," Vinny says around a mouthful of the cake.

A sharp whistle cutting through the night gets Elsa's attention, though. So she goes out to the upper-level deck, where Matt and Jason just whistled down to Lauren and Celia. Elsa waves to them, too, as they cross the yard, Celia carrying her guitar case. And what it does, when Celia waves up at her, is bring sheer relief. Because earlier, she was so unusually quiet during dinner, Elsa worried. Might Celia be doubting their partnership to run the Ocean Star Inn?

But that one casual hand-wave allays Elsa's fear. She rushes into the back room as the two women return. "Celia," Elsa says. "Everything okay?"

Celia sets down her guitar and hugs Elsa. "Yes. Yes, I'm fine," she says into her ear before backing up a step. "I just had some misty memories, that's all."

"That's what I thought, dear. This old place is filled with them, no?"

Celia nods. "Beautiful ones, though."

When the rest of the gang wanders back inside and starts oohing and aahing over the waiting desserts, Lauren pulls at Celia to sit in a booth with her and Kyle.

"Gather round, everyone, and have a seat!" Elsa calls out as the friends shuffle about and jockey for their favorite spots. Dibbed seats go back years in time, to when *they* were the teens hanging out here. It's obvious when Kyle hitches his thumb at Vinny, who's apparently sitting in Kyle's long-reserved spot. Vinny forfeits his seat, but not without a friendly shove to his beach chum as he does so. Not much has changed, Elsa can see that, in the camaraderie of the room.

"Cliff?" Elsa asks. "Are we ready?"

Cliff fills the last of the wineglasses before giving her a thumbs-up.

"Okay, then," Elsa says as Cliff moves by her side and offers her a glass. Elsa raises it to make a special toast. "To the days ahead here at the Ocean Star Inn. May there be blue skies and smiles for all who stay in these rooms."

Cries of *Salute!* and *Cheers!* ring out, after which Maris and

Eva both hug Elsa and give her their gifts.

"A chalk assortment for your *inn*-spiration walkway," Eva tells her as she presents her with a festive, ribbon-wrapped bucket that is packed tight with fat, colorful pieces of chalk. "Enough to write many happy greetings for your guests."

"How thoughtful!" Elsa says while spinning the bucket and perusing the colors. She then sits in a booth with Cliff beside her, and Jason and Maris across from her. "And what's this?" Elsa asks when Maris hands her a large leather-bound book adorned with a huge blue bow.

"Your very first reservation ledger. I know you'll reserve rooms online, but it's nice to have this at the front desk, too." Maris opens it on the table between them. "Some of the dates have been filled in with guest names already. So if you don't mind passing it around, we'll complete each reservation."

"*Perfetto!*" Elsa runs an open hand across the blank calendar page, then lifts the ledger and nods to Kyle's table. "Kyle? Would you do the honors?"

Jason passes the ledger to Kyle behind him, who opens the long cover and pages through to September. Lauren leans close beside him, whispering in his ear as she points to the week. As he writes *Bradford* in the allotted weekend dates, adds the number of guests and reason for stay, Elsa hurries over and bends close to read what he writes.

"Really?" she asks, standing straight and raising her leopard-print reading glasses to the top of her head. "Your ten-year wedding anniversary is coming up?"

"Sure is." Kyle slaps the ledger shut. "And I just booked a room here for it."

Amidst the whoops and hollers, Elsa hears someone—Vinny, she thinks—yell out *You made it!*

"Damn straight, Vincenzo." Kyle loops his arm around Lauren's shoulder, pulls her close and gives her a long kiss. "Best ten years of my life. It's also all we can manage for a vacation next year, with the new house and all."

"Advance warning. Stay away from *that* room that weekend. Might break a noise ordinance," Nick advises everyone, bringing more lively banter about heavy breathing and sleepless nights.

"Hey, man." Kyle glares across the table at Nick. "Where's *your* reservation?"

"It's in there." Nick spins the ledger around and opens it to the May page, then takes the pen from Kyle. "My reservation is for late May, when … Wait for it." He holds up the pen until the room goes silent. "Drumroll, please … I graduate from college."

"Woo-hoo!" Maris calls from behind him.

Nick fills in the dates, saying, "Family's coming in from out of town and I'll need a couple of rooms."

"Finally, dude." Matt holds up his glass in a toast from his booth. "After years of classes, schedules, homework, you did it. Made it to the finish line."

"It's about time," Kyle adds, tipping his glass to Nick's. "Cheers to you."

"Hey," Nick informs them after sipping his prosecco. "When I get that B.A., do you know what it stands for? Badass!"

"Ooh, you wish," Vinny says as he forks off a hunk of tiramisu. "But nice try," he adds around the sweet cake.

Eva walks over and grabs the book to bring back to her booth. "Speaking of parties," she says as she squeezes into her booth beside Taylor. "Tay's sweet sixteen is next year, in the spring. But what she wants is a summertime-by-the-sea event."

Taylor claps her hands and opens the ledger. "Maybe when school gets out." She flips her long blonde hair back, then points to the blank page.

So Eva picks up the pen and writes *Gallagher Party* on that milestone weekend. "I'm booking a girlfriends' sleepover in late June. Here, at the Ocean Star Inn."

"All right!" Taylor exclaims, tipping her juice glass to her father's wine.

"Sixteen?" Kyle asks over his shoulder. "Remember what we were doing at sixteen?"

"Whoa, hold it, Kyle," Eva warns him. "Don't be giving her any ideas!"

"Tay's such a good kid," Matt says of his daughter. "No worries, right Tay?"

His daughter snags a mouthful of gelato and tiramisu combined. "Not yet, anyway," she says with a wink.

"Smart kid," Kyle admits.

"Weren't we just sixteen?" Lauren looks over her shoulder and smiles at Taylor. "It feels it, sometimes."

"Okay," Cliff announces from his seat across the booth as he quickly drags his spoon through the last of his chocolate gelato. "Pass it this way, Eva."

The leather-bound ledger makes its way across the booths until Elsa slides it to Cliff. "*You're* booking a room?"

"You bet I am. For the Fourth of July, and here's why." Cliff opens the ledger to July just as Elsa squeezes back into the booth beside him, leaning close. He stretches out his arm and cuffs his shirtsleeve in exaggerated preparation. "As the new beach commissioner, I'm allowing fireworks on Stony Point Beach for the first time, right in front of the Ocean Star Inn."

The Beach Inn

"Nice work, Commish," Jason tells him. "You're going all out."

"Well," Cliff says to Elsa as he writes his name on the Fourth of July, "I'll need to spend the night in that turret room your architect designed." With a nod, he glances up at Jason. "Way up high. To keep a handle on the fireworks situation on the beach. I'm sure once Jason's crew is done building that turret, I'll have the best view in town."

Elsa leans over and kisses his cheek, then brushes her fingers through his hair.

"It'll be even better," Cliff tells her, "if a certain innkeeper might join me there."

In the dimly lit room, Maris then reaches across the table and pulls over the ledger. "Jason and I are booking a room for the holidays, next year. Christmas Eve at the Ocean Star Inn!" She turns to the December page and writes *Barlows* on the appropriate arrival and departure dates. "Doesn't it sound exquisite? A grand Christmas tree, and twinkly lights in all the starfish-adorned windows." Jason pulls her close and kisses the side of Maris' head as she talks. "Maybe a Christmas Eve candlelit stroll on the snow-dusted boardwalk, beside the sea?"

"Psst," Eva whispers. She's turned around in her booth seat behind Maris and hangs on her every word. "Put *us* on that reservation, too," Eva says, motioning to Matt and Taylor and herself.

And as Maris does just that, Elsa notices Vinny and Paige making their way to the jukebox. "This calls for a dance," Vinny announces over his shoulder as he drops in the coins. He presses the jukebox keys for his selection, and by the time the record falls into place, he's already hit the dance floor, rolling up his shirtsleeves while waiting with Paige for the music to begin.

All it takes is the first guitar riff to get the whole gang on their feet. Elsa's actually amazed at how the song works like magic, taking hold of Maris and Jason, Eva and Matt, Kyle twirling Lauren onto the floor. Even Nick takes Celia in his arms and starts a-swaying. The fun part is the way they all get down to Springsteen singing about glory days, and the good old times, and sitting around with a drink and stories. Not a beat is missed as they strut and stamp the floor, and clap along, and change partners, too.

What it all does, the dance, is weave some invisible thread between them—Kyle dipping Eva, Matt grooving with Maris, Jason holding Lauren in his arms. In the shadowy light of the room—as they stomp on the wood floor, the screen door open to the deck—Elsa time travels. Suddenly she sees them twenty years ago, all in their teens—the girls' hair long and flyaway, their faces sun kissed, dancing barefoot in their jeans and tees, laughing away their youth. Tonight, the song simply frees them again as they dance in the glow of the jukebox amidst their sweet summer memories.

It apparently moves Cliff, too. He nudges Elsa and nods to the floor. "Glory days?" he asks. "If we don't get out there," he says, hitching his head in the direction of the jukebox, "we won't have any."

She hesitates, though, with a pang of guilt, a brief sadness at having such a carefree good time when she lost her son just over a month ago.

Until she looks at the faces of all of Sal's close friends, each one lit up with familiar comfort, and happiness, that comes only from being right here, at Stony Point, in this little corner of the world he truly loved.

Until she hears—somewhere in that stomping on the old

wooden floor, in the chorus of all the voices singing along, in the music and laughter of this glorious day that's destined to be one for the books—two words. *Sorridi, Ma.*

Granting her son's whispered wish, she smiles and follows Cliff to the dance floor. And when Vinny plays the same song once more, doesn't Elsa shrug her shoulders, swing her lace-covered arms and shimmy low, then take Cliff's hand in the glow of the jukebox and settle into his arms as he grooves with her in Foley's old back-room hangout.

⌒

"Lauren," Celia says after the dancing subsides. "Give me a jing-a-ling?"

Lauren grabs the crescent tambourine from a shelf, brings it to the front of the bustling room and raises it with a good jangle.

"Excuse me, everybody," Celia calls out once the room quiets. Some of the friends sit at their booths, swapping seats like a game of musical chairs: Jason and Kyle, drinks in hand, come in from out on the deck; Eva and Maris sit with Paige and Vinny, looking like they're engrossed in a quick card game; Elsa and Cliff chat with Taylor in their booth.

So Celia simply waits a moment until Lauren pulls over a stool for her. "I want to play you all a very personal song," she says then, while sitting on the stool and settling her guitar on her lap. "In honor of Sal. He would be *so* happy if he were here this special night."

When Kyle lets out a whistle, Celia glances to the large, driftwood-framed photograph hanging on the wall near the jukebox. It was taken in August, after a homecoming party for

Maris and Eva. In the photo, everyone in this room sits around a bonfire on the night beach. Lauren kneels beside Kyle with her head on his shoulder; Matt and Eva are off to the side; Maris sits in front of Jason, leaning back into him as he kisses the side of her head; and Sal. Sal, who had just waltzed Celia barefoot across the sand as they danced beneath the stars. Sal, who sits in the sand and leans back on his hands, watching her strum her guitar. One shot caught them all in, well, certainly a glory-day moment—with a full red moon hanging low in the sky behind them.

And here they are again, everyone except for Sal.

So Celia summons his presence. "I know Sal wanted this beach inn to be the premiere destination on the Connecticut coast. We talked about it often," she says, her voice low. "Sometimes, after we talked long into the night, he asked me to play a particular tune, especially if he was feeling a little tired."

What she notices now is that someone could drop a pin and they'd all hear it. The room is that quiet in its longing for Sal, sweet Sal. Knowing that she's pregnant, Celia could almost place a hand to her stomach; the urge is so strong, it feels instinctual. Surely reading her sad thoughts in the silent pause, Lauren squeezes her shoulder, then walks past to sit beside Kyle.

Crossing her legs on the stool, Celia plucks at a few strings as she tinkers with tuning the guitar, then looks out at the dusky room. If she squints just right into the dust particles floating in the glow of the jukebox light, does she decipher a vague silhouette? Maybe standing way in the back, leaning on the pinball machine while watching her?

"Okay, I'm ready now," she says, looking beyond them all

to the rear of the room. "This one's always for you, Salvatore."

A sea breeze floats through one of the windows as she draws her pick across the strings. The familiar tune rising from her guitar brings tears to her eyes as she remembers changing the words this past summer, special for Sal. Remembers him lying on her sofa, half dozing, with a smile on his face.

Twinkle, twinkle ocean star ... How I wonder what you are.
Floating on the sea, so light ... Like a diamond, shining bright.

As she sings, her beach friends lean into each other: Matt with his arm around Eva; Cliff taking Elsa's hand across the table; Maris resting her head on Jason's shoulder; Kyle leading Lauren out of their booth to barely slow dance as Celia improvises, her strumming taking the tune to sad new places for several minutes before bringing it back around to her lyrics.

Twinkle, twinkle ocean star ... How I wonder ...

She pauses with misty eyes, glancing out the screen door toward the distant sea before finishing.

How I wonder ... where you are.

twenty-eight

LATER IN THE EVENING, WHEN everyone's settled in the booths and working on seconds of her cream-cheese-filled, cocoa-dusted tiramisu, Elsa makes her move. First, she closes the old wooden storm door to the deck, seemingly to keep out the cold air now coming through the screen. No one would suspect it's to conceal the surprise guest she invited with the help of her niece Maris. Then Elsa leaves the back room, hurries to her kitchen and opens a drawer. To complete this magical night when all the stars finally align in her life again, she touches her etched-gold star necklace with a silent wish. This one? For Jason. Finally, she lifts the necessary items from the drawer.

On her way back to the party, a bluesy song finishes up on the jukebox, over which she hears the steady murmur of friendly voices, all mixed with the clinking of forks to dessert dishes. Jason had shut off the ceiling lights a while ago, and Maris brought Mason jar candles to each booth's table, so the atmosphere is quiet and intimate.

Which is exactly what Elsa was waiting for. Mood matters, and this is the perfect mood to spring her surprise on the now-subdued group. Holding the papers retrieved from the kitchen, she walks in and stops beside the booth where Cliff sits talking to Kyle, Lauren and Celia. In the booth behind him, Jason and Maris sit with Eva and Matt, wineglasses and dessert dishes between them. In the room's far corner, Nick and Taylor challenge Vinny and Paige in a rowdy game of pinball—the flippers flipping, the score beeping and dinging. And somehow, the talk in the old Foley's hangout room weaves from one area to the other as they all listen in and chat together.

Elsa lifts a fork and clinks an empty wineglass on her table. "Before the party ends," she announces as the pinball in play rolls to a stop and the booths quiet, "I want to share a very special reason that I gathered you all here. A reason *beyond* keeping the beach inn."

It's apparent she now has their undivided attention when the pinball players quietly break up the game. Together, Taylor, Nick, Paige and Vinny squeeze into the last empty booth and take a cautious seat.

At that point, Elsa lifts the multipage document in her hand and waves it briefly, getting the gold bangles jingling on her wrist. "First, I want to thank you all for your *pazienza* these past few weeks while I worked through my emotions. My wise nephew-in-law—I'm looking at you, Jason—recently told me that grieving is okay, because it comes from love." As she says it, Elsa sees Maris leave a kiss on Jason's whiskered cheek, then touch his hair. Love, love, it's everywhere Elsa looks tonight. "Anyway, Jason told me that it's *love* that gives us the strength to go on. For me," she says, her eyes filling with tears, "it's not just the love for my son, Salvatore. It's far more than that. It's the love in this room tonight, from my beautiful *famiglia* and friends, that gets me through many dark days. Today? Today is a good day, but I know there are still difficult ones ahead."

Unable to contain herself, Eva scoots out of her booth and rushes to Elsa, giving her a quick hug and kiss before returning to her seat beside Matt.

"Much of grief, and sadness, is like the tide here at Stony Point, the way it comes and goes. So your Operation Make Elsa Smile," Elsa continues with a wink to Cliff, "meant the world to me. Everything you've all done these past weeks ... taking me kite flying, painting *en plein air*, bringing egg sandwiches and building nighttime campfires. The sweet home movies. Well, it worked. All of it." She smiles and catches a tear that escapes. "Because yes, I can finally, *finally*, smile ... looking at all of you."

As Elsa gets choked up and presses a hand to her mouth, Cliff starts to go to her. But with a now-teary smile, she motions for him to wait.

"I stand before all of you holding the real estate contract I signed to put my cottage, my *inn*, on the market last month—just days after losing Sal." Elsa glances at her signature on the contract that effectively was selling out her life. "You see, I lost my son, and lost myself, as well." She looks to Kyle with a nod, and he raises his wineglass in a silent toast. "Rash decisions," Elsa tells him directly. "Oh, you were so right, my friend. My decision to sell this grand old cottage was very rash, a decision coming on the rebound of the worst pain I've ever felt after laying my son to rest. But thanks to all of you, yes, I've changed my mind and will *not* be selling this soon-to-be beach inn. So without further ado ..."

A lone whistle breaks the silence as she slowly raises her real estate contract once more. A whistle from Nick, then another from

Matt. Then applause—sparse at first—as Elsa starts the long, slow ripping of the legal document. That single shearing sound cuts through the dusty room. As her hands tear the real estate papers neatly in half and ceremoniously save the beach inn, more applause and cheers and whoops come from the shadows. Cliff is first to get out of the booth. He gives her a tender kiss, then presses back a wisp of her hair—his smile wider than anyone's.

Except maybe for Celia's, as she rushes to Elsa and hugs her, too.

But the happy excitement lasts for only a minute, only until a sudden knock sounds at the now-closed door leading to the deck. Kyle goes to open it, but Elsa grabs his arm and stops him in the nick of time.

"Before *I* open the door," Elsa says while turning to everyone there, "we need to ..." She stops when the chattering voices wondering who's on the other side of that door interrupt her. "Please! Listen up!" she yells. When that doesn't work, she tries something she's never done before: hooks two fingers in her mouth and attempts a sharp whistle. When that ends up sounding more like a fuzzy hiss, she snatches a fork and raps it on a glass again. "*Jason*," she calls out over the din. "Jason! We need a moment to talk. About *you*."

And that does it. People stop in the candlelit room, slowly sit again in the tattered restaurant booths, and look from Elsa to Jason—who turns up his hands and shrugs in his booth. "Me?" he asks.

"Yes." Elsa walks closer to where he sits. "You are like a son to me, and I care deeply about your decisions. Tonight, I'm wondering if you will make good on a promise."

It happens then. Murmurs fill the room: *Promise? What promise?*

Kyle turns in his seat and slaps Jason's shoulder. "What's going on, bro?" he asks.

But with a wary look, Jason's eyes stay on Elsa, all while Maris leans into him and whispers something in his ear.

"Not long ago," Elsa continues with a small smile, her voice lowering, "you stopped by here and tried to convince me to keep this grand old cottage—Foley's, this house of memories for all you kids. During our heated discussion that morning, I turned the tables and asked what it would take for *you* to sign that CT-TV contract and commit to a cottage renovation television pilot."

"*Gesù, Santa Maria*," Jason says first as his eyes drop closed for only a second. Until he squints at Elsa while shaking his head.

"What?" Nick asks, rubbing his goatee. "What's going on?"

"What the hell'd you promise?" Kyle asks from behind Jason.

But Jason ignores it all and watches only Elsa.

"And when I asked you what—*specifically*—it would take to get you to finally sign your contract," Elsa says, leaning closer to Jason before motioning her hand for him to share it with the room, "you were *very* clear when you said ..."

Jason still doesn't move as he admits the words. "*You ripping up yours.*"

So Elsa raises her eyebrow and drops her ripped-up real estate contract on the table in front of him, then pauses to smooth a few wrinkles from the fabric of her black jumpsuit before walking to the door—her each deliberate step clipping on the creaky planked floor. To make a show of the moment, she sweeps her lace-covered arm toward the doorknob before opening it to Trent from CT-TV. Holding a big white

The Beach Inn

envelope, he briefly pauses, steps into the room and walks straight to Jason's booth.

Again, every voice is silent as all heads turn to watch Elsa personally challenge Jason's promise. Okay, though she's sure to keep a twinkle in her eye, there's no mistaking one thing: A promise is a promise. She returns to Jason's booth, sits beside him and first looks directly at him with a nod to the CT-TV contract that Trent pulled from the envelope and set on the table.

When Jason looks from the document, back to Elsa, she smiles—yes, smiles—and hands him her finest Italian pen.

twenty-nine

ONCE ALL HER GUESTS HAVE left and Elsa's alone in the quiet cottage, she presses back the white curtain at a window, straightens a starfish leaning on the pane and softly sighs. Because it's time for her to mark the return of the beach inn, finally, in her own way. To accept all that's come to pass.

So she changes into black leggings and a fringe-trimmed flannel tunic, picks up her new chalk bucket, finds her floral-print foam kneepad and goes outside. With that low crescent moon and thousands of stars twinkling above her, she kneels on her stone patio. Decorative solar lights glimmer from between the sweeping ornamental grasses and hydrangea bushes. Large white conch shells dot the edge of the patio. She remembers the day Sal installed the lights, saying the illumination made it a nice spot to linger at night. And so he added a wood-slatted bench there.

As Elsa chooses a fat piece of glow-in-the-dark chalk from the bucket, a sea breeze brings the sound of distant waves to her. The splashing is clear and rhythmic as those waves break on the beach. It beautifully reminds her of how time goes on, like the tides she'd mentioned earlier, and she takes comfort in the feeling. Though still sad, she's supposed to be *here* now, at Stony Point. Continuing on without Sal. It'll be okay.

After one more glance up at the starlit sky above the sea, she writes across her inn-spiration walkway, in sweeping cursive, a private message to her son: *Twinkle, twinkle ocean star.*

When she sits back on her haunches and reads the line, someone comes up behind her and drops a sweater over her shoulders. She turns to see Celia standing there wearing her long burgundy skirt and cropped top, still. "It's chilly, so I brought you a sweater."

"Oh, Celia!" Elsa quickly brushes away a tear before reaching for Celia's hand as she helps her to her feet.

"I saw your lights on outside, from the guesthouse, and thought I'd visit for a bit." Celia gives Elsa a gentle hug, then steps back.

"What a beautiful night, no?" Elsa asks.

Celia sweeps her fingers across a fading hydrangea blossom beside the walkway. "It is."

"This past month, I didn't think beautiful nights were possible anymore. Tonight, Salvatore must be smiling down on us." Elsa snaps off a few of those pale violet hydrangea blossoms and gives them to Celia. "Especially now that Jason signed on for his cottage reno show."

"And the beach inn will be his pilot episode!"

Elsa brushes back a strand of hair. At the end of this long, emotional evening, she feels fatigued. "Except I'm not sure I'm camera-ready," she tells Celia.

"Oh, Elsa." Celia sits on the wood bench and sets the flowers there. Behind her, the sweeping beach grasses seem to whisper in the night's breezes. "You're so beautiful. Just like Sophia Loren! The cameras will love you."

"We'll see." Elsa gets back to her chalked inn-spiration message. As she swirls a blue line beneath the words, she says over her shoulder, "I'm really happy that everyone was here tonight, everyone so dear to me. And to Sal."

"Me, too. I can never leave."

After a long moment, Celia stands and hovers behind her. Elsa sees a glimpse of her long skirt fluttering as she steps closer.

"What are you writing?" Celia asks.

When Elsa looks up at her, Celia is pressing her hair back as she bends lower to see. So Elsa moves aside and tells her, "A line from the pretty song you sang tonight. It sounded so peaceful, your voice so soft." She smiles at Celia, thinking how she still seems sad. Or distracted. Something. "I could picture my son listening to your every inflection. The way you strummed your guitar and sang the song tonight, it sounded like, well … like a sweet lullaby." Elsa turns back and fusses with the lyrics she'd written as Celia is silent behind her. The night seems to cloak them there, alone with the memory of Celia singing her song.

After another long moment, Celia pats Elsa's shoulder. "It actually *is* going to be a lullaby."

"What?" Elsa looks up from her walkway message, then slowly stands while brushing chalk dust from her hands. "What are you saying?"

All the while, Celia is nodding. "I found out this morning, but didn't want to tell you in front of everyone. I'm pregnant." She whispers through a teary smile, "I'm going to have a baby. Sal's baby."

Elsa takes a sharp breath as she drops the piece of blue chalk and presses her hand to her heart.

"When I left here a few weeks ago and went back to Addison, it felt like the summer never happened," Celia continues. "I was just so sad, and I never even suspected. But now ..."

"Celia!" Elsa rushes forward and takes up all of Celia's thin frame in a tight hug as she rocks her back and forth. "Celia, Celia, Celia!" She steps back and brushes her fingers through Celia's straight auburn hair. "A baby? Are you *sure*?"

"Oh, yes." Celia nods right as tears fall from her sad eyes. "I am. You're going to be a grandmother."

Elsa tips her head, taking in Celia's words. Tears are never as painful as when they mock with their mixed emotions. Her son is gone, and yet his child lives. As tears spill from Elsa's eyes, oh her heart could split open with this sadness and joy at once.

"But I have to tell you something," Celia admits. "I'm so scared, Elsa."

"Scared?" Elsa pulls her sweater closer over her shoulders.

"Yes, scared. Scared of everything that will happen now. I mean, a baby!"

"Come over here." Elsa takes her hand and walks her to the bench where they sit side by side. She gives Celia another hug, whispering close, "Don't be afraid, Celia. Don't be afraid. Sal loved you *so much*, and I do, too. Everything will be okay, I promise. Do you know why?" She pulls back and smiles through her own tears to see Celia shaking her head. "Because the best place, the *very* best place to start over ... is by the sea."

Finally, Celia gives her another smile. It's small, but it's genuine as can be. "That's the first thing you told me when we met, remember? When you invited me over for a lemonade last June?"

"Of course I do. But you're not starting over alone. I'm here, your beach friends are here." She takes Celia's hand and clasps it in her lap. "And Sal's here, Celia. He really is … in the sea breezes. It's what he loved the most about Stony Point, dear, being in this sweet salt air."

There have been times in Elsa's life when the beauty of a moment is so intense, it hurts. When the immensity of the beauty leaves pain in her heart, and makes it hard to even breathe as she takes in the moment. Capturing fireflies with her sister thirty-five years ago during a summer sunset at the lagoon; seeing Sal walk around the corner of her shingled cottage early last summer, looking weary from life on Wall Street, coming home to Connecticut. And now? Now, this. His baby.

"Look," Celia says, pointing to the night sky. "I used to skip stones with Sal, and he would tell me how the spray of the water looked like a shooting star, just like that one."

Elsa watches a shooting star streak across the sky, leaving a faint, sparkling trail in the darkness. Sitting here this magical night with Celia, knowing she'll be having Sal's child? This, this is one of those rare moments.

A moment as fleeting as the fading tail of a shooting star … when life is as sad, and sweet, as it could possibly ever be.

thirty

THE BEACH IS DARK; THE boardwalk lights shut off now. Maddy runs along the weaving high tide line with her nose to the damp seaweed. Behind her, Jason follows on the cool, packed seaside sand—ground unlike any other on earth. Which is why he wanted to take this late walk before removing his prosthesis at home. After a tiring evening, the firm sand here always soothes his weary gait. Above, the faint light of the low crescent moon falls on the rippling water of Long Island Sound. There's a silhouette of a small anchored boat out beyond the big rock, and it reminds him of Sal, and the way he drifted alone in his rowboat so many summer nights before he died.

A cool October breeze skims off the water now, and Jason hikes his black sweatshirt up around his neck. No one else is out here; the cottages on the hill are mere shadows, closed up for the off-season. It's a solitude he relishes tonight, after signing the CT-TV contract. Though he's glad to have given over his signature right in the old Foley's hangout room—with all the friends' history ingrained in those walls—his life is about to take a new turn. So this beach walk is a simple way to hold on to some of the past. To stand still, thinking of his brother, Neil, and how he'll bring his influence to the show.

Ahead of him, waves break along the sand. He listens, knowing they always break, no matter what. No matter when.

Where've you been?

Jason turns and squints down the empty beach, toward the rock jetty. He looks out at the moonlit water, then raises his eyes to the starry sky above it. The sea, the stars. On the night he left this all behind a month ago, he'd vowed never to look at the stars again. Not until he could somehow find his way back to the sea.

Back home.

Just like his father did, finding his way home from the jungles of 'Nam. *It's those stars that saved me. They looked the same as if I'd been in my own Connecticut backyard*, he'd say of the stars he could make out through the Southeast Asian trees. *They kept me going until I could see my home stars again.*

When Jason starts walking toward the rocks, the foghorn moans from out at the Gull Island Lighthouse.

I said, where've you been, bro? Talk to me, man.

Instantly, Jason's eyes fill with tears. "Shit." He looks over his shoulder and glances into the shadows on the beach. "I've been right here."

A wave breaks, hissing up onto the sand at the same time he finally, finally hears his brother's long-awaited voice. *No, you haven't. No night walks, no dog. Nothing. You've been so goddamn gone, Jay.*

Again, though the sight is blurry through his tears, Jason looks to the stars. "Past month's been hell," he quietly says. "Had a tough time. Felt a little like Dad must've, in the jungle." Jason thinks of the battles he's faced in just one month: losing and missing his cousin Sal; an unfortunate entanglement with Celia; butting heads with Michael Micelli; trying to save Elsa's beach inn; keeping his marriage afloat; rescuing Neil's dilapidated shingled shack from the onslaught of a coming winter.

"I've been fighting off my own enemies," he tells Neil. "Sidestepping mines, escaping skirmishes ... mostly unscathed."

As he walks, he nears the stony point at the far end of the beach. A shadowy patch of woods rises beyond, where a sudden breeze whispers through the pine branches.

What have I always told you? Jason hears murmured at the same time. *It's what Dad told us about why he came here after Vietnam. The sea, Jay. The sea and its salt air.*

Jason takes a long breath, filling his lungs with that sweet elixir. "Cures what ails you." He stops at the rocks and waits, then turns to head back down the beach, toward the boardwalk. "You still out there?" he asks, his words hushed.

No voice comes to him as he walks along the driftline. There's only Maddy, splashing in the water beside him. The German shepherd prances through a breaking wave, then runs up onto the sand with a happy bark.

But no Neil in the breeze. Nothing but darkness.

Until Jason feels a shove from behind. A hand pushing against his shoulder, maybe, hard enough to cause him to stumble, then regain his footing in the sand. He glances back. Or was it just his foot catching on a cluster of seaweed? When he looks up, Maris is approaching from the boardwalk. Her long hair blows in the wind; she wears a corduroy peacoat and thick sweater over her jeans; the dog is now at her side.

"I brought you this," she calls out while holding up a warmer jacket. "Where've you been?"

It's uncanny, having heard above the splashing waves those same words from Neil, only moments ago. *Where've you been?* Had his brother actually been waiting for *him*? Was it really *Jason* who had left for all this time? Not hearing his brother's voice—or even sensing his presence—for so long, he'd believed for the past month that Sal's death somehow took Neil's spirit, too.

But now, he knows. It didn't. Sal's death took his *own* spirit to some dark place it wasn't supposed to go. And for the past month, Jason did it; he struggled and fought to find his way out of the jungle, find his way back to his home stars.

Maris waits in the sand, watching him. He walks to her and touches a wisp of her silky hair. After he does, she helps him put the jacket on over his sweatshirt, then tucks his father's Vietnam dog tags beneath his shirt collar.

"Feel better?" she asks, running a finger along his cheek. "It's cold out here."

Jason nods, then steps even closer and hugs her on the night beach, beside the sea. His arms reach around her shoulders and hold tight; his hands stroke her hair. "Thank you," he whispers against her ear before stepping back and cradling her face. His fingers barely skim her neck, and he looks at her for a long moment. "For not giving up on me these past weeks."

"Oh, Jason," Maris says, her words as soft as the hissing froth of the breaking waves. Her smile, gentle.

A light breeze lifts off the water; he feels it brush his face, his hair. And so he leans in and kisses her as lightly, his lips barely touching hers, his fingers tracing her jaw.

After a moment, he takes her hand and they head toward the boardwalk. He helps Maris step onto it from the sand, then

The Beach Inn

gives a whistle back toward the water to beckon Maddy. The dog bounds out of the shadows and onto the boardwalk ahead of them. Off to the side, the few remaining boats in the little marina rise and fall with the currents, creaking against the pilings to which they're secured.

As Jason walks with Maris over the planked boards, he feels the grit of sand beneath his step and remembers the special times he actually used his leaf blower to clear the sand off the boardwalk: for Elsa's morning business meetings this past summer; for the epic home-movie night only days ago; for his own seaside wedding reception last year.

Maris stops to gather the tote and flashlight she'd left behind just minutes before. "I was sitting here, waiting, when I didn't see you," she says while picking up her things. "Where were you?"

"Right here, sweetheart," he tells her, motioning to the beach scarcely illuminated by the low crescent moon. He glances out at the dark sea, before slipping his arm around her shoulders and pressing a kiss to the side of her head. "Right where I'll always be."

They start walking home then, crossing the sandy boardwalk to make their way to the narrow footpath winding up the hill.

A footpath leading to the bluff on the end of Sea View Road, where silver-tipped waves slosh against the rocks and where seagulls cry early mornings when sunrises paint the coast gold.

A footpath leading to where Jason's gabled cottage stands overlooking Long Island Sound as the night's stars shine above the salty water. A cottage where lamplight spills from paned windows. A cottage with hurricane lanterns and framed photographs on the mantel, clustered around a conch shell and pewter hourglass there. A cottage where many nights, a sea breeze lifts the curtains as Jason takes his beautiful wife in his arms beside the old, glowing jukebox.

With Maris by his side now, he reaches the top of that footpath.

A footpath leading to a very fortunate life, indeed.

The beach friends' journey continues in

BEACH BLISS

The next novel in The Seaside Saga from New York Times Bestselling Author

JOANNE DEMAIO

Also by Joanne DeMaio

The Seaside Saga
(In order)
1) Blue Jeans and Coffee Beans
2) The Denim Blue Sea
3) Beach Blues
4) Beach Breeze
5) The Beach Inn
6) Beach Bliss
7) Castaway Cottage
8) Night Beach
9) Little Beach Bungalow
10) Every Summer
–And More Seaside Saga Books–

Summer Standalone Novels
True Blend
Whole Latte Life

Winter Novels
Eighteen Winters
First Flurries
Cardinal Cabin
Snow Deer and Cocoa Cheer
Snowflakes and Coffee Cakes

For a complete list of books by *New York Times* bestselling author Joanne DeMaio, visit:

Joannedemaio.com

About the Author

JOANNE DEMAIO is a *New York Times* and *USA Today* bestselling author of contemporary fiction. The novels of her ongoing and groundbreaking Seaside Saga journey with a group of beach friends, much the way a TV series does, continuing with the same cast of characters from book-to-book. In addition, she writes winter novels set in a quaint New England town. Joanne lives with her family in Connecticut.

For a complete list of books and for news on upcoming releases, please visit Joanne's website. She also enjoys hearing from readers on Facebook.

Author Website:
Joannedemaio.com

Facebook:
Facebook.com/JoanneDeMaioAuthor

Made in United States
North Haven, CT
15 April 2022